SLITHER

Her scream shocked through him.

'Mary, what—?' For a moment he sat paralysed, then he jumped up from his armchair and dashed around to her side of the desk.

She screamed again. A long, sobbing, terrified scream.

Several small worms, about four or five inches in length, were spilling out of the opened package which lay on its side on the pink blotter. They wriggled over the desk towards her. One of them was already attached, leech-like, to the heavy white flesh of her forearm. She stared at it, screaming, making no attempt to pull it off, but just screaming.

Also in Hamlyn Paperbacks
by John Halkin

The Unholy

SLITHER

JOHN HALKIN

Hamlyn Paperbacks

A Hamlyn Paperback

Published by Arrow Books Limited

17-21 Conway Street, London W1P 6JD

A division of the Hutchinson Publishing Group

London Melbourne Sydney Auckland
Johannesburg and agencies throughout
the world

First published in Great Britain by Hamlyn Paperbacks 1980
Reprinted 1980, 1981, 1982 (three times) and 1984

Printed and bound in Great Britain by
Anchor Brendon Limited, Tiptree, Essex

ISBN 0 600 20018 3

'The worm is not to be trusted . . .
. . . there is no goodness in the worm.'

Antony and Cleopatra

1

With a sudden flick, whiplike, three of the worms reversed direction in the sewer and sped towards Matt's hand. They were at least eighteen inches long, like snakes, as fat as his wrist, dead straight and as swift as arrows. They looked just as dangerous too, their skins glowing with a weird beautiful luminosity even under the glare of the lights.

Matt had been groping around in the sludge for the light meter he'd dropped. Before he was able to pull his hand out of the water the first worm's teeth bit sharply into the ball of his thumb. He staggered back, gasping with shock at the pain.

It didn't let go. It didn't even curl or wriggle. Those sharp teeth held him vice-like, tightening.

He tried his best to straighten up on that slippery, narrow ledge where he was perched but he was too tall. The buttress curved forward as it met the vaulted roof of the sewer and there wasn't enough room for him to stand upright. Around the foot of the buttress three deep streams of effluent met together, swirling and foaming. One false step and he'd be in it up to the knees. The other worms, four of them now, had already gathered there, waiting for him.

'*Ah!*' The cry escaped from him involuntarily as a fresh wave of pain shot through his right hand and arm.

He stared at his hand, disbelieving. The worm hung there, occasionally convulsing but for the most part motionless. It was forcing its teeth deeper and deeper into that pad of flesh, biting it in just the same way that he might attack a roast leg of chicken. *Eating it!* But what sort of animal devours living flesh? And from a human being?

For a few seconds he was paralysed, all will-power gone, until the rational part of his mind told him urgently he must fight back, do something to save himself, survive.

With his left hand he grasped the worm just below its head. He couldn't pull it away, that was too painful, so instead he squeezed it with all the force he could muster in order to get its jaws open. The worm gulped and undulated between his fingers, straining to free itself from their throttling pressure.

Then it tried a new tactic. Its eyes moved and sought his in a hard relentless challenge. He caught his breath and for a moment felt himself weakening; then he willed himself to look away and tightened his grip. In a last spasm of resistance the worm unexpectedly curled upwards and attempted to lash against him, uselessly. And suddenly it slackened. Its jaws relaxed and he prised them apart. The mouth was red with his blood; shreds of his flesh clung to the teeth.

The dead worm dangled limply from his fingers, its eyes now two stony, lifeless buttons. He became aware the others were watching, waiting, and he flung the corpse down to them contemptuously. In a flash they'd surrounded it, greedily tearing at it with their teeth, and diving down to grab any piece that dropped.

After the recent rains the effluent was as clear as pure drinking water and he could see every move. He stared at them, fascinated and horrified, for a brief moment forgetting his wounded hand. But his blood dripped down, and each time the worms whipped around to suck it into their mouths before it could dissolve. Then they looked up for more, expectantly.

His eyes misted; he felt himself swaying. 'Mustn't faint,' he told himself firmly. Aloud he suddenly shouted the words, '*I . . . must . . . not . . . faint!*'

His voice echoed and re-echoed through those long Victorian London sewers until it lost itself somewhere in the distance. He was alone down there on his buttress island surrounded by the deep channels of effluent. With one great stride he might have crossed back to the safety of the walk-way where his camera stood on its tripod, the lights on their stands, everything normal as it should be. But he couldn't do it. Something inside him screamed he'd never make it.

That's just what the worms wanted, what they were waiting for. . .

Everything was in a haze, unsubstantial, shifting. . . The

narrow ledge where he stood offered no firm foothold; it was covered with slime and he was afraid to move in case his feet slid from under him and. . .

That's how the accident had happened in the first place. He'd felt himself slipping, grasped at the brickwork of the buttress for support, and dropped the light meter. It had slithered across the ledge and into the water. Only had it a week, too; a birthday present from Helen. Must have cost her. . . Well, now he'd have to leave it there.

'Anyone around?' he called out.

Anyone around, around, ound, nd. . . the tunnels were alive with murmurs, whispers, mocking him . . . *ound, ound, nd. . .*

But there *had* to be somebody. . .

'Anyone?'

Matt knew it was his own stupid fault, the whole thing. Matt Parker, TV film cameraman, aged thirty-six and beginning to feel it in his bones. He should never have accepted this film in the first place. All his instincts had screamed out against it the moment he'd heard it involved spending a week in the sewers beneath the City of London. It was not even a feature film. No re-make of *The Third Man* or that sort of crap – he'd be so lucky! No, just another bread-and-butter TV documentary about urban growth through the centuries, starting with a section of Roman wall and ending eight tedious episodes later with shots of concrete jungle graffiti.

Low budget, of course. Educational.

But then, Matt thought bitterly, he was a low budget, bread-and-butter sort of cameraman. In spite of it all. As a kid, from the day he'd first come across the existence of films and cameras he'd thought of nothing else, done a gruelling paper round every day before school to save enough money for a secondhand 8mm. Kodak, and carried on with the papers afterwards to pay for film stock and everything else he needed. When eventually the opportunity came to join a TV company as a trainee assistant film cameraman he'd jumped at it.

Opportunity? He'd lived film every waking minute of the day, even dreamed about it at night, only to find others promoted ahead of him, picked out for the big drama productions while he was left with run-of-the-mill documentaries shown at off-peak hours. 'You're a first-rate cameraman,' they'd told him not all that long ago. 'Just the sort of person we need for some of our less experienced directors. Keep them on the right track. Stop them making fools of themselves. You know what you're doing. They don't.'

Well, cameramen can't be choosers, as he'd said to Helen when he'd told her about the sewers.

His own bloody fault.

And now he faced a slow, painful death. Or, if he survived, a vegetable existence, mutilated and unrecognizable. Perhaps even unable to walk, his arms and legs stripped of flesh, dehumanized.

'I need help!' he called out in desperation, hearing the fear in his own voice. 'Help!'

Help, help, elp, lp ... the tunnels replied. The vaulted Victorian brickwork looked like the set for some horror movie. His own lights dazzled his eyes, emphasizing the darkness beyond.

It would be another fifteen minutes or so before the crew came clattering back. 'Ready, Matt?' they'd call out. 'Can we go for a take?' Andy Page, the latest young director, hardly out of his university nappies, would rub his hands together and try to give the impression he was in charge. They'd joked about him that morning, he and the crew, while his back was turned. *From bright young directors and things that go bump in the sewers, Good Lord deliver us!* someone had intoned. Oh, if only they'd come back early. Or if only he'd said no.

Helen had put her foot down, told him not to, but he'd argued it was his job. Somebody had to do it. She'd looked unconvinced, worried.

'Why you?'

For Matt, working in cramped spaces was the ninth circle of hell. And it didn't get any better. Maybe it was his height – six feet two in his nylon socks and bearded with it. A short, tidy red beard, fastidious, Shakespearean. He spent hours in front of the mirror trimming it almost hair by hair. Freckles, too, across his nose and cheeks. What he hadn't told Helen was that he seldom used the lift these days, fearing he might betray the panic he experienced every time the doors slid shut. Didn't tell anybody, but walked up the five flights regularly.

And now the tunnels seemed to close in around him, alive with their own directionless murmurs, drips, shiftings and slitherings, sighs and whispers, somewhere beyond the lights in the velvet blackness.

They were hunting him, six of them now. Their mean little eyes were on him, waiting for the next drop of blood which had already soaked through his handkerchief and was collecting on his fingers. Any minute now ... the little bastards were well aware of it, he knew from the way they watched ... their heads above the water, swaying slightly, marking him as their prey. Two of them swam around, prowling backwards and forwards, patrolling... Were any others on their way? Had they sent signals?

He kept his hand up to try and reduce the flow of blood, using his buttoned jacket as a sling. The pain spread, throbbing and raw. Cramp seized the muscles of his arm.

He'd just finished lighting the next shot which was to start on the brick vaulting and pan across to reveal the anchorman – Charlie, as usual – going on about cholera in nineteenth-century London. If he could remember the words. Charlie was one of those TV presenters who can convince the world they are instant experts on everything, always providing someone else has written the script. This time he was going to have his work cut out trying to appear at ease with the dripping walls and the stench. But, no doubt, viewers would find it all very exotic as they watched in their cosy living rooms; they wouldn't be able to smell it, nor feel hemmed in by those narrow walls.

Then someone had suggested a break for coffee before the take. And a breath of fresh air.

'Great!' Matt had agreed. 'You go ahead, I'll follow. I'll just check this buttress.'

The director had wanted it in the foreground of the shot but it seemed to absorb all the light he could give it and offer nothing back. Matt was preoccupied with the challenge; for a moment his claustrophobia no longer worried him. He'd have to cross over to it and take a reading.

No problem, though. One stride, the full stretch of his long legs. . . A shorter man couldn't have done it.

So why couldn't he get back? He was afraid, yes, but. . . He must brace himself. Discipline himself. If only he weren't so tall he could stand upright, give himself a better balance. And if only the ledge weren't so slimy.

He glanced down. They were watching him. Maybe they could even read his mind.

'It's a matter of will-power,' he told himself angrily.

Will-power, power, ower, er. . .

He ignored the echoes coming at him from all directions and worked out what he had to do. Extend his leg carefully over the stream of effluent, then try to shift his weight, his centre of gravity, so that. . .

No.

Cowardice, was it? Or commonsense? Nothing was going to make him move from that ledge before help arrived. One small slip and his foot would be in the water. Their teeth would find his ankle. Or the calf of his leg, perhaps. With six of them attacking together it wouldn't take much to bring him down, force him to his knees, pull his face into the stinking water. Then they'd have a feast of vengeance for their dead comrade. They'd gnaw their way through the wall of his stomach, or into the heavy flesh at the top of his legs, up his colon, penetrating his intestines. . .

They'd keep him alive as long as possible, enjoying the flow of blood through his veins and capillaries, savouring it as a sauce to their meal.

Their cunning eyes observed him as they bided their time, knowing he hadn't the strength to last out. He shifted cautiously inch by inch until he was facing the buttress, his legs apart for a better grip, his arms around the brickwork, his head forced to rest sideways on his hunched shoulders by the low curvature of the arched roof. His hand still bled through the handkerchief; the blood gathered into a great blob which fell on to the slimy ledge where it rolled and slipped into the water, like a raindrop down a window pane.

The loss of blood was weakening him. He felt his knees beginning to sag. His right arm was practically useless. The walk-way was so close, almost within reach, yet he was convinced he'd never get there, not without a firm, dry jumping-off point. It was absurd, this situation.

Though he should try. He'd no alternative. The longer he left it. . .

He edged his way slowly around the buttress, looking down at the ledge, searching for a foothold. The worms moved around with him, determined not to lose sight of their prey. But quietly. Without fuss. As if they knew time was on their side.

Those eyes had thoughts behind them, he could swear. And a hypnotic attraction. Yet they'd nothing of the soft sympathy of a dog's eyes; nor the self-centredness of a cat's, full of character; they betrayed no personality at all, only an alertness.

His foot slipped.

It skidded across the sloping ledge, the edge of his shoe scoring the slime, and almost touched the surface of the water. There was an immediate commotion as all six worms swung around to reach him simultaneously. It was a miracle he managed to save himself that time. Cheated them.

'Get my breath back,' he muttered, his heart thumping away.

Yet in pulling himself back up he was forced to place too much weight on the other foot and that also began to slide. His arms had to hold him up, embracing the bricks, his fingers desperately digging into the gaps left by the crumbling mortar.

For a few seconds he thought he'd succeeded. And a few seconds were all that should have been necessary, for it couldn't be that long now before the rest of the film crew returned, surely it couldn't be long. . .

But the fingers of his mutilated hand had no strength in them. His feet searched wildly for a firm hold but his shoes wouldn't grip; their soles were coated with slime from the ledge. Slowly he felt the bricks of the buttress beginning to scrape against him as he slid towards the water. And he saw Helen's face, reproachful, *I asked you not to go*. . . Then their daughter Jenny looking up at him, smiling.

The effluent filled his shoes, covered his ankles, soaked through his trouser legs. He waited, resigned, for the sharp teeth. No point in struggling. Just let it happen, the self-surrender of every hunted prey. It would be over more quickly that way.

But they didn't bite. Why not? Where were they?

He was up to his knees, trying instinctively to get a footing, to stand straight, but without success. He slipped, and then pitched forward into the diluted effluent. The worms swam around him, investigating, nudging against him, then turning to try some other spot. Suddenly he understood why. They were puzzled by his clothing! They wanted naked flesh.

Their bewilderment gave him a quick surge of hope. He tried once again to scramble to his feet or pull himself up on to the walk-way. Too slow. Much too slow. A couple of the worms, attracted by the blood, started work on the fingers of his right hand. He screamed with pain and fright, thrashing about clumsily as he tried to shake them off, too panic-stricken to realize what he was doing.

A third worm brushed against his face. He recoiled. Its teeth cut into his cheek. He heard himself shrieking again and again.

'*No! Get off! No!*'

The tunnels took up his cry, bouncing it off their walls, amplifying it, throwing it back at him as yet another worm took the lobe of his ear and a fifth found the soft flesh beneath his chin.

Gasping, spluttering, his mouth filled with the effluent supplied by all the drains of London, his chest torn by razor-sharp pains as he breathed some of it in, he managed yet one more shout before consciousness left him.

It was not a high-pitched shriek this time but a deep bellow, like a bull in the agony of death. Then the world slipped away: Helen, Jenny, the dissolving tunnels, the pain... Release.

2

Aubrey Morgan felt decidedly pleased with himself as he stood in the men's washroom at Television Hall, humming tunelessly and running a comb through his thinning blond hair.

'Eaten by *what*?' he'd demanded, unable to believe his ears. 'Snakes?'

'That's what they looked like,' young Andy Page had told him, 'but someone here says they're worms. Giant worms.'

He'd phoned in from the foreman's office somewhere among the complex of London sewers, scarcely able to control the excitement in his voice when he described how he'd found the cameraman slumped unconscious in the sewage while the worms fed on him. Then, to Aubrey's surprise, he added simply: 'I filmed it.'

'You—?'

'I've got it in the can. I thought maybe News would be interested.'

News was. A smart cookie, that young director. Who else would have thought of filming the worms before jumping in to rescue the poor sod? It could be a scoop. Aubrey smiled contentedly at his own image in the mirror, a plump round face with baby cheeks and heavy brown horn-rimmed glasses which gave him that intellectual look. Young Andy Page was one of his own recruits. If the pictures were really good there'd be an outcry in the press, maybe even questions in the House of Commons... Excellent publicity – and Aubrey believed firmly that exciting television meant taking risks.

Which explained why he was Controller of Programmes at the age of thirty-three.

He was putting on weight, though. His midriff already betrayed what he whimsically called 'the bulge of success'. Have to keep an eye on that. Start jogging, perhaps. He smoothed down his chunky salt-and-pepper sweater and went towards the lift.

Mary Keating was waiting for him in the viewing room. She nodded as he entered, fumbled in her handbag for a cigarette and lit it nervously. Her untidy hair was streaked with grey, her face lined. She'd risen to the position of Managing Director via children's and family programmes in a career famous for the long hours she put in. According to rumour, the price she'd paid for this fanatical dedication was two broken marriages and an unknown number of desperately unhappy love affairs. Now she lived alone with only three demanding cats for company.

'Al's coming, is he?' she demanded impatiently. 'I've not all that much time.'

Al Wilson, Head of News, came into the viewing room as she spoke. 'Sorry I kept you waiting,' he apologized briefly. 'Things to see to. We'll be ready in a second.'

He must be getting on for fifty-five, Aubrey reckoned as they sat there, silent. Still showing no signs of grey. Apart from an early stint in Korea as a war correspondent he'd been a desk man most of his working life in one newsroom after another. Copy-taster, deputy news editor, and so on up. He was reputed to have worn the same shapeless blue suit all those years. Nobody'd ever seen him in anything else.

The loudspeaker crackled. 'Ready.'

Al pressed the talkback key and told the operator to go ahead. The lights dimmed immediately.

The first few seconds of the film were unsteady. The camera scanned the sewer walls, seeking out its subject; then it settled on the prone cameraman, zooming in on his face. Two fat worms – is that what they were? – guzzled at his cheek. Aubrey could think of no other word for it.

From Mary came an exclamation of disgust. The colour pictures were vivid and gruesome. Enough to trigger off a national panic, Aubrey thought. He recognized the victim as someone he'd worked with often enough in his own early days as a director.

When the lights went up again they all sat in shocked

silence, none of them wishing to speak first. Mary Keating looked pale.

'I ... I think Andy Page showed great presence of mind,' Aubrey ventured cautiously, testing the water. 'He was the first on the scene. Everything was set up – lights, camera... He saw the opportunity and grabbed it.'

'Anyone else might've helped the poor man,' Mary said sharply.

'The rest of the crew were only a few seconds behind,' Aubrey defended him. Then, thinking he'd gone too far, he took off his glasses and began to polish them on a clean hand-kerchief. 'Not a very human reaction,' he admitted. 'But professional.'

'We can't use those pictures.' Her tone was final.

'We can't *not* use them,' Al intervened briskly, jealous of any encroachment on his own territory. 'We'll hold the film back for the later bulletins, but the public has a right to—'

'Al, would you like *your* children to see pictures like that?' she insisted.

'Kids should be in bed at that hour,' Al argued. 'After all, we showed people burning to death in Vietnam, executions in Nigeria, God knows what else... What's so different about these worms, except they're nearer home?'

Mary shuddered and drew on her cigarette. 'Why do we call them worms? They're more like snakes.'

'Aren't they snakes?' Aubrey asked.

'Seems not.' Al scratched the side of his jaw which as always at that time of day was covered with dark stubble. 'We've done some research.'

He'd a folder of press cuttings in his hand and began a brief summary of what was known. The worms had first appeared in the sewers just over a year earlier, though no newspaper had given them much space.

'To tell the truth,' Al commented drily, 'it was the same month as the royal wedding and most papers couldn't find space for them. It'll be a bit different after tonight.'

Aubrey glanced through the cuttings. 'But these are much

smaller,' he objected. 'A few inches long, according to this paper. They're not the same.'

'I rang the sewer foreman. He insisted they are the same. They grow, just as we do. He's known them several sizes. Says they keep the rats down.'

'That's all very interesting,' Mary broke in testily, 'but we can't transmit those pictures into people's homes. And imagine his wife seeing them. He was married?'

'Is,' Al corrected her. 'She's with him now.'

'I understood he'd died.'

'No, I called the hospital. They're not too optimistic, though. He's in a bad way.'

'Al, I don't wish to interfere in your department. You've a lifetime of experience behind you. But think of what it'll do to people.'

'I'm not going to withhold hard news.'

'Just the pictures.'

'I'm sorry, no.'

Aubrey watched, fascinated, as Al's face flushed red with annoyance, then turned white, the veins bulging out on his forehead. A few seconds later the sharp lines softened once more as he regained his self-control.

'Mary, what if it happens again?' He spoke gently, almost affectionately. 'This is the first record of worms attacking human beings. It might not be the last.'

'You're making unjustified assumptions.'

'I'm making a news judgment. This is an important story. How many of those things are living down there? How widespread are they? What if they come into the open and attack our children? If we show the film there'll be a public outcry and something may be done. On the other hand, you know as well as I do if we don't show it. . .' He shrugged.

Mary thought about it. 'I know I shan't watch,' she said at last, surrendering. 'And I doubt if I'll sleep tonight.'

Helen Parker looked at the bandage-swathed figure in the hospital bed, still unable to grasp what had happened. Or even feel certain this was really her husband; it could be anybody.

The face was almost totally covered. Only the nostrils, the tip of the nose and the closed eyelids remained free.

She hated herself for feeling so neutral, so unmoved. 'Matt?' she said, leaning over him.

No movement. He was lifeless, swaddled in those bandages like an Egyptian mummy in some creepy film.

'He's lost a lot of blood,' the white-coated doctor told her, an Indian with bright intelligent eyes which his glasses magnified slightly.

'Is he going to live?'

For a moment the doctor didn't answer; then he said: 'There's a good chance.'

'And an equally good chance he won't?'

She straightened up, brushing back the short blond hair from her cheeks. How could she be so calm, she wondered.

They'd telephoned her at work – must've got the number from the agency – to tell her Matt had been attacked by worms. Down a sewer somewhere. It'd sounded so ludicrous, she'd laughed aloud. 'You're joking,' she'd said, thinking Matt had put them up to it. She'd questioned the man at the other end closely for some minutes before allowing herself to be convinced.

The office manager had been reluctant to let her go. 'This really is inconvenient,' he'd fussed. He was a sharp-featured little man with dandruff on the stooped shoulders of his cheap suit. 'I particularly asked the agency to send someone reliable. This typing is most urgent.'

'My husband's been rushed to hospital,' she repeated.

'That's why you laughed?' He made no attempt to hide the fact he didn't believe her. 'I heard you laugh. The whole office heard you.'

'I . . . he . . .' She couldn't very well tell him Matt had been attacked by worms. 'Oh, for Chrissake!' she'd exploded in fury. 'I've no time to talk – he's lying there unconscious. Phone the agency to send someone else. I'm off.'

'Temps!' he'd almost screamed as she pushed past him. 'You can't trust any of them. Fly-by-nights, every single one. Well, don't think I'm going to pay for today, because I'm not. There'll be no money for—'

She'd slammed the door on her way out, cutting short his hysterical abuse. The frosted glass had rattled in its frame. In the street she'd grabbed the first taxi. Then, at the hospital they'd let her wait for two hours before bringing her into this private room in the surgical wing.

Yet in spite of the row in the office she now felt nothing but calm ... not resignation, no, that wasn't true. But indifference almost. They'd grown apart, she and Matt. Even left the house in the morning these days without a kiss, the once-obligatory peck...

And in bed? It was weeks since he'd last reached out for her; and then, as so often, she'd muttered something about wanting to get to sleep. He'd turned his back without another word.

But she still loved him, she tried to reassure herself as she looked down at him lying long and straight in that hospital bed; it was too short, as always. Of course she still loved him. Only she couldn't identify *her* Matt with that prone figure plugged into the various machines which registered he was still alive. The only evidence that he was still breathing.

The drip-feed bottle above the bed hiccoughed.

'You should be going home, Mrs Parker,' the Indian doctor was saying. 'Try to get some rest. If there's any change, we'll ring you, I promise.'

'Yes ... thank you...'

Yet she hesitated. Jenny would be waiting, of course, collected from school by one of the neighbours. She'd want to know why her Daddy was in hospital, what was wrong with him. What could she tell her? An accident?

'Doctor, is—?' She stopped short, then rephrased her question brutally. 'How much did they eat?'

The surprise showed on his face; his voice became professionally understanding. 'You could of course spend the night here if you wished. I'm sure Sister would find you a bed and something to help you sleep.'

'How much?'

He seemed for a moment uncertain what to tell her. 'The main injuries are around his face and neck. One of his ears. His hands. Wrists. He's going to need more surgery.'

'And his fingers?' She'd noticed the unusual shape of the bandaging.

'He's lost a couple.'

'But he won't be maimed? I mean, badly? He's not going to spend the rest of his life in a wheelchair or—?'

'We've no reason to think anything like that. If he can get over this initial twenty-four hours—'

'Why's he still unconscious?'

'Loss of blood. Shock.'

'He did lose a lot, didn't he? You mean there could be brain damage? Please let me know the truth.'

'The truth is we're hoping to save him, Mrs Parker. Some of your questions are just unanswerable at the present time.' He took her arm gently. 'Now if you'd like me to have a word with Sister?'

'I hardly recognize him,' she said wonderingly. 'He could be anyone.' Once more she leaned over him. 'Matt? I'm going now, Matt, to see Jenny.' She looked up, suddenly embarrassed. 'It's all right, Doctor, I know he can't hear me but. . .'

'Mrs Parker, that might be just what he needs, the sound of your voice,' the Indian doctor smiled. 'Drugs and surgery can't do everything.'

3

Much to Aubrey Morgan's satisfaction the news of the attack on Matt Parker demonstrated once again the immense impact of television. Words alone would never have triggered off the near panic which seized Fleet Street, but colour pictures of those hungry worms feeding off living human flesh caused the editor of every mass-circulation newspaper to scrap his pre-planned front page and lead with the Matt Parker story.

Aubrey spread out the papers on his desk and gloated over the headlines. GIANT WORMS FEED ON MAN was the most sober; A DIET OF WORMS was the most tasteless. One paper made the whole story sound like a gimmick with NOW IT'S MAN-EATING WORMS! But his favourite read MAMMOTH WORMS EAT TV MAN IN SEWER – GRUESOME NEWSREEL SHOCKS NATION.

They all carried pictures, black-and-white off-prints prepared the night before in anticipation of the flurry of phone-calls from Fleet Street after the first screening at ten o'clock. Even the *Financial Times* carried the story, expressing concern at the hidden dangers beneath the City, the financial centre of the world.

It was a possible angle, he mused. Of course, everything depended on how widespread the worms were. That was one of the questions he'd have to put to the tame professor he was expecting, but ever since the first transmission there'd been an endless stream of calls, many of them protests – Mary handled those – but quite a few from people who claimed similar experiences.

Birmingham, Liverpool, Plymouth, Worcester, Bath... He flicked through the typed list.

A man from Isleworth complained his dog's nose had been nipped in the River Crane.

A woman teacher might have seen them in the mud of the Avon Gorge beneath Clifton suspension bridge.

A girl student reported she'd been bitten on her left breast while bathing nude in the Cam at Grantchester and was willing to show viewers the scar if the fee was right.

Yet all of these had been small worms, none longer than about four inches. Only one man asserted he'd stumbled across really big ones. *Giant buggers like the bloody Loch Ness monster*, the girl taking the calls had typed primly. She'd added a note of her own: *Speech slurred; probably sees pink elephants too.*

The blue phone rang and Aubrey extracted it from beneath the papers. 'Yes?'

'Andy Page on the line.' His secretary's cool voice.

'Put him on... Andy? Good, now listen. I had a word with – Rodney, isn't it, in charge of your series?'

'Townscape, yes.'

'That's the title? Mm. Look, I'm arranging for someone else to take over from you.' A moment's silence at the other end. 'Hello?'

'I'm sorry ... yes...' The boy was embarrassed.

'Thought we'd been cut off. So I want you to drop what you're doing and get here right away.'

'It's the union, is it?' He sounded worried and apologetic. 'I was warned there'd be trouble.'

'I don't follow you.'

'About me operating the camera.'

Aubrey became impatient. 'I haven't the faintest idea what you're talking about. We're planning a special documentary about these worms. Investigation in depth, implications, all that jazz. If you don't think you can handle it...'

'And drop Townscape?'

'Do I have to spell it out? We've got the whole population shit-scared about worms. They're talking nothing else in the pubs, the buses, the launderettes. Every leading newspaper carries the story. Worms that eat living human beings – and you're the man who filmed them! Well, congratulations, but don't let it go to your head. This is a tough assignment and you'll find plenty of people against you. Peak-hour viewing,

Saturday night if we can get it.'

'Who do I work to?'

'Me. Directly to me. Now your replacement for that educational crap ... er...' He found the name scribbled on his pad. 'Jacqui Turner. She's already on her way out to you, so grab a taxi and get here. Like now.'

He slammed the phone down. Bet that put the fear of God into him, he thought. Right, young Andy Page, let's see how you shape up on this one. A tricky assignment, so he'd keep the reins in his own hands. Present the programme, too. Since he'd been promoted Controller of Programmes he'd been too much out of the public eye. High time he made a comeback on the small screen. *Written, produced and presented by Aubrey Morgan...*

Carole came into the office; neat, calm, not a hair out of place. The most elegant secretary in the building, and she knew it. 'We've found that map you asked for.'

It showed the whole of England and Wales, stopping short just north of the Scottish border. She fixed it to the display board and began sticking in coloured pins to indicate worm sightings, red for full size, blue for their smaller cousins. He'd need a chart of dates as well; an animation sequence perhaps...

Aubrey's face broke into a smile of satisfaction as he saw the programme taking shape; it'd be the biggest thing since his famous documentary on child prostitution. No problem about audience ratings that week.

'We're in business, Carole my darling, we're in business again!' He slipped his arm around her as she stepped back from the board. 'Mmm, you *are* gorgeous this morning!' As she turned he kissed her full on the lips.

'I need more coloured pins,' she said, matter-of-fact.

He let her go. She never responded, was never even ruffled. It was water off a duck's back. In fact, kissing a duck might have been more interesting. Tall, slim, self-contained Carole. Daddy was a major-general; she'd once been photographed for *Tatler*; breeding oozed from every pore, assuming that she possessed such vulgar apertures.

The phone rang and she answered it, 'Mr Morgan's office.' With that voice she ought to be working for a dentist. 'I'll tell him.' She put the receiver down and said the herpetologist had arrived.

'Yes?'

'Your professor,' she added by way of explanation. Plus a superior smile.

Professor Jones had been taken to Presentation Suite A where one of the make-up girls was busy spraying lacquer on his mop of unruly hair. 'I wish you wouldn't put that stuff on me,' he was protesting when Aubrey got there. 'I'll only have to wash it out again.'

The girl, an Irish red-head, smiled at him, puckering her lips. He stared back at her as though at one of his dissected lizards. He wore brown corduroy trousers and a fawn sports jacket with leather patches on the elbows. His hands were surprisingly small for a man of his height.

Aubrey introduced himself and said he'd be conducting the interview.

'I don't know what I can tell you,' the Professor replied apologetically. 'I was sent the remains of one worm, rather the worse for wear. Admittedly it bore a superficial resemblance to the worms we investigated last year, but it was three times the size.'

'The sewer foreman is convinced they're the same, and he's probably seen more than most people.'

'Nevertheless, he is a layman.'

The Professor stood up and followed Aubrey into the studio without even bothering to nod his thanks to the red-headed make-up girl. Behind his back Aubrey winked at her; she pulled a face in return.

'Sorry I was a little late,' the Professor was going on. 'I'd a few urgent matters to deal with before I came out. I'm afraid I can't give you much of my time.'

The floor manager led them to two low chairs arranged on either side of a cheap coffee table. The Professor sat down uncomfortably, shifting about to find the best position for his long legs, then deciding there wasn't one.

'Stand by!' the floor manager called.

On cue, Aubrey began his usual smooth introduction, explaining that Professor Jones was a herpetologist of international standing who'd made a special study of sewer worms when they'd first appeared only twelve months ago.

'But why,' he asked, 'are they called worms at all when they look like snakes?'

'Oh, not to the trained eye!' The Professor picked up one of the stills they'd prepared. 'If you examine this picture you'll see they have eyelids, which snakes do not. Also – here – an eardrum, clearly visible. No doubt about it, these are lizards – limbless lizards, like the slow worm or blind worm. In fact' – he warmed to his theme – 'we know many different kinds of lizard, some with four legs, functional legs, some whose legs are reduced and practically non-existent, as well as these which are completely limbless. I could mention the *Anops kingii* of South America and other amphisbaenids such as the *Leposternum microcephalum*, and in Britain the familiar *Anguis* which everyone knows.'

'The ang—?'

'Slow worm,' the Professor repeated testily.

'Do any of them eat flesh?'

'Several reptiles are carnivorous.' He seemed surprised at the question. 'The most well-known perhaps are crocodiles, alligators, pythons. . .'

Aubrey let him go on without interruption, at the same time making mental notes of where to edit the interview. At last he managed to slip in a question about the worms which had attacked Matt Parker. Had anything like them been seen before?

'My department did a brief study last year at the request of the Ministry of Agriculture on quite small worms of a very similar appearance. . .'

'Could they have grown?'

'That's certainly possible. The ones we examined last year might not have been full-size, though at the time everyone assumed they were. I'm not prepared to state categorically they were essentially the same as the worms which almost killed your cameraman, though superficially they look alike.'

'So in your opinion we might be faced with the menace of two different species of carnivorous worms rather than just one?' Aubrey pressed him.

'I said nothing of the sort. That's just the kind of cheap sensationalism I don't want to be associated with. That word "menace" – there are many creatures in the animal kingdom far more dangerous than the worms, big or small. These are. . .' He paused, flushed with annoyance. 'They're no more of a menace than ferrets.'

'But you think there are two species?'

'At present I've insufficient evidence to come to any conclusion.'

'Why are we suddenly seeing them now? They're not in any of the textbooks. Up to a year or so ago no one even knew of their existence. Have they only just evolved?'

'Evolution doesn't work that way.' The Professor smiled condescendingly. 'It takes millions of years. We know of over six thousand different species of reptile living today, and only in 1979 a colony of giant worms up to ten feet long was discovered in the Pacific and—'

'Worms like ours?' Aubrey interrupted him, excitedly.

'Of course not.' He looked mildly surprised. 'Thought I'd made that clear. But very, very interesting all the same. You see—'

'I'm sorry, could we stick to our sewer worms? It's been suggested no one ever saw them before because they lived at the bottom of the North Sea or the Bristol Channel, and that, now they've been disturbed by the oil drilling, they've moved inland.'

'Impossible. They couldn't live so deep under water. They breathe air, same as we do – though what with the carbon monoxide and lead we pour out from our car exhausts, we're much more dangerous to them than they are to us. If you television people really want to stir up a scandal, do a programme on how we pollute the air we breathe.'

Aubrey nodded. 'But it doesn't do to underplay this,' he argued. 'A man's in hospital.'

'One unlucky man. That hardly constitutes a national crisis.'

No worse than ferrets, mused Aubrey as he accompanied the Professor down in the lift. We can cut directly from that statement to shots of the worms devouring Matt Parker's face. Guzzling like pigs at a trough. A good strong contrast to make the viewers sit up in their armchairs.

'We'll be using a minute or so of that interview in the News later today,' he explained as they reached the ground floor. 'But the full version will go into the documentary we're preparing.'

'One interesting thing about these sewer worms,' the Professor said before they parted, 'is reproduction. Frankly, we just don't know. The blind worm is viviparous – gives birth to live young, doesn't lay eggs as most reptiles do. But so far we've not managed to find a female sewer worm. They've all been males. If you collect any during your investigations, do give me a ring.'

'Of course,' Aubrey promised. This gave him a new angle. What do sewer worms do about sex? 'Maybe we could come and film the dissection?'

'That might be possible.'

He waited until his guest was through the revolving door before returning to the lifts. Mary Keating had sent a message to the Presentation Suite that she'd like a word, and this was as good a time as any to discuss the documentary with her. He'd need her agreement before he could really go ahead, and she could easily object. 'No worse than ferrets,' he repeated to himself as he strode around the curving corridor towards her office: that was the clinching argument.

'Well, I warned you!' she announced grimly the moment he opened the door. She was looking at him over the top of her reading glasses. An untidy mess of letters and telegrams was spread out before her over her large executive desk. 'I've just had the Chairman of the Independent Broadcasting Authority on the phone.'

'Complaints?'

He chose the most comfortable armchair and settled himself in it. From the look on her face it was going to be one of those long sessions. Her midget, balding teddy bear stared back at him from its usual place next to the intercom. Near it was an unopened package from Fortnum and Mason tied with ornate ribbon.

'An unholy row, and coming right from the top,' she was saying. 'Protests from the Viewers' Assocation, the Protection of Children Group, two bishops . . . oh, and look at these!' She held them up.

'Letters? Already?'

'Delivered by hand. I shudder to think what the post will bring. Three Tory MPs and two Labour all say they're tabling questions in the House of Commons.' She glanced down at one of the letters. 'No, I'm wrong. The Labour lady intends to demand an emergency debate.'

'At least they're taking the threat seriously.'

'The threat? Oh, from the worms? No, it's the propriety of showing it on TV they're arguing about. Bringing violence into the home.' She began to shuffle the papers together.

Aubrey watched her for a second. 'At least one person sent you something nice.' He indicated the Fortnum and Mason package. 'Chocolates?'

'I imagine so.' She looked slightly surprised at his abrupt change of topic.

'Your birthday?'

'No, they just came addressed to me. When I produced Tiny Toddlers I used to get lots of little presents. Aubrey, we've a meeting with the union this afternoon at three. They're demanding full compensation for Matt Parker.'

'But the Company's hardly responsible for—'

She cut him short. 'And they want Andy Page's head. For handling the camera.'

'Oh my God!' He took off his horn-rimmed glasses and began to polish them vigorously on his handkerchief. 'Trouble. I was going to use him on—'

'Don't touch him!' she snapped. 'Leave him where he is, at least till we see which way things are pointing. Compensation for Parker could amount to thousands, perhaps hundreds of thousands, we just don't know yet.'

'He was insured.'

'The insurance company will dispute it. They'll want to know what he was doing there by himself when the rest of the crew had gone off. But whatever they say, we need to work out a strategy for this afternoon's meeting. If necessary, we'll have to let the union have their blood sacrifice.'

'Andy Page? Well, he asked for it.'

She reached out for the Fortnum and Mason package and started to undo the ribbon. 'I've invited Al Wilson, Jimmy Case, Veronica and Max—' Her scream shocked through him.

'Mary, what—?' For a moment he sat paralyzed, then he jumped up from his armchair and dashed around to her side of the desk.

She screamed again. A long, sobbing, terrified scream.

Several small worms, about four or five inches in length, were spilling out of the Fortnum and Mason package which lay on its side on the pink blotter. They wriggled over the desk towards her. One of them was already attached, leech-like, to the heavy white flesh of her forearm. She stared at it, screaming, making no attempt to pull it off, but just screaming.

Aubrey caught hold of her high leather chair and tried to tug it clear of the desk. Before he could shift it a second worm launched itself at her from the blotter. If only she hadn't been wearing that short-sleeved dress... The worm dropped on to the heaving bodice and started to squirm purposefully towards the low V-neck.

Again she screamed, shuddering with horror, but not defending herself at all.

Her secretary ran into the room, a thin wispy woman in her late thirties, prematurely grey. She stood there goggling at Mary, at the worms, and whispering, 'No! Oh, no . . . no. . .'

'Come and help, for Chrissake!' Aubrey bawled at her, but she stayed rooted to the spot.

By now he'd managed to pull the chair back from the desk but gradually Mary slipped down from her seat till she was collapsing to her knees on the thick carpet, paralyzed with hysteria. He caught her under one arm, trying to hold her up, but she was too heavy for him.

'For Chrissake, help me!' he yelled again at the secretary. 'No . . . no. . .' She was backing towards the door. 'No. . .'

He shoved the heavy chair to one side and dragged Mary across the room as far away from the desk as possible. At least half-a-dozen worms writhed over it, making for the edge.

Over towards the window he lowered her gently to the

carpet where she lay with her dress riding high above her knees and her bare arms spread out defencelessly. The thick flesh of her forearm was puckered and red where the worm was still feeding on it. A thin stream of blood moved rapidly down her skin.

He caught the worm just below the head, holding it between his fingers and thumb and squeezing hard. Something snapped, and it went limp. He was surprised at how easily it'd died. For a few seconds he stared at its lifeless body lying in the palm of his hand; then, feeling sick, he flung it away from him and turned back to Mary. Blood from her arm was staining the carpet, but she was unconscious.

More people were rushing into the room now, demanding to know what was happening. He shouted a warning to them as he searched for the second worm. It had reached the V-neck and was already burrowing into the soft flesh between her breasts. As it gorged itself, its tail still protruded, swaying slightly as if with pleasure.

Aubrey hesitated, uncertain. Then someone brushed him aside – Veronica Dale from Personnel – and hooked her fingers into the top of Mary's dress and ripped it open. They had to cut the strap of her bra and hold her breasts apart before Aubrey could get a grip on the worm's neck. When he pulled it away it left a raw, bleeding patch the size of an old penny; the exposed bone of her rib-cage was clearly visible through the blood.

The little worm wriggled between his fingers as he stood up. It was a greenish colour, in every way a miniature version of the worms on the newsreel of Matt Parker. Holding it over the metal waste-paper bin, he gradually crushed the life out of it.

'How many are there, for Pete's sake?' someone was shouting. 'How many are there?'

'What's the panic?' he grinned; suddenly Aubrey was enjoying himself. 'They're easy enough to kill. That one over there – stamp on it!' He snatched another from the desk top, squashed it between finger and thumb, and dropped it contemptuously into the waste bin. 'Don't let them bite you first, though! One of you ring for an ambulance.'

No more of a menace than ferrets! The Professor had been right. As if to prove it to himself, Aubrey watched one of the worms slithering across the carpet towards Mary, making straight for the flabby white breast which hung out of her torn dress.

Before it could strike the ground he ground it to death under his shoe. As a boy he'd killed caterpillars the same way.

4

'No more of a menace than ferrets,' Matt repeated bitterly to himself as he stood stripped to the waist in front of the washbasin. Three months he'd been in hospital while they'd tried to rebuild his face. Several operations . . . skin grafts. His buttocks still felt sore whenever he sat down; he'd never understand why they'd had to take it from that part of his body.

'Nobody'll know one end of me from t'other,' he'd joked with the nurses, trying to hide his resentment. And failing.

What if his face turned out to be horrific when they removed the bandages, a mass of pink scar-tissue like Frankenstein's monster, not resembling a face at all? It was a recurring nightmare. He imagined himself released from hospital and making his way home alone through hostile streets, on foot, arriving at last, the street, the house, putting the key in the lock, opening the front door, only to find no one recognized him, not even his own daughter . . . she screamed when she saw him, covered her eyes.

That was the real reason he'd insisted on Helen and Jenny being there that afternoon when they cut the bandages off. Helen had refused at first, saying it wasn't fair on Jenny; she was only nine after all and. . .

He'd had to plead with her, but he understood well enough. She was as scared as he was.

He stared at himself in the mirror above the washbasin, wondering. Only a few more hours. Would his beard grow, or would he remain permanently scarred and smooth-cheeked? At least his voice was now almost normal again, or so the speech therapist had told him.

The whiteness of the bandages made his eyes seem darker and more penetrating, like the hypnotic gaze of the sewer worms. Or had it been merely his fear that had made them seem that way? While filming in Kenya he'd observed the same disabling fear in the eyes of wildebeeste attacked by lions.

Yet he could swear these worms had some ruthless power. Those last moments before losing consciousness his mind had keyed into theirs and. . .

Fuck! What the hell did it matter now? He dried himself on the rough towel and went back to his bed. He'd a file of press clippings collected by Helen, and he turned them over again for the thousandth time. Two or three days' hysteria, and then the topic was elbowed off the front pages by revelations of a politician's homosexual love life. Anything to boost the circulation figures.

As for TV, someone had planned a documentary special on the worms, but that was dropped after the woman managing director had received a gift of half-a-dozen of the smaller variety sent to her in a fancy chocolate box. In its place they'd screened a full-length interview with Professor Cledwyn Jones, the well-known herpetologist. According to one clipping – Matt'd been too ill to watch TV himself that evening – he'd assured the populace that 'they're no more dangerous than ferrets.'

But then, Matt excused him, the Professor had never encountered any alive. That was the point. Otherwise he'd have known they were vicious, ruthless, and regarded human beings solely as convenience food.

There was nothing like being eaten alive to concentrate the mind.

It didn't do to talk about it too much, though. Once, when Matt was trying to get his thoughts straight, he'd risked confiding in a fellow patient. For the next few days he'd been aware of amused, pitying glances in his direction, till the hospital psychiatrist had called him in for a chat. Since then he'd kept quiet about them.

Helen and Jenny arrived early, as he'd hoped they would. The longer they spent talking together before the bandages were removed the better. It was desperately important to him that Jenny should be sure the man behind the strange new face was the same person she'd known all her life. He noticed she wasn't in jeans today but had allowed her mother to talk her into wearing a neat summer dress. Dolled up for the great occasion!

'New?' he asked.

'Yeah.' She shook the long, blonde hair back from her shoulders. 'Daddy, what are you going to look like when they take the bandages off?'

'Much the same as before, with any luck.'

'I can't really remember before,' she commented. With her forefinger she was tracing the veins over the back of his hand. 'Does it hurt not having those two fingers?'

'No, not any more.'

Helen pulled her hand away. 'Of course you can remember what Daddy looks like,' she scolded nervously. 'She's just saying that, Matt. Your picture's on my bedside table.'

'I think I've forgotten myself,' Matt joked, trying to ease the tension. 'Jenny, what have you been up to since I saw you last? Haven't your holidays started yet?'

'Ages ago, and I've been playing out with Sandra and Barney and...'

As Jenny chattered on, Matt looked across at Helen. She'd had her hair done, he noted; still bright blonde, but the darkness at the roots had gone. It was much shorter, hardly reaching the lobes of her ears, and fluffed out elaborately like a wig. Must've cost her a bomb, though he couldn't say he cared for it much. If the doctors were satisfied when they removed the bandages, they'd be discharging him soon. A matter of days now. Going home, trying to live together...

For a second her eyes rested on his and he knew she feared it as much as he did.

'And then we went swimming,' Jenny was going on happily, 'all of us together—'

'Swimming?' His voice was sharp. Anxious. 'Not in the river?'

'No, in the baths!' Jenny defended herself hotly. 'I never said the river, Mummy, did I?'

'She's a very good swimmer,' Helen snapped. 'If you'd spent more time with her last summer, you'd know that.'

'I'm sorry,' he apologized, relieved. 'Sorry, Jenny. Going to the baths is fine, but not in the river. Not even paddling in a stream. Just keep away from those places.'

'Why?'

The nurse came to fetch him before he could answer.

But, hell, he had to warn them somehow. All over the country schools were beginning their holidays. Kids would be playing by streams, ditches, sewage outlets on the beaches. . . The worms could be in any one of them, lying in wait. He'd no hard evidence, of course. Only that gut feeling which had stayed with him since their minds had gen-locked into his just as their teeth had bitten into his flesh. The psychiatrist had tried to convince him it was a symptom of shock; sooner or later, with any luck, he might overcome it.

No, this was no hallucination. This was real.

'Well, Mr Parker, how are you feeling?' The surgeon shook his hand and patted him reassuringly on the shoulder. He was a youngish, athletic-looking man who was beginning to put on too much weight. The best specialist for this kind of operation in the whole of Europe, someone had told him. Rumour had it New York had offered him ten times his British income plus all the facilities he needed but he'd turned them down. 'And this is Mrs Parker, is it?'

Matt introduced Helen and Jenny. He began to explain once again why he'd like them to be present. The surgeon held up his hand to stop him.

'Of course you'd like your family near you,' he agreed. 'Now, nurse. . .'

They placed him with his back to Helen and Jenny while the nurse clipped through the bandages. Carefully she lifted the dressing away. Matt kept his eyes on the surgeon's white coat, bulging over his stomach.

'Mm, yes . . . yes. Now, Mr Parker, would you like to see yourself in a looking-glass, or would you prefer to turn round to face your wife and daughter first? It's just as you wish. Feel free. Take your time.'

The surgeon's expression betrayed nothing. Matt took a breath, then slowly turned to look at Helen.

For a few moments she said nothing. Then, unhappily: 'Oh, Matt!'

'I think it makes you look . . . *special*!' Jenny announced brightly. 'Like a soldier back from a war. You should have a V.C.!'

Unexpectedly, Helen took a couple of quick steps towards him, hugged him tight, then kissed his new face. 'We'll have to get used to it, won't we?'

Matt took the looking-glass the nurse was holding out to him. His mouth was slightly lopsided, but it'd been that way while he still wore the bandages so he was already accustomed to it. His face itself was longer and gaunter than he remembered it; one cheek was pinker than the other, as though made of different material, and puckered. There were more scars on his neck and throat.

Yet it was all natural flesh and blood, he thought. Flesh which the sewer worms would devour only too eagerly, given half a chance.

'You have to realize, Mr Parker,' the surgeon was saying, 'the whole of your cheek on that side had been practically eaten away. We've had to build it up from nothing.'

'You've done a good job,' Matt said dully. 'And I never was much of a beauty.'

'Later on we could try some more cosmetic surgery. . . Er, nurse, I wonder if you could rustle up some cups of tea?'

The nurse smiled and left them. Jenny took hold of his hand, pressing herself against him affectionately. 'It's a funny face but I think I like it,' she decided. 'My teacher said we must be grateful you're still alive. Daddy, where did the worms come from?'

It distressed Matt when he left hospital to find most people had come to accept the worms as just one more natural hazard in the same class as jellyfish, wasps, hornets, scorpions or sharks – nasty to have around, but unlikely to affect them personally. He tried to convince anyone who'd listen that they were more calculating and deliberate in their attacks on human beings, but very few seemed to understand.

Until, that is, they realized who he was. Then they switched on expressions of sympathy he could well have done without. 'Try to forget,' was the most general advice. But how could he when every glance in a mirror brought back the memory?

'I'm worried about you, honestly,' Helen confessed as she snuggled up to him in bed on his fourth night home. 'You think about nothing else. They've become an obsession. Oh, I'm not blaming you but I'm worried.'

Even down at Television Hall, when he dropped in to remind them of his existence, he found them preoccupied with other things. When he mentioned worms their eyes glazed over. They just didn't want to know. They talked about a major drama series for the autumn, preliminary plans for the Christmas variety shows, anything to get away from the topic.

Bluff, heavyweight Jimmy Case, the film operations manager, spared five minutes to shake his hand heartily and say how glad he was Matt was out of hospital at last.

'No need to rush back to work, Matt. Have a holiday while the weather holds.' His teeth were nicotine-stained and his beer-flush redder than ever. 'Seaside or somewhere.'

Matt felt unexpectedly reassured to see him again. 'We've a cottage down at Westport,' he said, 'and I think Helen's planning for us to go down there.'

'Well, take it easy. There'll be plenty of work lined up for you when you get back.'

'We should be doing something on sewer worms,' Matt informed him. 'A documentary. I don't know if anything's planned, but I'd like to be involved if there is.'

Jimmy reached out for a cigarette from the open packet on his desk; the gesture was automatic and he didn't even have to look down. 'I'm glad you told me,' he commented at last, blowing the smoke out in a long stream. 'If you're really sure – though if I were in your shoes I'd stay clear of them. There's nothing on the cards, though, not that I know of. You could try one of the education producers.'

'Andy Page?' Matt demanded sarcastically.

'Oh, they suspended him after your little do. Talk about callous? There were you in trouble, practically dead, and all he could think of was filming it. He's in Australia now, they say. Good riddance. Then of course we had that little episode when some joker sent Mary Keating some worms in a box – you heard about that? Aubrey Morgan's been doing her job while she's been away. I'm told she's taking early retirement. Oh, it's all been happening, Matt, all been happening. Never a dull moment.' He stood up and moved to the door as if to make it quite plain the interview was over. 'Anyway, it's great to see you on your feet again. Don't forget that holiday, eh? We'll need you on top form when you come back.'

It was hopeless trying to interest anybody, Matt decided once he was outside in the corridor again. Maybe the hospital psychiatrist was right. And everybody else. Maybe he was still suffering from shock and should try his best to forget them. He stood in front of one of the notice boards, pretending to read the pieces of paper while he wondered about it.

Only one way to find out, he thought.

5

The sewer foreman was a short, dark-haired man of about fifty with a deeply-lined angular face which warned all comers he could be a tough bastard when the mood took him. He recognized Matt the moment he stepped into the office.

'You're . . . ay, that poor bloody cameraman! So you're out of hospital then? That's fine! It's great to see you!' He shook Matt's hand warmly like a long-lost friend, then stepped back to look at him. 'They didn't improve your appearance any, but at least you're in one piece, that's something. I'll never forget when they carried you out on that stretcher. I've seen men wi' their faces blown off, their guts hangin' out, but nothing shocked me like the sight o' you after the worms'd been at you.'

'It's about the worms I've come to ask you,' Matt said.

'Ay, but you know, I can't remember your name! You'll have to remind me. Ay, that day, I've dreamed of it often, but I never think o' you by name. *That poor bloody sod*, that's how I think o' you. But now . . . Max, is it? Matt?'

'Matt Parker.'

'We were never properly introduced anyhow. I'm Angus Hume, sewer foreman. Now if we want to talk, there's a pub round the corner an' I'm just about ready to wash the taste o' the sewer out o' my mouth.' He led the way to the door, taking his hat from the peg. 'Gets into your spittle, that's the truth of it. Takes a couple o' good pints to kill the taste.'

The Crown was a small street-corner pub, probably unchanged since it was first built a hundred years earlier. The burly landlord began to draw the first pint the moment he saw Angus coming in through the door. Matt was introduced and his hand gripped in a giant fist.

'Pint for you too?'

'Please.'

'They did a good job, those surgeons.' The landlord stared at him critically. 'The way I heard the story, you'd no face left. Wonderful what they can do these days.'

'They built one side up,' Matt explained.

Talking about it this way seemed more natural than people averting their eyes, which was the more usual reaction. He fished in his pocket for some money but Angus was ahead of him, slapping a pound note down on the bar.

'My round,' he insisted.

'Wife says I should 'ave my nose done,' the landlord confided as he turned to the till. 'But it doesn't worry me, so why bother? Scars o' battle, I tell her, but she won't listen. The way she goes on, you wouldn't believe I was still boxing when she married me. But they change, don't they, women?'

They sat at a little round table in a corner. Angus took a first, long draught before another word was spoken, then he set down the glass with a sigh of contentment and started to fill his pipe from an old, worn pouch.

'Turned to the pipe when I started in the sewers,' he said, carefully pushing the tobacco into the bowl with his forefinger. 'Never tried it before. In the army I smoked fags. Always fags.' He turned the pouch over and returned it to his pocket before lighting the pipe. Every movement was slow and deliberate. 'Now what can I do for you, Matt? You didn't come back just to pass the time o' day.'

'No,' Matt admitted. 'But you must have more experience of worms than most other people.'

'Ay, I thought it might be that. Well, ask your questions, Matt, though I warn you I know nothing more than I've already told the reporters.' He took another long pull at his beer and laughed. 'We had 'em in here that night they took you to hospital, falling over themselves to buy us drinks, an' half o' them pissed as newts by eight o'clock.'

'They saw the worms themselves?'

'None to see. Some dead, the rest sleeping off a good meal – *you.*'

'But on a normal day. . . ?'

'Saw some today,' Angus confirmed. 'I'll tell you something. The first I came across were little 'uns, about the length o' your hand. Eighteen months ago, that'd be. I've been ten years down those sewers, mind, ever since I came out o' the army, an' I never saw none before that. These little 'uns – well, a couple o' my mates got nipped, nothing much, no more'n a rat'd do to you. But now they're bigger we watch out. Ay, well, you know about that.' He drained his glass. 'You don't see many rats in the sewers these days, that's one thing you can say for 'em.'

Matt went to the bar for another couple of pints and the landlord leaned across to him confidentially. ''Ere, them worms gets bigger every time 'e talks about 'em. If 'e's tellin' the truth – an' 'e's straight, mind, is Angus – it's my opinion somethin' ought to be done. You pass that on to your TV people.'

But back at the table, Angus made it clear the authorities had taken some temporary measures pending the result of an inquiry. They'd put down lumps of poisoned meat. That'd worked for a couple of days, but then the worms had returned in force.

'Ay, it was like the buggers knew what we'd been about an' weren't having any. They've calmed down again now, but I've never known 'em quite so vicious as that week.'

'Can I see them?'

'Ay.' Angus was uncommittal.

'Take some photographs.'

'If anyone's a right to, you have.' He drew on his pipe. 'Not tonight. Not tomorrow. Wednesday. About eleven o'clock. I'll take you down.

Wednesday was the day Helen planned they should drive down to the cottage at Westport and Matt had some trouble persuading her. He said nothing about going to the sewers but suggested there were a couple of jobs needed doing on the car. She remained unconvinced till she saw him change into his overalls and go out to start draining the oil from the sump. Luckily the phone rang with an offer of a day's typing at a nearby insurance office. The money was good – they often paid her a bonus over and above the agency fee – and that clinched the matter.

Matt waited till both Helen and Jenny were safely out of

the house before trying to ring Professor Jones at the University.

It was his third attempt and he half expected the bored operator to say, yet again: 'Sorry, no reply.' But this time he was put through to a woman in the secretariat who explained that the professor was away on a motoring holiday in southern Europe and not expected back for two months.

'This is vacation time,' she reminded him condescendingly. 'No one's here except for those doing summer courses for foreign students.'

'Then who feeds the animals?' Matt demanded.

'Animals?' She sounded genuinely astonished.

'Reptiles. In his laboratory.'

'They're all dead.'

'Dead?'

'In jars and things,' she added. 'I don't think the professor ever has any living specimens. But maybe Albert can help you better. He's the lab assistant. I'll have you transferred, if that's any use.'

Matt felt he was walking on quicksand. 'Would he like some living specimens? I mean, if he's studying worms and their habits he'll—'

'I'll have you transferred.' A series of clicks and metallic groans. Then: 'Could you transfer this call to 568?' More clicks. Then an ominous silence.'

'Hello?' said Matt. 'Hello?'

No answer.

At last he put the phone down, defeated.

When he arrived at the sewer foreman's office just before eleven o'clock on Wednesday morning, Angus eyed him with mild amusement. 'It's a wee trip down the drain we're planning,' he commented drily, 'not an expedition to climb Everest.'

In addition to his camera, extra lenses and a couple of battery-operated lamps, Matt had brought a picnic ice-box and a pair of heavy gauntlet gloves made of imitation leather. He remembered the worms hadn't bitten through his ordinary clothing but reckoned that genuine leather, being skin, wouldn't put them off in the same way. He'd no wish to experience their sharp teeth for a second time.

In the office he pulled off his shoes and changed into rubber waders. Angus, in gum boots, led the way down a dank, stone staircase into the vaulted sewers.

It was all he could do to hide his sudden spasm of fear as the sour smell caught his nostrils and he heard once again the echoing whispers of the tunnels. The old panic rose within him. The walls seemed to shrink menacingly, pressing in on him from all sides.

But the gleam of torchlight on the effluent brought back the vivid memory of the pain and terror of the worms. His claustrophobia receded as he became more and more determined to hit back at them.

'Ne'er a sign of any this morning,' Angus observed, flashing his lamp along the flowing stream of water. 'Looks like we're out o' luck.'

'Let's try some of this.' From his pocket Matt produced a flat whisky bottle containing a red fluid, and emptied half of it into the sewer. 'Blood.'

'Where d'you buy bottles o' blood, for Chrissake? Or d'you tap your own veins?'

Matt grinned. 'I thought of that. No, I went through yellow pages and phoned round the kosher butchers till I found one who'd sell it to me.' He stared down at the effluent. 'No worms, though.'

'We could try the next tunnel,' Angus suggested. 'D'you genuinely think blood'll attract 'em?'

'Mine did,' he answered grimly, remembering how they'd sucked in each drop as it hit the water.

They went to the next tunnel and he poured out some more blood. Its redness dissolved into a faint pink stain, then disappeared. They waited.

No worms. A few scraps of paper, discarded plastic containers, patches of foam, but no worms.

Then Angus grasped his arm. 'Down there!' he whispered. 'Two o' the bastards, their heads poked up over the water like bloody U-boats.'

Matt nodded. 'We'll give 'em one more taste.' He emptied the rest of the bottle and watched the blood spread through the effluent. 'They like it, see? Coming upstream for more.'

'Ay, drinkin' it like it was best bitter, the little buggers.'

Matt flicked open the clips on the ice box lid. Inside, he'd two string shopping nets, each filled with raw meat and attached to a long cord. He threw the first into the effluent and handed Angus the cord, asking him to wind it round his fist and hold it taut. Then he switched on the lamps and adjusted their angle.

Already the worms were speeding towards the meat in the net, their heads ducked beneath the surface. Angus pulled the net up, forcing them out of the effluent if they wanted to eat, which they did. Matt snapped off six quick exposures one after the other without pausing.

They were beautiful, undulating slivers of constantly varying shades of green, glowing brightly, intensely, like dangerous angel worms. A much better name for them, Matt thought – angel worms. He changed the lens for a tighter shot.

'Jus' look at 'em, little buggers!' Angus was saying, delighted. 'Like hungry hyenas.'

Four more worms – no, five! – shot through the water towards the bait, as though the first two had sent them an urgent summons. It had been the same pattern when they'd attacked him, Matt recalled, as if they had telepathic communication. It'd make them doubly dangerous. Doubly fascinating, too.

He took more pictures, working his way steadily through the film. One with its mouth open, poised to bite. Another with its teeth clamped into the raw meat. One staring directly into the lens, its eyes hard and challenging. Relentless. It was a relief when, for a split second, the shutter cut them off from view.

Angus was playing with them, holding the cord at arm's length, moving the bait this way and that, sometimes above the water, sometimes sinking into it. 'A great shame you're not taking movies this time!' he declared. 'I could make 'em dance for you!'

'Don't underestimate them, Angus. Last time they made *me*

dance. And never look in their eyes. Once they get their eyes fixed on you, you'll be stepping down into that water, doing just what they want.'

'Man, you're exaggerating!'

'Don't you believe it.' He took the last two exposures, then closed the camera and returned it to its case. 'You can drop the cord and let them have the rest of the meat now.'

They both watched, intrigued, as the worms gorged themselves on it as though they'd not eaten for weeks. Their skins glistened, one second green, the next purple, the patches of colour shifting and merging as they thrashed about in the water. The string bag was in shreds and two worms fought over the last morsel of meat. The others remained almost motionless, their heads upright as they waited to see what he'd do next.

Matt hadn't planned anything other than the photographs, but he was aware there was unsettled business between the worms and him. As he looked down at them he knew what he had to do.

He tugged on the gauntlet gloves and took the second string net from the ice-box.

'Let's give them some more,' he said, passing the cord to Angus. 'Same routine. Keep the meat just above the surface.'

Before Angus could reply Matt had lowered himself into the effluent. Immediately the worms began nudging against his legs.

'Are you crazy, man?' Angus cried.

'Keep the meat on the surface,' Matt snapped at him, irritated.

'I'd never have come down here if I'd known this was what you had in mind,' Angus protested, but he did as Matt asked.

The worms didn't bite. The rubber of his waders puzzled them. One by one they abandoned him in favour of the meat in the string net. He took a slow step towards them, carefully, then stopped suddenly to catch one in his gloved hand.

It wriggled as he held it up. Grinning, he tightened his fingers, squeezing till he felt its head collapse under the pressure. Then he slung the body into the ice-box and turned to scoop up the next one. Contemptuously.

Angus was staring at him, his eyes wide. 'Are you mad?' he was whispering. 'Is it revenge you're after?'

Matt was too busy to reply. He squeezed the second worm to death, threw it into the box, and set to work on the third. Vaguely in the back of his mind he imagined he'd take them along to Television Hall, slam them down on someone's desk and force them to take an interest. Failing that, a newspaper perhaps.

As he killed the fourth – it had swum willingly into his hand – he became aware the others were still feeding on the meat in the string net. They made no joint attempt to defend themselves, which suggested their telepathy might not be all that strong after all.

The fifth seemed to accept death indifferently, almost mockingly; perhaps it knew something hidden from him. Matt's wild mood suddenly sagged; he felt uneasy.

'Get out, man, get out quick!' The panic in Angus's voice was warning enough. 'Take my hand!'

Matt grabbed his arm and climbed back on to the walkway. Something glimmered at the far end of the tunnel, he couldn't quite make out what. He swung one of the lamps around.

The stream of effluent was thick with sewer worms, their heads raised above the surface, watching him as they assembled. More and more joined the rear of the throng and lined up with them.

'Like an army!' Angus said, his voice oddly hushed. 'We've walked into an ambush.'

Matt snapped down the lid of the ice-box; that was one thing he wasn't going to leave behind, whatever happened. He slung the camera around his neck and grabbed the case of lenses. Angus gathered up one of the lamps, but they abandoned the other.

'Now follow me, man, an' keep close,' Angus instructed urgently, speaking quietly as though the worms could overhear. 'Careful how you put your feet. The sewers can be treacherous.'

Matt followed him as he dodged through the low archway leading into the neighbouring tunnel. The torchlight beam showed sewer worms gathering there too. They were motionless, their heads raised, their eyes alert.

'Ay, you can sit there,' Angus muttered. 'Time's on your side, isn't it? Or is it you're not ready yet?'

'Why d'you say that?' Matt demanded. His words echoed through the tunnels, betraying his fear; once again he felt the walls moving in on him.

Angus didn't bother to answer. They went to a third tunnel, doubled back, then into a fourth. Fewer worms watched them now, but still enough to observe their movements. And report back?

Even in the bubbling effluent at the foot of the steps they found a patrol waiting for them. As if posted there.

But it wasn't until they were safely in the Crown with two large scotches in front of them that Angus began to explain what he really thought.

'I sensed 'em coming,' he said soberly. 'A change in the sound o' the tunnels. If you've been down there as long as me, practically living down there some weeks, your ears get tuned in to every little noise. But it was you killin' 'em brought 'em out. Why you had to do it, I don't understand; everything was fine till then. It was you they came for, Matt.'

'The food attracted them,' Matt tried to bluff.

'Put it that way if you like. Once they'd had a taste o' you. . .'

It wasn't what Matt had meant, but he didn't argue.

'If you ask me, it was like watchin' an army, the way they turned out. Battalion strength.'

6

Matt said nothing to Helen about his trip down into the sewers, still less his encounter with the worms. Something about her manner warned him to keep quiet. Since he'd come out of hospital he'd had the feeling she was being ultra-cautious about how she behaved towards him, as though they'd stuck labels all over him – *Fragile: Handle With Care!*

As though the hospital psychiatrist had been talking to her.

At times he wanted to shake her awake. 'Helen, this is me, remember? Matt! Your old Matt! Matt and Helen – *you know*! The old firm!' But it wouldn't work, and the realization hurt him like a long-standing deep wound.

'It'll be better when we get down to the cottage,' she had repeated several times during the past few days. 'You'll see. It'll get your mind off them. I do understand, Matt. Honestly.'

He'd secured the ice-box with wire before tucking it into the boot of his ten-year-old Morris. Helen had watched him, puzzled, but he'd offered no explanation. The last thing he wanted was for either Helen or Jenny to open the box accidentally and find the dead worms inside. *If* they were all dead.

As they drove down he was aware Helen was glancing curiously at him from time to time, and it irritated him. He'd have to talk to her about the worms soon, he knew: describe his feelings while they were attacking him; why he'd returned to the sewers; the whole threat he was convinced in his guts was facing everyone, yet couldn't prove.

Ideally he could have talked while he was driving, keeping his eyes on the road to avoid looking at her; but with Jenny playing happily on the back seat it was impossible. He'd have to wait till they got to the cottage. She'd be in a better mood then, anyway. She always was, at the cottage.

They'd stumbled across it whilst on holiday at Westport

three years earlier and she'd fallen in love with it right away. From a distance it was picturesque, snuggling cosily into the hillside. A closer view had revealed several slates missing, half the windows broken and the walls in need of re-pointing. Brambles tore at their legs in the large, overgrown garden. In the kitchen the single tap shuddered and swayed precariously at the end of a loose section of lead piping.

'It'll need a bit of work,' she'd commented seriously.

The money had been hers, left to her by her mother, but she'd insisted on the deeds being drawn up in their joint names. That's how things had been between them at the time – so close they voiced each other's thoughts; every absence a wound which only healed when they were together again.

Maybe it was the cottage itself which killed it. Every holiday, almost every available week-end, they worked down there repairing the roof, replacing the guttering, painting the woodwork... She even coaxed a loan out of the bank manager to pay for the installation of a bathroom. A fisherman's cottage it had been – born, lived and died there. That fired Helen's imagination. 'We'll come and live here ourselves one day,' she'd announced when they were dead beat after re-doing the kitchen. 'We need roots.'

Matt carried the first couple of suitcases into the cottage before taking the wired-up ice-box down to the larger of the two garden sheds where he'd fixed himself up a workbench and darkroom.

'What's in it?' Jenny asked inquisitively.

'Oh ... specimens.' He was deliberately vague, and not too sure himself what he intended to do with the worms. 'Things I want to photograph. Maybe I'll show you later on.'

Through the open shed door he could see Helen was listening, but she said nothing. Why not?

'Come on,' he added, 'let's go and help Mummy to unpack. Then we'll walk down to the harbour and look at the boats, just you and me.'

It was one of their established rituals, that walk down to the old harbour on their first evening at Westport, yet this time Matt felt uneasy about leaving Helen alone. If she untwisted the wires to look in the box? As he'd put it down on the workbench he'd heard a scratching sound from somewhere. It needed only one of the worms to be still alive for. . .

No, he told himself, that was ridiculous.

Jenny ran slightly ahead of him through the uneven lane between the houses, making straight for the steep, cobbled street which led down to the sea. The handful of shops had mostly closed already – grocers, butchers, fishing-gear specialists – and there were very few holiday-makers about. Probably at this hour the Westport landladies were serving up their evening meals and the campers were tending their Calor-gas stoves.

But the craft shop was still open, with its clusters of open sandals hanging like strings of Spanish onions outside. Usually Matt didn't give it a glance, but this evening he stopped to look curiously at the handmade leather bags and snakeskin belts. An idea was forming slowly in his mind.

'That bag's crocodile skin!' Jenny told him excitedly, cutting across his thoughts. 'We learned about crocodiles at school. Some countries have special farms where they breed them for the skins.'

'Aren't they dangerous?'

Inside the shop a girl was tidying up ready to close for the day. She was tall, with straight dark-brown hair drawn back and tied with a ribbon; typically she wore a peasant smock of dull yellow ochre with a brown sash. She looked up and smiled at him through the display of coloured scarves and raffia hats. Or was it at Jenny?

'Not if you keep out of their way,' Jenny was saying, as practical as her mother. 'Let's see the boats.'

He let her pull him away from the shop window in the direction of the harbour. She chattered about all she intended to do that holiday, but he only half listened. Westport seemed so peaceful, it was almost unreal. The smell of the seaweed, swooping seagulls, fishing nets draped over the walls, the winking of the lighthouse on the horizon as the sky darkened, the murmur of the waves against the rocks. . . Slowly he felt the tensions inside him easing.

Of course the sea had always held dangers – the lifeboat on the slipway was a reminder – but they were familiar because they'd always been there. They were older than man himself. The worms were a new threat.

'Daddy?' It was almost as though she could read his thoughts. 'When the worms ate your fingers, did they eat the bones as well?'

The question shocked him back to reality. 'No, just the . . . just the meat.'

Helen was bound to tamper with the ice-box. Suddenly he was convinced there must be at least one worm alive inside. Never underestimate them, that was the golden rule. He remembered how easily the last couple had seemed to die. *Seemed to.*

He took Jenny's hand and hurried her back up the cobbled street, through the lane with its tiny fishermen's houses and quiet stream, till they got to the cottage. The shed door was closed. Through the open window he saw Helen cooking supper in the kitchen.

Much to her surprise he kissed her on the cheek as she was trying to open a packet of bacon, and she flushed with pleasure at the gesture.

'I've been thinking about the living room,' she told him above the sizzle of the frying sausages and the scream of the boiling kettle. 'We could leave it till later and do the garden first. After all that time in hospital, you need fresh air.'

She'd not been near the shed, that was obvious. Relieved, he started to lay the table. 'I've a film to develop later this evening,' he mentioned casually. He'd show her the pictures and raise the subject of the worms that way, he decided.

'May I help you?' Jenny asked eagerly.

'Oh, you'll be in bed long before I'm ready.'

After their meal he helped Helen to tidy the cottage and put things away. It was almost eleven o'clock before he went out to the shed. She had gone up to the bedroom; from the garden he could see her shadow on the curtain.

Not a sound came from the ice-box. He stood in front of it, listening. Maybe he'd been imagining things earlier; maybe not. He thought of Angus having to go down into those sewers every day, and some of the remarks he'd made.

But first things first. He washed the bench down and cleaned the whole place thoroughly, then refilled the reservoir with fresh water. Helen would find nothing odd about him working this late at night. As a darkroom, the shed was only makeshift, not even completely lightproof in the daytime.

He developed the film first, rinsed it, and hung it up to dry. Good clear pictures, most of them. Turning next to the ice-box, he began methodically to remove the strands of wire with his pliers. He collected them all up and threw them in the rubbish box before pulling on his gauntlet gloves and snapping open the clips which secured the lid.

Then he stopped for a second or two, apprehensively. His stomach muscles cramped. He'd the odd impression that Angus was looking over his shoulder, a sardonic grin on his face.

He raised the lid.

The worms lay curled up at the bottom of the box, inter-twining and overlapping each other like Laocoon's serpents. They were motionless, a glorious splash of luminous colour against the dull white of the plastic, every imaginable shade of green and purple merging into each other.

Still he hesitated, but at last he plunged his gauntleted hand in among them and grasped one. Carefully he extracted it from the coils of the others, shaking it slightly to free it. Between his fingers it felt supple, almost alive. He placed it on the sheet of white blotting paper he'd spread out on the bench in front of him.

Its jaws yawned open, then suddenly snapped shut again.

Startled, Matt was about to bring a heavy file down on its head when he paused and poked it with the end instead. No further movement. He rolled the worm over. Still nothing.

Laying a rule alongside it, he switched on his lamp and photographed it from several angles. In length it measured nineteen-and-a-half inches. The head was elongated, with long narrow jaws. He forced them apart and ran the tip of his gloved finger over the sharp teeth; surprisingly, a few felt loose. Between them were several decaying shreds of meat.

Its skin was tough and scaly. He wondered if they sloughed it off, or if it renewed itself patchily, a bit at a time. Even in death its colours had a scintillating brilliance; he'd never seen anything like it before, except perhaps certain stones or a rare seashell.

Opening the ice-box once again he took out a second worm and started to compare them. Were their skins identical or individual? He examined them methodically, inch by inch, and was so absorbed in the task, he didn't hear the shed door open.

'Oh no!'

It was the note of fear in Helen's voice that shocked him more than anything else. She was staring at the worms on the bench, her eyes bulging.

'Matt, it's not worms, is it?' And you've brought them here?' She clutched her dressing-gown about her and took a step back. Her hand shook. 'How could you?'

'It's all right,' he tried to calm her.

'All right?' she screamed at him hysterically. 'Matt, don't you see it can't be all right? We came down here to forget these things. They're in the past.'

'Helen—'

'I suspected you'd something like that in the picnic box.'

'They're dead.'

She shook her head violently. 'They're not dead, Matt.'

'Of course they are.'

'Not in your mind. You dream about them, don't you? I know you do. You toss and turn, you moan, sometimes I hear you crying, whimpering like some animal in pain.' She was still yelling at him, all her pent-up emotions flooding out. 'I lie awake listening to you, d'you understand? Now you go and do this to me.'

'Helen, I'd like to tell you about them.'

'The doctors explained you might be like this but I thought—' She bit her lip anxiously, attempting to control herself. 'I'll have to ring them up, Matt.'

'Why?'

'They told me to.'

'Not before we've had a talk.'

'Don't you see you're ill, Matt?' she pleaded with him. 'The doctors will help you.'

'Helen, listen to me!' He stood with his back to the door, refusing to move till she'd heard him out. Then he told her how he'd gone back to the sewers to take some photographs – 'And to prove I could, I suppose,' he admitted – and all that had happened down there. The army of worms massing in every tunnel, what Angus had said, the lot.

Her face was anguished. He went to her, putting his arm around her. 'What really made you do it?' she asked. 'Oh, Matt, they look horrid. Those teeth . . . the colour like slime. . . We've got to burn them. We can't risk Jenny seeing them.'

'But I think they're lovely!' Jenny stood in the doorway in her pyjamas. 'I couldn't sleep when you two were quarrelling. Are those the worms which ate you? Aren't they beautiful?'

'Jenny, don't touch them!' Helen cried out.

'They're dead,' Matt repeated wearily. 'And, Jenny, we weren't really quarrelling. Your Mummy's worried, that's all.'

'About the worms?'

'That's right.'

Helen was looking at them both helplessly. She must have been to bed already, Matt thought; perhaps even slept. Her short blonde hair stuck out untidily at the sides; her dressing-gown clung awkwardly to her figure, making it more obvious that she'd been putting on weight around the hips.

'Have you developed your pictures yet?' Jenny asked.

'Yes. Helen. I thought . . . well, we need to earn more money and if we can sell the pictures to magazines. . .'

'Of dead worms?' Scorn. Disbelief.

'They were alive.'

'But why did you bring these dead ones here?'

It was a logical question. He glanced at Jenny. Her hand, clean from the bath and slightly rosy, was resting on the back of one of the worms. He remembered what she'd said about the crocodile farm and the thought he'd had outside the craft shop.

'For the skins,' he said. 'They could be made into belts or something.'

Helen was unimpressed. 'That colour? Who'd buy that colour? Like cats' eyes in the dark.'

Her voice had softened, though. She'd constantly nagged at him over the years to show some business initiative. The TV company, she'd often declared, was merely exploiting him. They paid him a miserable salary and gave all the big reputation-building jobs to other people. It was up to him to make his own way, wasn't it? Then she'd go on to quote her own father who'd started half a dozen small businesses in his time.

'I like the colour,' said Jenny.

'And it's high time you were back in bed.' Helen took refuge in scolding her. She propelled Jenny towards the door. 'Matt, don't stay up all night if you can help it.'

She left him with a feeling of emptiness and bewilderment. He'd neither won nor lost, but could he really talk to her now? As for trying to sell the skins, it had been a passing idea, nothing more. Now he'd have to go through the motions at least, if only to avoid being shunted off to a mental home, certified insane.

With a sharp knife he removed the heads of the two worms, then slit them down the belly and began cleaning them out, dumping the guts and bones on an old newspaper. The stench from the gobbets of half-digested meat made him feel sick. As thoroughly as he could, he cleaned the skins, trying to remember what he'd learned a few years ago while working on a short film about taxidermy. It hadn't been much.

When he went up to bed, Helen was still awake. She lay with the light on, staring up at the ceiling, her eyes red. An open paperback lay on the rug within reach, but he guessed it had only been a pretence at reading. She didn't even turn her head as he came into the room.

Stooping awkwardly under the low rafters, he got undressed and slipped into bed. No response when he leaned across to kiss her. He switched the light out.

Helen was breathing unevenly. Outside, the breeze quietly rustled among the trees. A dog barked somewhere far away. From the cottage came the occasional creak as it settled down.

He reached out for her, thinking he should make a gesture at least. She rolled over towards him, snuggling into his arms and sobbing unrestrainedly. No point in saying anything. What good could words do? He held her close. Gradually the tears eased; the crisis passed.

She was the one who started to make love, desperately searching in the darkness for his mouth, forcing her tongue between his lips, digging her fingers into him as though trying to unbury something she'd lost.

Gently he caressed her, but she broke impatiently away from him, sat on the edge of the bed and pulled off the night-dress over her head. To see better, she opened the curtains and stood for a few seconds at the window, her full breasts in silhouette against the starlit sky. Then she crawled back to his side of the bed.

For just over a week now he'd been out of hospital; on his first night home they'd attempted to make love, a perfunctory ritual with neither of them very interested. But this was different.

She found his hardened sex, running her spread fingers over it, moving up to his stomach, then down again; up to his ribs, exploring him with her hands, her lips, her tongue, till at last he swung over her, towered above her – her face expectant – and lowered himself into her.

She moaned and clung to him. 'Matt . . . Matt. . .'

And it was more than mere sexual pleasure. He could just see her eyes in the dim light. The barriers which had grown between them, neither knew how, began to dissolve. They recognized each other at last. Turned back the clock, or so it seemed. The old firm. . .

They had breakfast next morning out in the garden, peeling off their sweaters as the warm sun dissipated the remaining wisps of sea mist. Maybe she was right, Matt was thinking; maybe his mind had become obsessed with sewer worms. And what was so different about them, after all? Nature contained many a threat. Puff adders, rattlesnakes, spitting cobras. . . Mankind had learned to live with them all.

The quiet was shattered by the splutter of a motorbike approaching through the lane. One final roar announced the rider's virility before he switched off the engine and came striding through the gate: a boy of about nineteen, swaggering, assertive, with what looked like a knife scar down one cheek.

'Telegram.'

He handed it over and sauntered off again, revving his engine several times before letting in the clutch and throwing up a shower of dirt in the lane.

'From Jimmy Case,' said Matt, showing it to Helen. 'Wants me to ring him.'

'If it's work, tell him you can't do it. You're not ready yet.'

'Depends what it is, doesn't it?'

They had no phone at the cottage, so he would have to go down to the post office. On the way he would pass the craft shop. No harm in trying, he thought. Without saying anything to Helen or Jenny he went into the shed and wrapped the two rolled-up worm skins in a sheet of old newspaper.

When he came out, Helen was standing by the kitchen door. She had a resigned look on her face.

'I'll see if they're interested,' he called out, tucking the parcel under his arm. 'Shan't be long.'

But he didn't hurry; it wasn't that sort of day. The sun had already taken the early morning chill off the air and the little fishing town was settling into a slow, lazy rhythm. Swarms of tiny flies hovered above the scattered patches of dog-shit and decaying rubbish in the lane between the houses. He brushed them away from his face. Even the stream seemed subdued.

As he turned into the cobbled street he glimpsed the sea beyond the harbour, dazzling like pure silver.

At the post office he found the telephone occupied by a large, buxom woman who gave the impression she'd settled down for a good long chat. Well, Jimmy could wait. He turned back up the road towards the craft shop.

The string of open sandals was already hanging outside the door and the girl was rearranging the display in the window. She'd a slight sprinkling of freckles across the bridge of her nose, he noticed. Quick eyes with long lashes. Full red lips, without lipstick. Today she was in a plain green dress of some rough folk-weave material, drawn in at the waist by a cord.

A bell tinkled as Matt pushed open the door. She looked round and smiled at him.

'These things are always untidy!' she laughed, pushing a wisp of hair back. She wore little cockleshell earrings, but her hands looked practical. 'Customers never put them back properly. Never buy any, either.'

'What do they buy?'

'Oh, sandals mostly. And sun hats.' She paused, then added disconcertingly. 'And what can I sell you? A belt? A key-case? Wallet? Look around. Take your time.'

'I really need some advice.'

A quick expression of disappointment. 'Oh, if it's accommodation you need, I'm afraid—'

'It's this,' he interrupted her. He pulled off the newspaper wrapping and unrolled one of the worm skins across the counter. Its colours sparkled with life.

'Oh! Oh, it's absolutely gorgeous!' she exclaimed enthusiastically. 'But what is it? I've never seen anything like it before!'

'D'you think there might be a sale for this sort of skin? I mean, I imagine you do most of this leather-work yourself?'

'Mm,' she nodded. 'But I wonder how easy this would be to work? It's some kind of snake, is it?'

'In a way.' He unrolled the second skin. 'Unusual, aren't they?'

'Very.' She picked one up, fingered it, examined it from both sides, then took it to the door to see it in direct sunlight. 'Not well prepared, are they? Somebody who didn't know what he was doing.'

'Me,' he admitted with a grin. 'But I've three more I haven't skinned yet. Do them yourself if you're interested.'

'How much?'

'What d'you suggest?'

'I'd be taking a risk.'

'I've taken a few already, getting them. They're sewer worms. Heard of them?'

She had. For the first time she seemed to notice his two missing fingers; then she glanced up at his face and suddenly flushed with embarrassment. 'You're that cameraman, aren't you? It was in the local paper – and how you'd bought the old fisherman's cottage up the hill. I'm sorry, I should've recognized you.' Her face reddened again, as though she'd said the wrong thing.

'What about the skins?'

'I'll be frank. It depends how they turn out. I'll not know till I've tried.' She hesitated. Then, in a rush, she admitted it'd been a bad summer so far, she couldn't risk laying out money on them, but if he'd accept a percentage – 'Twenty-five?'

'Maybe I'll shop around a bit.' He began rolling them up again.

'There's nowhere else in Westport.'

'London?'

'Make me an offer,' she invited.

'Fifty-fifty and no haggling. I get the skins, as many as you need, and you do the rest.' He remembered the worms' hard little eyes staring intelligently at him in the sewer; there was something satisfying about the thought of fishing them out one by one to be made into decorative belts or women's evening purses. 'Only I'd expect you to peddle them around Harrods and Liberty's, not only down here.'

For a moment she regarded him pensively; then suddenly she grinned with a flash of white teeth, welcoming the challenge. The tip of her tongue appeared for a tantalizing second. 'My name's Fran,' she introduced herself. 'Frances Whyte.'

'It's agreed, then?'

'Agreed.'

7

In October that year there was a heat wave. The teachers were on strike in Middlehampton, otherwise Tim and Annie would both have been in school. As it was, they walked disconsolately along the unkempt grass verge running the length of the high wall which surrounded The Cedars and wondered what to do. During the summer holidays there'd been no problem. They'd found a spot where they could get over the wall quite easily; the house was shuttered and closed up; no one had bothered them.

To a stranger's eye, they might easily have been twins. Tim's hair was straight, and longer than Annie's; hers was curly. But they were both ten years old, the same height, dressed in identical blue T-shirts and faded jeans. For as long as they could remember they'd lived next door to each other.

The garden of The Cedars had been ideal for them, with plenty of trees as well as lawns, an orchard and a vegetable patch which an old gardener came in to tend once or twice a week. They'd built a rough shelter for when it rained; stole tomatoes from the greenhouse when they were thirsty; connected up the hosepipe when the sun was too hot and pranced about naked in the spray. Occasionally they'd talked about filling the empty swimming pool, but never risked it.

Now the owner was back.

On the first day of the strike they'd gone over the wall as usual but immediately had to duck down behind some bushes at the sound of voices. When they'd peeped out they'd seen a bronzed, active-looking man in light fawn trousers and a black open-necked shirt practising putting shots on the newly-mown lawn. A brand-new Jaguar, vivid red, reflected the brilliant sunshine glaringly on the drive.

'Something in the City,' Tim's father had said, whatever

that meant. 'Stinking rich. Spends his summers swanning around the Med on a yacht.'

Tim and Annie whispered together hurriedly and decided to beat a retreat, but as they moved he spotted them. In a loud, imperious voice he demanded to know what they thought they were doing, didn't they realize this was private property, they were trespassing, it would serve them right if he set the dog on them. Tim took a step forward, defending himself hotly, declaring they weren't harming anything, they weren't stealing, *honestly...*

A girl appeared behind the man, inquiringly. She wore a black bikini and long, blonde hair down to her shoulders. Beyond, Tim noticed the unaccustomed sparkle of the water in the filled swimming pool.

'Darling, let them go. They've learned their lesson!' Her voice was soft with a touch of laughter in it; as she looked at Tim and Annie her lips twitched.

'Right, but don't let me catch you here again!' the man bawled, and he stood watching them as they climbed out the same way they'd come in.

As he remembered it two days later Tim's lips tightened. They'd known it couldn't last for ever but the man, whoever he was, had no need to shout at him like that. He stared at the wall. Somewhere on the other side... His foot caught in a tangle of grass and fern; he kicked it free, savagely.

'We ought to get our own back,' said Annie, speaking his thoughts. 'And I know how.'

'How then?'

'Biters!' She added: 'They'd make 'em jump, and nobody could prove it was us.'

She explained her plan.

Tim's face lit up with a mischievous grin. 'That'd show 'em!' he approved grimly. 'That'd just show 'em!'

'Make 'em jump!' Annie repeated.

They dashed back home, excited, for their wellies and fishing nets. Tim appropriated a large glass jar from the garden shed; he tied some string around its neck to make a handle.

'Where are you off to?' his mother demanded, leaning out of the bedroom window, her face harassed as usual.

'Out!' he called back.

They'd first come across the tiny green worms they'd dubbed 'biters' one day back in the Easter holidays when they'd had to look after Annie's younger sister, Joan. That was a bore as usual, specially when she'd insisted on 'exploring'. They'd decided on the woods beyond the rubbish dump.

The village where they lived was already part suburb, swallowed up by Middlehampton where their fathers worked. In one direction were farms, with miles of cabbages and row upon row of greenhouses; in the other a petrol station with broken, rusting cars in an oil-stained field behind it, and the municipal rubbish dump which they skirted in Indian file.

Then Joan discovered it was more interesting to play in the stream – in reality, little more than a trickle of water at the bottom of a ditch by the side of the dump. She paddled happily for two or three minutes before they'd had to pull her out screaming. Two green biters had attached themselves to her leg, one on the calf and the other lower down on the ankle.

Fortunately her reaction had been immediate, and they were able to pull them off before much damage was done. They'd had no choice but to take her home, wash the wounds and stick Elastoplast over them; they'd also drilled her not to mention the biters in case they got into trouble for letting her go in the ditch. They'd made up some story about her being cut by barbed wire hidden in the long grass.

'This is where we saw 'em last time,' Annie announced, staring down into the water. 'But I can't see any now.'

It was a fairly clear spot where the water was almost transparent. Farther along the ditch were a couple of rusting tin cans and a twisted bicycle wheel. A slight breeze came from the direction of the rubbish dump, carrying with it an acid smell of ash and decay.

'There!' He began to climb down the sloping side of the ditch to get nearer. 'Hey, they've grown bigger. Whoppers!'

'Be careful!'

'They can't bite through my wellies.'

They found one, about six or seven inches long. Before it spotted them, they'd swooped it up in the fishing net and dropped it into the glass jar.

Another, also by itself.

But no more until they moved farther along the ditch when unexpectedly they came across three of them together. Annie netted one, but Tim's wriggled out again before he could transfer it to the jar. This was even more fun than they'd imagined; and the knowledge that these green worms could bite back added extra spice.

'*Ouch!*' Annie had some trouble getting one of them into the jar; she tried to help it along with her free hand but it bit her through the net, which she dropped. She sucked her finger, grimacing, but her eyes laughing. Some, she seemed to imply, deserved to go free.

The jar looked quite full when they stopped, and it was as much as Tim could do to prevent the worms escaping. He screwed down the metal lid in which he'd punched several air holes, then held it up to examine them.

'Don't like their eyes,' Annie commented with a deep shudder. 'Like they was cutting into you, an' they're only the size o' pins!'

The risk that the jar might be discovered if they took it home was too great, so they hid it in a rain gully at the foot of the long wall surrounding the estate. After tea, when it was getting dark, they came out again to look for it. Annie found it. Tim climbed on to the wall first and she handed it up to him, then followed.

One by one they dropped noiselessly down on to the soft earth. Everything was quiet. No sign of a dog either; in fact they were convinced he'd been bluffing and didn't own one. Annie went forward first, then beckoned Tim to follow.

The house showed some signs of activity. There were lights in several of the rooms, and occasionally a shadow against a curtain. But no one was looking out and it seemed the way was clear across the lawn to the swimming pool. They ran across together, lightly but not quickly. At the edge of the pool Annie held the jar while Tim unscrewed the top; once it was off she tipped the jar over and shook it.

A series of mild plops told them the worms had dropped into the water.

Tim fumbled to get the lid back on again before they

dashed for cover among the bushes, crouching down, listening and waiting... Not a sound.

Just as they were about to move to the wall the garden was suddenly flooded with light from car headlamps whose beam swung around as though searching for something. They pressed themselves down against the ground, scared of being caught out now. It wasn't the red Jaguar either, which they'd seen still parked in the driveway.

The powerful engine purred and then cut out. The lights died. The quiet clunk of expensive doors. Then:

'Darlings, how nice of you to come!'

Tim and Annie waited till the guests were inside the house before making their getaway over the wall. Once they were on the road again, running along towards their homes, their hearts sang. They laughed, danced, pushed each other.

'Boy oh boy, when they go swimming tomorrow morning! Oh boy!'

At The Cedars the party was going with a swing. Andrea watched as Gordon raised himself from the carpet, tummy upwards, a glass of champagne balanced on his forehead, gingerly manoeuvring himself to the point where he could begin to stand up. An informal party, he'd called it, just for the five of them. His idea of informality was a close-fitting white sweater with spotlessly new jeans which looked as though they'd been specially tailored for him.

But at his request Andrea had put up her long blonde hair, using the diamond hairpins to hold it in place. She wore a simple, clinging dress in green, with nothing underneath. The other two girls who'd arrived with Vincent – Tina and Gail – also revealed the 'naked look' whenever they stood against the light. It was going to be one of those evenings.

She imagined it was all laid on for Vincent's benefit. An important American client, Gordon had called him. His accent, though, was more central European. Fifty if he was a day, she judged. More like sixty. He wheezed when he laughed; his ridiculous little moustache bobbed up and down.

Tina and Gail squealed with laughter at Gordon's antics.

From an escort agency, probably. Odd the types they chose. Tina was on the plump side, with full breasts which bounced every time she moved; Gail was the opposite and had that skeletal look, every bone indentifiable.

More squeals. Gordon was on his knees now. Andrea moved to the sofa and sat up on the back with her bare feet on the cushion to keep out of the way. Christ, he was a bore! If only she'd realized. . .

She remembered the two children they'd caught in the grounds that morning. He'd been at his most pompous, bawling the poor kids out as though they'd committed some mortal sin climbing over *his* wall, leaving their footprints in *his* soil, disturbing *his* woman at her sunbathing. . .

That was the key to him: possession.

She could walk out at any time, of course. No need to stick around. But go back to what? It was over four years now since she'd left university with a degree in literature and a head full of nonsense only to discover that shorthand and typing would have been more useful. So she'd gone through the routines: secretarial course, job at the BBC, meals in the canteen, sharing her dreams with the producer she worked for, moving in with him, moving out again a year later, and finally throwing up her job in order to temp. Hundreds had trodden the same path before her.

Then, sent along as a temporary typist to Gordon's office in the executive suite of a city skyscraper, she'd found a different door opening. He'd been quite blunt about it. Couldn't give a damn about her brains or her shorthand, but she was good to look at, sense of style, lively, pleasant . . . The rewards could be very big, he told her. To prove the point he counted out a thousand pounds in cash and pushed it across to her.

She'd taken a week to think it over. In her shabby Tooting Bec bedroom she'd stripped off in front of the wardrobe mirror. Her body was good. She was proud of her hair. She had fluent French and Italian. She could drive, swim, dance, ski, play tennis and fuck – all of them well. So why waste her life over a typewriter?

'Oh!' Squeals of laughter again as Gordon almost lost his balance, then recovered it, but not in time to prevent the champagne spilling down his sweater. Tina's breasts quivered like jellies; Vincent's moustache went into contortions. Andrea flashed them a broad smile, politely.

'Time it was washed anyway!' Gordon blustered, getting up and peeling the sweater off. 'Ouf! I'm hot! What weather for October!'

He touched a couple of switches on the wall. The curtains parted with hardly a sound; greenish lights flooded the swimming pool on the lawn.

'A swim, anybody? The water's heated.' He glanced meaningfully at Andrea. 'Think I'll go in.'

Obediently she stood up on the sofa. 'Me too!' Balanced on the cushions, she reached behind her back with one hand, found the zipper and drew it gently down. Her green dress tumbled to her feet. She stood there naked.

Vincent's eyes bulged; his over-large abdomen trembled beneath his white shirt.

'The water's lovely,' she coaxed him, stepping down from the sofa. 'Aren't you coming in?'

Tina's breasts had escaped from her dress even before she'd touched her zip; she helped Gail as Gordon opened the French windows.

They crowded down to the pool with Vincent wheezing excitedly behind. Gail jumped in first, followed by Gordon, then Tina and Andrea. Vincent remained on the edge bathed in green light, the glory of his manhood shrivelled and retiring.

'Vince, darling, do come in!' Tina summoned him in a little girl voice. 'It's lonely down here without you.'

He squatted for a second or two on the side, then lowered himself into the water. As he did so, there was an anguished scream from Gordon. He began thrashing about, his face agonized.

'Gordon, what's—?' Andrea never finished her question. She drew in her breath sharply as the pain shot through her thigh. 'Get out, everybody! We have to get out!'

A second intensely sharp pain gripped her belly, low down near the top of her right leg. She reached under the water, fearful of what her fingers might find.

Tina let out a piercing scream, then tried to scramble for the side but lost her footing and fell back again. Gordon moaned loudly like a heifer in labour. Gail shrieked with hysteria, splashing about, then sinking, rising to the surface spluttering and shrieking once more, then sinking again. . .

Adrea's fingers found the source of the sharp pain on her abdomen, something long and thin clinging to her. She couldn't visualize what it was, but nor could she remove it. Pulling at it felt like cutting into her flesh with razors. 'Must keep calm,' she told herself. 'Must keep calm.'

Ignoring the others, she moved steadily through the water to the steps at the corner of the pool and climbed out. As she turned she caught sight of Tina standing waist-deep at the shallow end, sobbing as she stared down at something hanging from her breast. It looked like a snake.

'Get out of the water!' she yelled to her again. 'Tina, get out of the water!'

Suddenly she knew what they were: she'd read about them in the paper – sewer worms! The one on her abdomen seemed to be chewing its way into her. Fighting her rising panic, she grasped it with both hands, squeezing and twisting, irrationally convinced she could wrench its head off. She was acting blindly, racked by the excruciating pain, panting, her cheeks wet with tears. The worm was tough and resilient; she couldn't make it let her go. Then suddenly it began a series of jerks in quick, unpredictable spasms.

She could taste the blood on her lips where her own teeth had bitten into them. Shifting her grip she twisted again, twisted and pulled. The jerking continued, till the worm gave one last undulating shudder and then slackened. It became limp between her fingers. She flung it from her, far across the grass among the dark trees.

Her hands were sticky with blood flowing from the wound in her belly. Her breath came in uneasy sobs. And there on her leg, steadfastly hanging on to the flesh of her inner thigh, was the other worm. Oh God, she hadn't the strength. . .

'Help!' Vincent was whimpering from the pool. 'Help me! Please!'

Even under the low green lighting the dark blood was visible, like clouds in the water. Vincent was by the edge, pathetically holding out a podgy hand to be pulled out. Gail – it must have been Gail – was floating face-down, with only her meagre white buttocks on the surface. Someone else, probably Gordon, was still thrashing about at the far end, but weakening.

'Help me!' Vincent sobbed. 'Oh, help me, please!'

Why she did it, she'd never know. Streaming with blood, the worm on her thigh still gnawing into her, she crawled painfully to the side of the pool, grasped Vincent's hand, and pulled him out. He collapsed on the grass, lying there naked and white, heaving with sobs.

But she couldn't see a single worm on him anywhere.

8

Matt heard about it next day while lunching in the pub with the rest of the crew.

Over the weeks since he'd been recalled from Westport he'd worked non-stop on one uninspiring programme after another. This one, at a Middlehampton brake-cable factory, was a survey of the state of British industry – the usual fare.

Not that he hadn't tried to sell his idea for a documentary on sewer worms, but they weren't interested. Fobbed him off with unconvincing excuses. Humoured him, in fact. Yes, they'd allowed him to view – after worried expressions of concern – the newsreel of his own face being eaten. He'd watched it with cold curiosity, unmoved; though that night he'd woken up screaming, bathed in sweat, having relived the whole experience in his worst nightmare to date. Luckily he'd been alone in the house; Helen had still been at Westport with Jenny.

During those same weeks he'd assembled a growing file of press cuttings, magazine articles and photographs. Whenever work permitted he'd contacted Angus and arranged to go into the sewers again – at first to take more pictures, but later to hunt for skins.

Fran was having a great success selling worm-skin belts to a top fashion designer for his autumn collection. Matching handbags, too. Matt had met her a couple of times in London to discuss business details, and she'd agreed that Angus should be offered a cut to keep him happy.

'Sewer worms, that's what they were! First anyone's seen in this district, but there's no doubt about it.'

Matt's ears picked out the words across the general chatter of the pub – a high-pitched, smug voice, slightly nasal. Sharply he looked around to identify who was speaking.

The man was standing at the bar. He wore a shabby raincoat and heavy glasses which enlarged his bulging eyes. 'Naked, too!' he was saying, shaking his head with disapproval. The tip of his tongue passed over his thin lips. 'Serves 'em right if you ask me.'

The landlord nodded. 'Dead?' He spoke the word as though he and death shared a special understanding. Maybe they did. On the walls were photographs and trophies from the Western Desert; his bearing was military, shoulders back, hair short.

'Two of 'em. The others are in hospital.'

Matt emptied his glass and went over to join them. The worms have claimed their first dead, he was thinking; but it had been touch and go that he hadn't ended up in the cemetery himself. A couple of weeks earlier he'd tried to make an appointment to see Aubrey Morgan, Controller of Programmes, now Acting Managing Director. 'Too busy at the moment,' Jimmy had reported back to him several days later. 'And as for your documentary, he says nobody has been killed yet, so the worms can't be as dangerous as you claim. Sorry, Matt. He's right, you know.'

The landlord held his glass at eye-level, slightly tilted, as he poured the Guinness. Matt turned to the man in the raincoat.

'Heard you mention sewer worms,' he said affably. 'I could tell you a bit about them.'

The man's eyes flickered up to his face, betraying the usual expression of curiosity about his scars. Matt smiled, unembarrassed. He used those scars shamelessly whenever he wanted to get someone talking. Especially about worms. It worked this time too without a hitch; it always did.

Rodney Smith, the man said his name was. Deputy editor of the local paper. He questioned Matt for a minute or two about his experiences in the London sewers before telling of the 'tragedy at The Cedars' as he called it.

His contact at the police station – he phrased it to sound both conspiratorial and highly important – had tipped him off that someone passing The Cedars late at night had heard screams and dialled 999. What they'd found there was beyond description. A mixed nude bathing party in the private swimming pool ... such goings on! Then, those worms!

He'd followed up the story through his contact at the hospital who told him of two young women brought in with unusual wounds on their bodies; also a middle-aged man, unhurt but in a state of deep shock.

His contact at the mortuary had filled in more details. A woman, very thin, probably drowned, but with bites all over her, like a ferret had been at her. The dead man was in a worse state. His genitals had been eaten away. Only a few shreds of skin remained.

'Couldn't have done it without my contacts,' Rodney Smith stated contentedly as he sipped the large whisky Matt had bought him. 'Then, I always did have good contacts. Half the battle in my business.'

Matt made a quick excuse and slipped away to rejoin the rest of the crew. He told them what had happened, keeping his eyes on Jacqui Turner, their director. She was still in her twenties, a slip of a girl, but eager to make her way in television and tough enough to do it. This was the kind of opportunity she shouldn't turn down; one spectacular scoop like this and there'd be no trouble about renewing her contract – they'd be only too eager. Pete, his camera assistant, brought her another Guinness. She shook back the dark, wavy hair from her face as she drank, her eyes fixed on Matt.

'We're ahead of schedule. We can fit it in easily,' he argued.

'Shouldn't we ask permission, or something?'

'I'll clear it with them. Have to ring them anyway about the rushes. If you agree.'

He went to the phone in the passageway at the rear of the pub, waited impatiently for the exchange to answer, then put in his daily reverse-charge call to Jimmy Case. It took some time to get through. Jimmy's voice boomed at him through the crackles saying the rushes looked fine, no problems, up to his usual high standard, and asked how things were going. Matt said he'd no problems either and asked for the call to be transferred to Newsroom.

'A local scandal that's just blown up,' he explained. 'A late-night swimming party, all starkers, two of them dead and three in hospital. My director wants to know, can Newsroom do with any pictures?'

'Sounds you're a bit late on the scene for pictures,' Jimmy

bawled down the line with a bellowing laugh. 'But I'll get you transferred.'

Deliberately he hadn't mentioned the worms because he knew just how they'd react. Jimmy, anyway. 'It's a bloody obsession with that man,' he'd once said. 'Everywhere he goes he sees worms. Must be bloody Freudian.'

Newsroom answered. No, Al Wilson was out at lunch. What was that? Worms? Two dead? Well, no promises, mind, but as they were on the spot. . . At first she seemed more interested in the sex angle, but then she said: 'Worms? But who put them in the swimming pool?'

'Who puts them anywhere?' he replied. 'Get there by themselves, don't they?' But as he went back to the table he began to realize she might have a point, something he hadn't thought of before.

Rodney Smith, still in his shabby raincoat, led the procession of cars in his own battered, snub-nosed Morris Eight. The Cedars turned out to be a medium-sized house set in its own grounds which were cut off from public gaze by a high wall. The gates were open and they drove straight in. Two children, about the same age as Jenny, stood on the grass verge watching them pass. Twins, Matt thought. At one time he and Helen had dreamed of having twins. Just twins. No other children. Then Jenny was born and they forgot about it.

A uniformed constable sitting in the porch of the house came forward to ask what they wanted, but Rodney Smith knew him and there were no problems. He pointed out the swimming pool. While Matt and Jacqui stared down into the water, his stocky, dour camera assistant, Pete, began to set up.

'I can't see any worms,' Jacqui commented, walking along the edge. 'What do they look like? Small snakes?'

'Sometimes small, but they come in all sizes.'

'About the length of your hand, these were,' Rodney Smith said. 'No telling if there's any more in the water. The ones I saw were dead.'

'Green?' Matt asked.

'Greenish.' He went back to the constable, who nodded and indicated the shed. 'Some of the dead ones are still here,' he called over to them. 'I imagined the police had taken them all away but it seems they haven't. I'll get them.'

For a moment he disappeared into the shed, then came out bearing what looked like an old metal oven dish. In it lay several dead worms, stiff and straight, their greenish-purple colour lacking the sparkle of the larger variety. Jacqui picked one up gingerly.

'Urgh! Like pricks with teeth!'

They filmed her holding it and describing, straight to camera, how last night's swimming party had ended in disaster when these sharp little incisors had found their prey. Matt had no idea whether Newsroom would use the item or not, but it would all come in useful for that documentary if ever he got permission to do it. He took a couple of close shots of her holding the jaws apart, then suggested she should crouch down by the side of the pool.

'Wish we could see some live ones,' she said.

Rodney Smith sniggered. 'Dangle your fingers in the water,' he suggested nastily. 'If there's any of 'em left, they'll soon show themselves.'

'For Chrissake!' Matt swore at him. That high-pitched, nasal voice was beginning to get on his nerves.

'I was only saying if—'

'Do it yourself!' Matt told him roughly. 'I'll film them having a go at your hand, and gladly.'

They were packing up to drive down to the hospital when Matt noticed the two children who had followed them into the grounds. He grinned at them. Encouraged, they crept forward; the constable was examining the sound man's Nagra tape-recorder with absorbed interest and didn't notice them. He was a hi-fi fanatic, it seemed.

'You with TV, mister?' the boy wanted to know.

'Yes.'

'We can show you live biters if you like.'

'Biters?'

'Them.' The boy pointed to the metal tray. The girl stared at him speculatively, but without saying a word. 'We call 'em biters.'

'Good name,' Matt approved. 'D'you find a lot round these parts?'

'If you know where to look.'

The girl joined in, 'If you pay the right price. You *are* with telly, aren't you?'

She drove a tough bargain, five pounds, but Matt was too eager to see the worms to argue for long. He called Jacqui over. She agreed, and took the two children in her car. On the way to the Council rubbish dump he stopped in front of a small cluster of three shops and bought some offal. 'For the dog,' he explained to the butcher.

They parked just beyond the petrol station and followed the children along the path which led past the dump. Rodney Smith scoffed at the whole exercise and became irritated when a loop of rusting barbed wire sprang out of the undergrowth at him, catching his raincoat. The sound crew decided to stay in the car whilst Matt and Jacqui did the recce. Pete remained behind too to reload the camera.

The girl, Annie, suddenly stopped and pointed. 'Down in that ditch. There's lots down there. Little 'uns.'

They balanced precariously on the sloping grass sides of the ditch, staring down at the clear water. Bent grasses trailed in it; tiny insects busied themselves above the surface.

'Nothing there,' Rodney Smith declared nasally. 'You kids having us on?'

'That's where we. . .' she stopped, then giggled '. . . saw 'em last. Innit, Tim?'

Tim confirmed her story. 'Yeah, 'bout here.'

Matt unwrapped the packet of offal, took a small piece and dropped it into the water. The others looked at him curiously. 'Bait,' he grunted, watching it intently. No sign of them yet. He selected another piece which he tore to crumb-size shreds before scattering it on the water a little farther upstream.

'Cast thy bread upon the waters, for thou shalt find it after many days,' murmured Jacqui; she'd once mentioned her father was a Baptist minister, four-square on the Bible. Then, breathlessly: 'And here they come.'

'Look at 'em! Look at 'em!' Rodney Smith's voice rose even higher in his excitement. 'Did you ever see anything like that?'

Matt went up the bank again and waved to Pete to bring the

camera over. They wouldn't be easy to film in this light. Too much reflection from the surface of the water, and their colouring almost merging with the bed of the stream. He tried from several angles and took some readings; it was vital he managed to get a couple of shots at least. Angus had told him about these small ones before, so had his press cuttings, but it was the first time Matt had seen them for himself. Were they a different species after all? Or, as Angus had often said, merely younger? And if so, why? He'd like to take a couple back with him as specimens. Perhaps that busy professor was back from his long holiday by now.

Pete came up with the camera. Matt quickly explained the shot. 'You operate,' he said. 'I'll feed the buggers to attract them.'

He tossed more offal into the water, a bigger piece this time, and several worms homed in on it hungrily.

Jacqui was crouching in the long grass covering the steep bank of the ditch. 'They're ruthless,' she was saying. 'Quite ruthless and vicious.' The sunlight caught an auburn streak in her dark brown hair tumbled about her bent head. Her checked shirt had parted from the top of her jeans, revealing an expanse of white skin and the knobbles of her spine.

'Jacqui, be careful!' he warned her, with a sudden premonition. 'Don't get too close.'

'I'm all right.'

He could hear the faint whirr of the Arri BL's motor as Peter filmed the worms. Just to encourage them he threw in more offal. To take a couple with him he'd need a container, he thought. He looked around. There must be something among all the rubbish. An old tin, perhaps.

But the local journalist had the same idea. Before anyone could stop him, he blundered in front of Jacqui, fell to his knees right at the edge of the water and snatched at one of the worms with his bare hand. A gasp from the two kids who stood higher up the bank, watching. A curse from Pete at having his shot ruined.

Yet the idiot had succeeded. Half-lying on the bank he held the worm up triumphantly, his fingers grasping it just below the head. His laugh was a high-pitched whinny. 'Ha! Used to tickle trout when I was a boy. The hand hath not lost its ancient cunning!' He dropped the worm into a rusting paint can he'd placed nearby.

Jacqui lay sprawled on the grass. His sudden move had knocked her off balance; she was lucky not to have slipped down into the water. 'You bloody fool,' she told him, 'charging about like that.' She spoke quietly and intensely; her face drained of all its colour.

He ignored her, intent on fishing out a second worm. Jacqui, still on her back and still furious, flexed her leg. It was patently obvious what she was about to do. One gentle nudge with her foot would be sufficient to topple Rodney Smith into the stream among the worms.

Matt touched her arm. 'No,' he told her softly.

She ganced at him and he witnessed the anger melting from her face. Her expression became mischievous; her eyes twinkled, exploring his.

'Chuck some more meat in, will you?' Rodney Smith called over his shoulder. 'Bit nearer the edge.'

'If you'd only get out of the bloody way – you're ruining the shot!' Pete snapped at him.

'Never mind.' Matt tossed a handful of offal into the water. The worms were in turmoil in their eagerness to get at it. 'Can you take him fishing the things out?'

Pete widened his shot. Again the motor whirred as Rodney Smith bent over the narrow stream at the foot of the ditch. Then he grunted, a quick sharp grunt, and pulled back.

'*U-uh, u-uh,*' he moaned in a mixture of fear and pain.

This time the worms had won. One had bitten deeply into the ball of flesh where his thumb joined his hand.

'One all,' came Jacqui's voice calmly.

9

When he got home Matt found a note from Fran saying she was coming up to London to see him. Business was flourishing and she'd already received more orders than she could handle. It seemed everyone in the fashion world was fascinated by the luminous quality of the worm skins and their subtle changes of colour triggered off by variations in the light. But it was time, she suggested, they drew up a more formal agreement. She'd already had a word with a solicitor.

Helen stiffened defensively when she saw who the note was from. She read it without comment, then handed it back to him. 'You'd better meet her,' she said drily.

'Come with me?' he coaxed her. 'Darling, this could be the opening we've been waiting for. We'll be able to afford things for the cottage, and take Jenny to France, and. . .'

'You go by yourself,' Helen told him wearily. 'She's your partner. Your . . . business associate.'

'That's all she is!' he replied warmly.

Helen looked at him, her eyes puckering into an expression of doubt. But she said nothing.

They met at the solicitor's office near Wigmore Street. He was her cousin, it seemed: a fair young man, very formally dressed, with blue eyes and a slightly turned-up nose. After a few preliminaries he read out a draft agreement he'd drawn up. Fran was a tough negotiator. She hammered away at every clause, not giving an inch of ground until forced to. Matt tried to control his rising irritation. Without his worms, he reminded her, she'd get nowhere. Then she'd smile her sudden acceptance of the point, her nose would wrinkle and the tip of her tongue would appear for a split second between her lips.

In the end, when all the details were settled, she invited him to lunch in a nearby restaurant while the agreement was being typed. She'd already booked a table, she said.

'Champagne? To celebrate?' She turned over the pages of the wine-list. 'Matt, our business is really taking off, do you realize that? And so far we've no competitors.'

She began to tell him about some of the people she'd met from the top fashion houses. Then, when the *sole meunière* came and she tasted it, she launched into an enthusiastic account of how she always bought fish straight off the boat at Westport, how she prepared it, and the fish parties she sometimes gave.

'I'm glad you like fish too.' Her eyes seemed to be exploring his face. 'My husband didn't. But then he was a shit.'

Matt refilled her glass, not knowing what to say.

'I've a lot of faith in you, Matt. You really seem to understand about sewer worms.' She reached out and touched his mutilated hand, then bit her lip with a quick frown and laughed. 'If only we'd a better name for them.'

'The kids called them "biters".'

'What kids?'

He told her about it; she listened, interested.

'You talk as though they've some kind of intelligence,' she commented uneasily. 'As though they could read our minds. That local journalist – you really think they *planned* to bite his hand, don't you?'

'I imagine. . .' He hesitated. 'You can surprise them once but not twice,' he said at last. 'Which makes them that much more difficult to hunt.'

She shivered, and fingered the worm-skin belt she was wearing with her simple brown dress. 'What if one day they take it into their heads to start skinning *us*?'

He took her hand and moved his thumb gently across her palm. 'It won't happen,' he tried to reassure her.

At Television Hall later that afternoon he heard that Annie was missing. It seemed the police had been around to question the two children about the worms in the swimming pool; naturally they'd denied all knowledge, but next morning Annie had set out for school and never arrived there.

'But kids are always running off somewhere,' Jimmy remonstrated with him when he tried to discuss it. ''Specially when they think they're in trouble. She'll be picked up somewhere. Not our worry, thank God. We've enough on our plates.'

He paused to light a second cigarette from the stub of his first, drawing the smoke deeply into his lungs. Killing himself, Matt thought. His fists were massive, for he'd been something of a boxer in his early days, but now even the short flight of stairs up to the bar left him breathless.

'Our revered Acting Managing Director has agreed to see you.'

Matt was startled. 'When?'

'Thought that'd please you!' Jimmy's chuckle broke up into a cough; his face flushed a deep red. 'Today, at five. Don't ask me what made him change his mind – your latest exploits, I shouldn't wonder. I know you rang beforehand, but I'd have advised you differently if you'd said it was worms.'

'Newsroom was interested,' Matt defended himself.

'Haven't used the film though, have they?'

'That big earthquake story knocked everything else off the screen.'

Jimmy shook his head. 'It's the worms, Matt. And your reputation. If only you could forget those bloody worms.' He rummaged among the papers on his desk and fished out a green form. 'Here. Your annual report. No doubt you'd like to see it before I send it off.'

Matt glanced over it quickly. The accident in the sewers . . . three months in hospital . . . not quite readjusted after his unfortunate. . .

'Maybe you should've had more leave,' Jimmy was apologizing even as he read it. 'But you'd been passed as fit by the doctors, we were very short-handed, and. . . We acted for the best.'

'Has the Managing Director seen it?'

'*Acting* Managing Director,' Jimmy corrected him. 'No.' He paused, fumbling for a third cigarette to cover his embarrassment. 'Look, Matt, don't take this the wrong way. These reports they're routine, intended to help you. . . We think very highly of your work, you know that.'

This conversation didn't exactly leave him in the right mood to sell his great idea for a documentary to Aubrey Morgan, Controller of Programmes, *Acting* Managing Director, and Lord God Almighty in Television Hall. But it was the only chance he'd be given, so he'd have to make the best of it. He'd thought it over often enough, worked out one or two gimmicks to help it along... Such as suggesting Aubrey himself as presenter. Flattery wins empires.

The carpeted, curving corridors of power were in a part of Television Hall he'd seldom penetrated before. The atmosphere was hushed, as in some private mortuary. Maybe this was how they disposed of unwanted staff, he speculated gloomily. Discreet, taped organ music, a noiseless exit through sliding doors, a quick moment of intense heat, and all would be over. That split second of fierce desire as the flames licked his body...

Or as worms cut into it with sharp little teeth – was that to be his destiny?

He'd be tumbled naked into an oval pit filled with sewer worms while all the Heads of Department looked on from the safety of an observation gallery, jotting down notes for their reports. *Not quite readjusted ... hardly up to the requirements of the job ... could do better...*

'Mr Parker?' A voice like icicles. 'You can go in now.'

The secretary was tall and slim, a fashion-plate. She crossed gracefully to the interconnecting door and held it open for him, smiling as he passed – but with her lips only; her eyes remained indifferent.

'Ah, you're Matt Parker! I'm so glad to meet you at last. Do come in!'

The moment he saw him, Matt realized he'd met Aubrey Morgan before. A young director he'd been in those days, straight out of university and sporting patched denim jackets, not the lemon-coloured jet-set sweater he was wearing now. They'd both been starting out at the same time, Matt as a camera assistant, shy and awkward, making more mistakes than most. He wondered whether he should mention it, but decided against.

'I'd hoped we could manage a chat long before this.' The

expression on Aubrey's face changed as he realized Matt's hand was mutilated; he released it hurriedly. 'But you've been on location and I've two jobs these days, my own plus the Managing Director's. You heard about her little mishap? Oh, do sit down.'

'The worms?' Matt lowered himself into a mock-leather armchair.

'In a chocolate box!' Aubrey tutted. 'Of course, the shop wasn't responsible. The police checked on that. No one ever discovered who sent them. Now they tell me you want to do a documentary?'

'Yes, I—'

Aubrey stopped him. 'You've certainly plenty of experience of worms. Even this week, I'm told. In fact, they've become quite a hobby with you, haven't they?'

Say it, man, thought Matt. *Say it – obsession!*

'And I know exactly how you feel. Handled them myself, you know, when they attacked Mary. Had to pull them off her, squeeze the life out of them before they'd release her, feel their skulls crack between my fingers. . .'

'You noticed their eyes?'

'A sobering experience. I began having nightmares about them afterwards. For weeks. You too?'

Matt nodded.

'Not surprising. Come and look at this.'

He took Matt across to a map displayed on the far wall of the office. On it were a couple of dozen tiny coloured pins.

'The distribution of the worms, based on reports which have come in to us since you were attacked. Quite a number at first, though they've tailed off a bit. Mostly small ones – they're the blue pins. The larger worms are red.'

'They're all over the country!' Matt examined the map eagerly. Seeing the places marked like this really drove it home how widespread they must be. 'East Anglia has quite a bunch . . . fewer in Yorkshire . . . and fewer still in the big towns.'

'Fewer reports,' Aubrey corrected him. 'There must be thousands of places where people have either not yet noticed them, or not bothered to write in.'

'Who's working on it?' Matt asked, trying not to betray his disappointment.

'Working on—?'

'The documentary.'

'There's to be no documentary,' Aubrey told him blandly. 'Board of directors won't wear it, not after that affair with Mary. It wouldn't be in good taste. Drink? Scotch?'

'But you can't waste all that material!' Matt burst out. 'And what about the public? Shouldn't they be told about all this?' He waved his hand at the map. 'Those pins ... sightings ... here, here ... here ... here ...'

'Small worms, ninety-seven per cent of them.'

'They grow. Next year most of those pins will be red.' He took the glass Aubrey was holding out and placed it on the desk untouched. 'You do realize they've some degree of co-ordinating intelligence? We can't afford not to take them seriously.'

'You think we're no longer safe in our beds?'

'They're dangerous,' said Matt. 'How dangerous I don't think we know yet.'

'Matt, when I saw the film of you being attacked in the sewers, my reaction was *Oh, Christ, now we're going to have worms crawling out of every gutter, snapping at our ankles* ... But that's the point. It never happened. Nobody's even died yet.'

'Those two in the swimming pool?' Matt objected heatedly. 'Aren't they dead?'

'Drowned. Not killed by worms.'

'They chewed the man's balls off. Isn't that enough?'

'Have your drink,' Aubrey replied patiently. 'Look, don't think we haven't looked into this. We brought Professor Jones here, a world-famous herpetologist, who told us the worms are no more dangerous than ferrets. No less, but certainly no more.'

'Ferrets work on their own. You don't get a whole battalion coming after you.' But Matt immediately regretted saying it. That familiar look of understanding had appeared on Aubrey's face. *Humour the man. Don't forget his terrifying experience in the sewers. Must've unhinged him.* 'Could I see the letters?' he asked in an attempt to cover himself. 'The reports of worm sightings?'

Aubrey handed him a file from the shelf. 'They're all here. Take your time looking through them. I've one or two things to do anyway. Just sit there quietly and have a read.'

He sat in the armchair with the file on his knee. They were mostly letters, though some were notes of telephone conversations. A nip here, a nip there – no major attack – often no more than a report that someone thought he'd seen one but wasn't sure. One letter, though, was more interesting than the others. He read it twice, then – Aubrey was in the outer office – slipped it out of the file and into his pocket. When Aubrey returned he was finishing his drink.

'My dear fellow, I'm afraid you'll have to excuse me now.' He bustled over to his desk and started selecting folders which he put into his briefcase. 'Late for a meeting already. But I'm glad we were able to meet at last. Very glad.'

The interview left Matt feeling irritated and isolated. He couldn't get the message through to anybody. To most people he was merely unbalanced. Fran regarded the worms as nothing more than a source of income, Helen didn't want to hear about them, and Angus – well, good old Angus accepted them as yet another inexplicable fact of nature. Survive, that was his philosophy.

Survive. . .

Matt stopped dead in his tracks, then turned on his heel and headed for the nearest phone. He rang Newsroom first. Annie? No news yet. He tried the Middlehampton police. Sorry, doing our best but. . . Very sorry.

So was he, he told them. He checked through his notebook, then dialled Rodney Smith.

'Hello, yes?' The nasal voice was unmistakable. 'Annie? Of course I've not been out searching for her. I've been sitting at home nursing a chewed-up hand. Those doctors shot me full of anti-tetanus and lord knows what else. I've an aching hand, an aching backside, and an aching head. Now you ring with some stupid questions about the girl who stood and laughed at me while I was in danger of. . .'

'She might be in trouble,' Matt interrupted.

'So am I. She's probably gone to her auntie's for all I know, scared of a good hiding. Serve 'er right, too. You know what I felt like? You know? Like something on a butcher's slab. Not a human being. Meat, that's what.'

Matt put the phone down without waiting for him to finish. As he drove back to his small terrace house in one of the grimier streets of Chiswick, his fingers tapped the wheel nervously. A thought nagged at the back of his mind, something one of the kids had said. . .

Big 'uns? No, that wasn't it, but something they'd said suggested they knew there were bigger worms.

Not in that ditch, of course, but perhaps in a nearby river? Or a pond? Maybe no more than a patch of swamp in a farmer's field. Worms didn't need deep water, but just enough to keep their skins wet, their bodies at the right temperature.

Annie could have gone out to get some for another act of mischief. Or vengeance for some imagined slight. Perhaps she had a grudge against the police for daring to question her. He remembered her tough, childish face and hard bargaining. She was well capable of popping a couple into a policeman's helmet.

At home he tried telling Helen about it as they shared the washing-up after supper, but she wasn't interested. Her eyes betrayed that hurt look which haunted her whenever he mentioned worms.

'Tired?' he asked gently.

'Wouldn't you be?' she retorted, brushing a wisp of blonde hair back from her eyes. She began putting the plates back in the cupboard. 'You realize you've been away practically a fortnight and ever since you got home you've talked about nothing but those bloody worms? You're scaring the life out of Jenny.'

'I warned her not to play near any ditches or streams.'

'Where's she going to find ditches or streams round here? It's getting us both down, Matt. That girl's very fond of you. She really used to look forward to you coming home, but not these days. It's worms, worms, worms – nothing else!'

She hung up the tea-towel to dry and went into the living-room.

Jenny was doing her homework and Matt sat at the table with her, wanting to help. She looked up and smiled at him, but said nothing. Her long hair was scattered like a veil over her shoulders. Same age as Annie, he thought uneasily. He had a sudden picture of her pressing back against a tree somewhere in the midst of a vast swamp, surrounded by large worms advancing on her, their heads elevated above the water.

They should be sending out search parties, people who knew what they were up against. . . That girl could be anywhere.

When Jenny went to bed he switched on the TV for the news. The nude swimming party was mentioned, with his shots of the house and pool, together with the report that one of the children allegedly involved had run away from home. Helen glanced across at him; it was almost a gesture of apology for her outburst. Then her expression hardened again.

'You saw Fran this morning.'

'At the lawyer's. You could've been there.'

'I'm sure you enjoyed yourself better without me.'

'Darling, it was business, nothing else,' he reminded her wearily.

'So you keep saying.'

'The orders are rolling in.'

'I don't understand you, Matt.' She spoke calmly enough, without obvious dramatics, but her bitterness was unmistakable. 'The way you talk about these worms, you'd think they were one of the plagues of Egypt, sent by God to punish us all for our sins. You're scared of them, aren't you? Yet you can't keep away from them – as though you're hypnotized! I think you're in love with them in some horrible, perverted sort of way.'

'I'm in love with you.'

'Are you?'

He went over to sit with her on the sofa and put his arm round her. 'Yes, Helen,' he told her seriously, 'whatever else is wrong. If only I weren't away on location so often.'

'That's your job.'

'We could move down to Westport – throw up the job.'

'And do what? Breed worms?' Abruptly she went to the TV and switched to another channel. 'It's not that I mind you going after skins. If that's all it was, I'd say good luck and get on with it. But you never talk about anything else, Matt, there are nights I lie awake worrying about your sanity. And my own.'

10

According to the radio the following morning, Annie was still missing. The police had contacted all known friends and relations, but without success. They were appealing for information from anyone who'd seen her.

Matt made up his mind as he put on his shoes ready to drive Jenny to school.

Helen had already left. Her agency had found her work that week typing a lengthy report on product control for a firm of management consultants.

'I hope Mummy changes that job soon,' Jenny said brightly as she settled in the car. 'She always comes home bad-tempered.'

Without telling her what he was planning, he dropped her off at the school gate, then returned to the house for his usual worm-hunting gear – waders, gauntlet gloves, ice-boxes, cotton wool and chloroform, a couple of heavy walking-sticks, a sheath-knife and a change of clothing.

Then he scribbled a brief note to Helen saying he'd been called out on a job and propped it up against the clock.

The phone rang as he was about to leave; he hesitated before answering it. If it was Jimmy. . .

'Hello, Matt?' Fran's voice – businesslike, but with a tremor of excitement which she was trying to conceal. 'I need another fifty skins, urgently! We've landed a big order from Harrods!'

'Harrods?!' He congratulated her; then, because she seemed to be assuming he could drop everything and go down to the sewers right away, he explained about Annie.

She understood immediately, questioned him, concerned, and then said she'd like to come with him. He refused, putting every objection he could think of – except the real one: Helen

– but she overrode them all. In the end he gave in and arranged where to pick her up.

He'd call at Television Hall on the way, he decided. Collect a camera and some spools of film. One never knew.

Rodney Smith knew the neighbourhood better than anyone else and it seemed sensible to call on him first. Maybe he'd even come out with them if he smelled a story. They found his address easily enough in the phone-book, but had to stop and ask the way several times before eventually they got to his cottage in one of the villages on the outskirts of Middle-hampton.

Half a dozen well-laden apple trees dominated the garden and from somewhere around the back came the murmur of hens. Thick ivy covered the walls and encroached on the windows, which looked as though no one ever opened them.

'Anyone at home?' The door was unlocked and Matt poked his head in; the air smelled stale. 'Hello?'

'Who is it?' The familiar, high-pitched whine came from upstairs. 'Say who you are. State your business.'

Fran glanced at Matt, then choked with laughter. She withdrew into the garden again.

Matt announced himself and was summoned upstairs where he found Rodney Smith in bed with a high fever, a muffler round his neck, his arm in a sling, a skull-cap on his head, and a half-drunk glass of water in his hand. On the bedside table was a scattering of different-coloured pills.

'After that girl, I suppose? Can't help you. Confined to bed, as you see. Doctor's orders. My contact at the hospital says I'm lucky they've no beds, or I'd be in there.' He took another sip of water. 'Refill my glass, will you?'

'D'you have a contact in sewage?' Matt asked.

'What if I have? If you think they've seen any sewer worms, forget it. I've checked.'

Matt pulled a chair across and sat down, tired of stooping under the low ceiling.

'Cards on the table, Matt. Your best policy if you want my help.'

Matt explained his idea briefly. Somewhere there must be other worms; the two kids had implied as much. In any case, the water in that ditch would connect up with other streams, or a river, but only people familiar with the neighbourhood would know where.

'If you're right, why has no one else seen the worms?' Rodney Smith demanded.

'They probably have, but it's only when people get bitten they start talking about them.'

'Could be.' Smith conceded grudgingly.

He thought it over for a moment, then told Matt that he would find a map in the curtained alcove in the corner of the bedroom, somewhere under the pile of newspapers on the shelf. Matt fetched it and spread it across the eiderdown. Rodney Smith, forgetting his fever, traced the course of the various streams and rivers that might be linked with the ditch which bordered the rubbish dump.

'This is where you might start.' He marked the place with a red felt-tip. 'Know how to get there? I'll explain. . .'

Before he left the cottage armed with the map and several pages of notes, Matt went to the kitchen for a jug of water and refilled the bedside glass. He also drew the curtains. The patient lay back in his bed in the darkened room, his eyes closed.

In the garden he found Fran munching an apple she'd stolen from one of the trees. 'He's ill,' he explained to her, 'but he gave me some idea where to go.'

The roads were empty but he drove slowly, anxious not to overshoot the various turnings Rodney Smith had described. He felt oddly contented that Fran had come with him. He hardly knew her except on a business level, yet being with her eased some of the tensions in his mind. They'd not talked much during the drive, just a few remarks now and then, but she'd told him a bit more about herself. She'd married young, and very much in love. During the eight years it lasted she'd given up her friends, her interests, everything, till one day she'd discovered he was involved with someone else. That had been the last straw. On that same day, she said, she'd ceased knuckling under and hit out. He was in Australia now, remarried.

'I sent the bride a condolence card,' she added. 'Deepest sympathy.'

At last they came to a dark, twisting lane where the treetops came together to obscure the sky. A few leaves dropped from the branches; one landed on the windscreen. He pulled up beside a five-barred gate. Beyond it was a lumpy, sloping field punctuated with patches of cow dung; over in one corner was a gleam of water.

'Boots,' Matt instructed. 'And gloves.'

By the time he'd pulled on his own waders and slipped the sheath-knife into his belt, she was tucking the bottoms of her jeans into red wellingtons. He wondered vaguely whether worms reacted to bright colours. Well, they'd soon know. They climbed the gate and tramped across the uneven field.

'Obviously no worms,' she declared emphatically as they approached the pool. 'Look at the cow shit! Would cows come here to drink if they had their noses bitten every time?'

'You may be right.'

'I am.' She was adamant.

He took the packet of offal from his pocket, waded in, and scattered some of it over the water. Then he waited. After a while, he tried again, scanning the surface for the slightest evidence of worms.

'You win,' he conceded. 'Now let's try the stream.'

It ran sluggishly through a ditch skirting one side of the field. Overhanging branches cut out much of the light, but he tested two or three different places with offal while Fran made her own search for Annie, calling out her name from time to time in case she was lying injured somewhere among the bushes. But they found no Annie and no worms.

Back in the car he studied the map once more before continuing along the lane till it joined a wider road. Eventually he stopped again and checked their position.

'Over there,' he pointed, folding the map. 'The other side of that field.'

Another stream, livelier and wider, but still no worms. They returned to the car and proceeded to the next place on the list. Again they drew a blank. There was no evidence that Annie had been anywhere near these streams and ponds – nor that they were inhabited by worms. After their fourth stop, Fran suggested diplomatically that they might be wasting their time. Matt shook his head stubbornly and drove on. Somewhere, he was convinced, they'd find a colony of worms.

And that was where Annie must be.

The last pond, according to Rodney Smith's instructions, was hidden away among the trees on a stretch of land belonging to the Electricity Board. What he hadn't mentioned was the high wire fence and warning notice. But the Board had obviously not been too interested in the wood where they'd built their sub-station; they'd cleared away the nearest trees but left the rest undisturbed.

They followed the fence around. Down one side it bordered on a ploughed field, though separated from it by a rough track leading to farm buildings whose rooftops were visible a couple of hundred yards farther on.

Staying with the fence, they soon left the track and entered thick woodland. The heavy undergrowth made the going difficult; it must have been many years since it was last cleared.

'This is it!' Matt announced grimly.

'How can you be sure?'

He didn't answer, but every nerve in his body warned him that the worms were somewhere nearby.

At first he looked out for a tree actually overhanging the fence, thinking Annie might have crawled along a branch and dropped down on the other side. What he found was much simpler. Close to one of the concrete posts but well hidden by the undergrowth, someone had broken through the mesh with wire cutters, no doubt some bright local lad seeking a quiet spot where he could take his girl friend. Annie could easily have known about it and gone there to hide. The corner of the wire mesh was bent back.

'Annie!' he called softly. 'Annie, it's me – Matt – the man from TV, remember? We've come to help you!'

No reply.

The breeze rustled in the branches. A twig snapped under his feet. In the distance a tractor engine throbbed steadily.

'Annie?'

Fran stooped to crawl through the makeshift entrance. Once on the other side she stood up and called out again.

A movement, perhaps?

No – only the wind. Matt dropped to his hands and knees to follow her through. The rusting wire scraped over his back and the fence rattled against its concrete posts. The noise seemed alien. Fran looked at him, disturbed.

'Annie?' he called, more quietly this time.

The whispering among the branches changed pitch as the wind grew suddenly gusty, but it settled down again. No birds – that was it! He couldn't hear a single bird anywhere in the wood.

Fran pointed out what appeared to be a path between the trees where the undergrowth was thinner. He hesitated, examining the ground. No animal droppings. Nothing wanted to live here except insects and. . .

They had to find out; no going back now. He nodded to Fran and indicated his intention of going first. In her red wellingtons and jeans she seemed unprotected, exposed. His own high waders and gauntlet gloves looked a lot safer – let them bite through that lot if they could!

Bramble tentacles snatched at their legs as they pushed slowly through the wood. Twigs reached out to scratch against their faces. Matt's height forced him to walk stooped where the trees grew close; he began to feel hemmed in and clumsy. Behind him he could hear Fran's unvoiced gasps of exasperation.

She seized his arm and he swung around defensively. If only they'd brought the sticks. . .

Through the trees on their left she had spotted the glimmer of water. It was still, almost stagnant, with patches of vegetation floating on it and a dead branch, half submerged.

As they approached, the ground became more uneven, broken in several places by damp-looking gullies. Somewhere not far away Mat was convinced the worms were lurking. Perhaps even watching them.

Out of the corner of his eye he caught an unexpected movement and turned quickly. It was only a leaf. They'd begun to fall late that year and most of the trees were still green. The thick foliage cast a deep shadow over the pond.

Attempting to conceal his fear, Matt smiled nervously at Fran. She grinned confidently, almost cheerfully. But then, he thought, she'd not yet encountered a live worm. Not yet been initiated.

Not till that moment.

They heard the sound of something squirming towards them through the undergrowth, following the route they'd just taken. Then he realized this was no sinister slithering, but something bigger.

'Annie?' he said, half believing.

'No, look, it's a dog!' Fran's voice was warm with relief. 'Oh, isn't he lovely!'

The dog trotted towards them, its eyes bright, its tail wagging with pleasure at meeting them. A fox-terrier, almost. Fran, delighted, squatted down to say hello, not noticing the two worms sliding out of the adjoining rain gullies.

'Fran, keep clear!' Matt yelled at her. He grabbed the back of her collar to pull her upright, desperate to get her bare throat and face out of reach of those jaws. She staggered against him, struggling and furious; it was as much as he could do to prevent them both falling. 'Fran, don't!'

'What the hell d'you think you're up to?' she began to protest vigorously. Then she stopped, her body tense and quivering with terror as she saw them.

The two worms must each have been three feet long, the biggest he'd ever seen. Their skins were a scintillating, menacing green with shifting hues of blue and purple rippling across them at every undulation of their bodies. They seemed to flow over the ground with a wave-like movement, elegantly, almost a ballet... Then they raised themselves and waited with heads poised, their eyes fixed on the cowering dog.

It was only a second or two before they struck, though it seemed much longer. Matt found himself willing the little dog to turn and run; instead it remained there paralyzed, as if its paws were rooted to the spot. All the anguish of Matt's own experience flooded back into his mind. Maybe he even achieved some degree of telepathic contact with the dog, for he became aware that it was pleading with him, its eyes fixed on his, pleading for. . .

But for what? The yelp was ear-piercing as the first worm's teeth fastened into the dog's upper leg, and the pain broke the hypnotic spell. Suddenly it was fighting for its life.

Fran gripped Matt's arm as they watched, her fingers digging into his muscles. 'Oh no,' she was muttering to herself, horrified. 'Oh no, Matt. Oh Matt, now I understand what you. . . Oh Matt, my love. . .'

He stood there helplessly, holding on to Fran and wishing there was something he could do to help the dog; but there was nothing. The second worm had wrapped itself around the writhing, furry body and was attacking the hindquarters. The other was still gnawing at the front leg.

The dog twisted, rolling over, snapping at the worms, trying to bite into them, though steadily weakening as its blood poured out. But at last it caught the tail of one between its jaws and held on, determined.

The worm released the fleshy part of the leg it'd been chewing and aimed at the dog's throat. For a time it was stalemate between them, though the second worm was still feeding on the hindquarters. Then the dog jerked and shuddered uncontrollably, till it suddenly relaxed into death.

As its jaws slackened their grip, the worm's tail – over a foot long – dropped to the ground. It was completely severed.

The mutilated worm immediately abandoned feeding on the corpse in order to investigate its shorn tail, examining it from all sides as though trying to work something out. Then, to Matt's disgust, it began to ingest the tail in a series of purposeful gulps.

'It's obscene!' Fran whispered, horrified.

'Let's move while they're still busy,' Matt said urgently.

'And Annie?'

'D'you really imagine she can still be alive?'

'Oh, the poor girl!'

'We can only hope it was quick.'

Even as he said it, Matt knew that death by the worm was never quick. The carnivorous animals he'd seen while filming in East Africa had usually aimed first at the throat to immobilize their prey before eating them, but worms preferred their meals alive, with the blood still flowing through the veins.

'Come on,' he said. 'Now, tread carefully, and for Chrissake keep your eyes skinned. If they spot us. . .'

11

He had to go back there, that much was obvious.

Fran sat in the car, her head on her hands, her face drained of all colour. He knew well enough what she was going through. Every encounter with the worms left him with the same feeling – even now. But that piece of rag tangled in the weeds by the pond nagged at him. He'd spotted it only as they turned to go, and had said nothing. Now he knew he'd have to go back there.

He'd tell her he was hunting – she'd asked for fifty extra skins after all – and to make that look convincing he began to lift some of his equipment out of the boot. Regretfully he left the Bolex camera in its box. These worms were twice the length of any others he'd seen, but he would not be able to manage everything. Having to crawl through that hole in the fence complicated matters. It made escape more difficult if he was in trouble. One day, he thought, he'd devise some sort of face mask.

Fran still had not looked up. She'd a generous spread of freckles across the back of her neck which he noticed now for the first time. He moved his hand to touch her, then hesitated.

'I... I'll be back shortly,' he said lamely. 'Will you be all right?'

Her head jerked upward and her face hardened with determination. 'I'm all right now. Where are you going?' Her eyes fell on the ice-box. 'Oh.'

'You said we need more skins. I'll not be long.'

'By yourself? Why?'

'I always hunt by myself.'

'With Angus,' she contradicted him.

'He's not here. And I take the main risk; that's my part of the contract – remember?'

'You're trying to protect me!' she laughed, getting out of

the car. She stretched up on tiptoe and kissed him, a quick peck, almost maternal. 'Isn't that sweet!'

'No, but—'

'Matt, love, I've recovered now. I'm as tough as old boots. It was just the sight of that poor dog. . . I'm always like that about dogs.' She ran her hand over her hair as if to tidy it. 'But if that's what worms did to Annie, I'm going after them with you. What should I carry?'

He regarded her uncertainly, knowing the risks, but she insisted. Handing her the two empty ice-boxes, he went back to the boot for the Bolex camera and the hand-lamp. With her help it might be possible to film the worms after all.

Neither of them spoke as they trudged back around the perimeter till they reached the woods and the hole in the fence. Before going through he bent the wire mesh back as far as he could to give maximum room. He also poked around in the undergrowth with one of the walking-sticks, just to make sure.

'Okay,' he said at last. 'We'll take the gear through.'

'Too far away from the water for them,' she commented.

'Who knows? They may not be as dependent on water as we think.'

It was already late afternoon and he decided to do the filming first, before the light went. He'd load with fast Eastmancolor; with help from the hand-basher he might get some decent shots.

They followed the same path as before, with Matt taking the lead again. The only sound they could hear was their own legs brushing against the undergrowth and the uneasy play of the breeze among the branches. It was turning colder, too.

One worm was still feeding on the carcase of the dog, now an unrecognizable red mass. Several flies shared the meal. Silently, Matt showed Fran how he wanted her to direct the light from the hand-basher and he started filming. The worm blinked up at them, then went on chewing; its skin glowed with a weird phosphorescence.

After a couple of shots he moved nearer the edge of the pond in search of other worms. They might be hiding anywhere in the gullies which were deeply scored into the soggy ground, but he was reassured by the thought that they'd not yet been known to bite through waders and wellingtons. Yet how long would this immunity last? He was convinced they'd begin to understand sooner or later.

The pond was still, revealing nothing but weeds and decomposing leaves. The piece of rag was clearly visible among the stems. He stared at it doubtfully as Fran played the light over the water. Where were the worms?

Taking some offal from his pocket he threw it into the water but the pond was so overgrown, it produced only the slightest of ripples. He tried some more a little farther off. Still no reaction; it remained untouched.

The slithering sound behind them was so slight it was almost not there at all. Slow . . . soft . . . sustained. A quick gasp from Fran as they both turned. Three worms approached from different directions out of the undergrowth. The fear twisted in Matt's intestines but he forced himself to raise the camera.

'Light,' he requested.

She tried to obey, and switched the lamp on, even, but at the same time she stepped back and slipped on the mud. A terrified moan escaped from her lips as she fell.

'Fran!'

Matt dropped the camera and grabbed her, catching her with both arms around the body. But the momentum of her fall knocked him off balance too, and his feet began to skid from beneath him. Desperately he fought to regain a firm foothold, aware of the three pairs of hard eyes observing him alertly, waiting for the right second to sink their teeth into him.

It was a miracle he managed to avoid dropping flat on his face. As it was, he was forced down on to one knee in the mud, still holding Fran upright.

'I'm all right! I'm all right, Matt!' she announced breathlessly, holding on to an overhead branch to steady herself. 'Look after yourself.'

As he released her the worms darted closer. His face was almost within their reach and they reared up to strike, their heads back like cobras about to spit venom. Their jaws opened wide. Hate and revulsion flooded through him at the sight of those sharp incisors.

He bent forward challengingly, madly tempting fate. 'Come

on, let's see what you can do!' he taunted them. Some insane mood had seized him and he dared them to attack. In the background he heard Fran pleading with him to get up. 'Come on!' he urged them.

Their heads shot forward but Matt was quicker. He grasped the nearest couple by their necks and stood up, one in each hand, laughing in triumph. They wriggled helplessly as he gripped them.

'Let's go!' he said to Fran.

The third worm nudged against the rubber of his waders, then backed away. He ignored it and began to march along that twisting narrow path between the trees, holding the worms before him high enough to keep their tails clear of the ground.

Fran stumbled on behind him, protesting against the risk. 'They're too long, too dangerous. . .'

'Just what we need!' he called back cheerfully, ducking to avoid a tangle of branches above his head. One of the worms snapped viciously at his nose; he jerked back, narrowly avoiding its teeth. She was right; he'd have to be more cautious.

When they reached the fence he instructed her on how to open one of the ice-boxes they'd left there and pour a generous helping of chloroform over the cotton wool he'd spread out inside. Then he dropped the first worm in and she slammed the lid down before it could escape.

He waited for a few moments for the chloroform to take effect. 'Okay,' he said when he was ready.

She opened the lid and he lowered the second worm inside. The first was sluggish but not yet completely overcome by the fumes. Its head rose slowly over the edge in an attempt to escape, but he knocked it back in sharply with the tip of his walking-stick.

'That's the first two safely put away!'

'You're not going back again?' Her voice betrayed her fear.

'You asked for fifty.' He spoke lightly, trying to disguise his own uneasiness. What he longed for most at that moment was to get his hands on the driving-wheel again, feel the accelerator under his foot, and forget this place ever existed. 'How else are we going to get them?'

'We came here to look for Annie, not to get ourselves killed.'

'Did you see that piece of rag by the pond. Or rather, *in* it?'

'Well?'

'It could've been Annie's T-shirt. She was wearing one that colour when I met her. That makes two reasons for going back to the pond. And there's a third: I can't leave the camera.'

She was obviously worried. Her face was pale and she bit her lip uncertainly.

'Look,' he said gently, 'there's no need for you to come with me. Why don't you wait outside the fence?'

She scorned his suggestion, picked up the hand-basher and said she was ready to move. Matt slung the second ice-box over his shoulder; the first, containing the worms, he pushed out through the hole in the fence where they could collect it later.

They both carried walking-sticks, expecting to be attacked by worms at any minute, but they reached the pond without seeing a single one. The sun was sinking lower in the sky; the shadows were lengthening. Fran swung the wide beam of the lamp this way and that, on the look out for the slightest glimmer of luminescent green, but she found nothing. Several blue-bottles circled over the dog's remains, but no worms.

'Fran, watch the water while I try to fish the camera out,' Matt requested.

He'd hung the ice-box from a branch, well clear of the ground, then waded into the water, intending to try to hook the camera out with his walking-stick. It lay on the mud at the shallow edge of the pond, but he wanted to avoid stooping down in case the worms were waiting for him.

'But where are they?' Fran asked, bewildered. She skimmed the surface of the water with the light, illuminating the patches of scum, the dead branch, leaves, stalks, flies and midges.

Matt decided he'd risk it. Using the walking-stick only to steady himself on the treacherous mud, he suddenly swooped down to grab the camera. No difficulty. And no worms.

'Makes me feel a bit of an idiot,' he declared ruefully. 'I never imagined it'd be that easy.'

'They're here somewhere,' Fran said, convinced. 'Something tells me. . .'

He held out the camera at arm's length to let the water drip from it; the plip-plip-plip as the drops hit the surface of the pond sounded as sharp as a bell. Ripples spread and dissolved. Any minute now he expected the alert head of a worm to appear inquisitively, but. . .

Nothing.

The trees took on a darker, gnarled shape against the pale sky. Quick shadows jumped about silently as Fran moved the lamp. Elongating. Shortening. Becoming suddenly fat and overwhelming; then shrinking to nothing.

Worms often draw back and merely watch, thinking their own thoughts, perhaps transmitting them for other worms elsewhere to hear. Matt began explaining this to Fran, how he'd frequently felt. . .

'*Don't*!' she snapped at him sharply.

He stopped short.

A little nervous laugh from her. 'Sorry, I'm a bit on edge.'

'I think we both are.'

The sickly odour of chloroform met his nostrils as he dropped the camera into the ice-box and closed the lid. Then he waded through the pond towards the rag he'd spotted, fishing it out with his walking-stick. He showed it to Fran.

'You told me they don't bite through clothing,' she objected.

'I'm never certain what they can do. These are much bigger than the others.' He put the rag in the ice-box with the camera. 'But you're right, you know. They *are* here somewhere, and not just one or two of them either. If we only knew where to look.'

Taking the hand-basher from her, he swept the beam slowly across the overhanging branches. Maybe these larger ones could climb trees – many snakes did – and were gathering above their heads.

Fran seemed to read his thoughts. 'Matt,' she pleaded, 'let's get away from here. *Please*.'

'Okay, but once we're back in the thick of those trees, keep going and don't stop whatever the reason. Make straight for the fence and through to the other side. I'll be directly behind you. And use your stick if you have to.'

He slipped the ice-box strap over his shoulder and checked the knife in his belt. It was already so dark among the trees, it was no longer easy to pick out the right path, but Fran stumbled on ahead of him, forcing her way through the undergrowth with the help of her stick. Twigs sprang back at him after she'd pushed past them, catching him in the face as he ducked under the low branches.

What were they waiting for? Why weren't they attacking? These thoughts throbbed away in his mind.

'Urgh!' Fran squealed suddenly. 'Something's. . .'

'Go on!' he ordered roughly, giving her a push. 'For Chrissake don't stop!'

'Something in my hair,' she retorted, in control of herself again. 'No need to shove like that.'

'Just keep moving.'

He switched on the hand-basher again. She was right – something small and dark was clinging to her hair. But it was round, not snake-like; and it wasn't green.

When they came to the fence she scrambled through first. He pushed the ice-box after her, then dropped to his knees and crawled through himself. Standing up again, he paused to look back. A shimmer of green among the branches? Perhaps. . .?

He played the light slowly over the dark group of trees from which they'd just emerged. The wire mesh threw giant, diamond-shaped shadows against the thick foliage. Yes, something *was* shining there like long, thin cat's eyes. . .

'Matt!' Fran urged him on.

Each carrying whatever they could, they lurched over the rough ground towards the farm track, not stopping till they reached it and could at last see the fierce crimson disc of the setting sun touching the horizon beyond the ploughed field. Then they looked at each other, relieved yet still afraid.

'Get that thing out of my hair,' she begged.

It was a bat, and her face broke into smiles when she saw it. 'Oh, only a bat!' She took it from him, then tossed it into the air and cried out with pleasure as it spread its wide wings. After worms, even an ordinary bat seemed attractive.

As she relaxed and looked up into his face, her full lips parted invitingly, her eyes tender. They kissed, and her fingers touched the back of his neck, moving slowly around to the scars on his face. 'I don't think I fully realized at first. . .' she said.

'Oh, Matt, what you must've gone through.' They kissed again hungrily, her body pressing against him, her tongue urgently seeking his.

After a time she broke away. Her hair was in a mess, her face dirty and scratched. 'Damn! Oh, damn!' she repeated, upset. She bit her lip and stared up at him ruefully. 'I wasn't going to get involved with another man. Not ever.'

12

Jimmy was furious. 'Worms again!' he exploded, scattering cigarette ash over the papers on his desk. 'Christ, I might have known it'd be worms! We had a job for you, hunted high and low, no one knew where you'd got to, no address, no phone number, nothing. You really landed us in the shit – and for what? Bloody worms!'

'A yard long,' Matt tried to tell him patiently. 'I filmed them killing a dog, poor brute.'

'Who authorized you?'

'I was out looking for that lost girl.'

'Who bloody authorized you to go filming more worms?' Jimmy yelled at him, slamming his hefty fist down on the desk. 'Wasting time, wasting film stock. . .'

Matt lost his temper. 'Waste? We've got the only film in existence of worms that size, and you call it waste! What's going on round here? Why are you trying to hush it up? Or are you all too stupid to see what's happening? *These worms are getting bigger month by month!*'

'So you say!' Jimmy's face was a flaming crimson. 'And you're the expert, aren't you?'

'By now – *yes!*' In his turn Matt banged the desk top with his mutilated hand and sent the overflowing ashtray spinning across the floor. 'I've never met anyone so blind, so block-headed. Come and see for yourself with your own eyes if you don't believe me. I'll show you—'

'Matt, you'd better not talk to me in that tone,' Jimmy warned him, suddenly quieter. Matt could almost sense him rumbling like a volcano before an eruption. 'You're in trouble, laddie, I can tell you that now.'

'For what – showing initiative? You don't like that, do you? Never did. Don't think I can't see through you, Jimmy. Anything likely to cause trouble, you avoid it – and to hell with the programmes.'

Even as he spoke Matt knew he'd made a false move. Somewhere beyond the open door sat Jimmy's clerk, Marilyn, listening to the row, memorizing every juicy detail to repeat at length later in the canteen. Jimmy couldn't afford to lose face.

'Matt, this isn't doing either of us any good.' He spoke calmly, almost considerably, as he fumbled among the papers on his desk, searching for his cigarettes. 'I suggest you go and have a cup of coffee, think things over, and then come back here in . . . maybe half an hour? Then we'll have another chat about it.'

'Okay, Jimmy.' Matt felt tired. The whole argument seemed so petty. 'We both need a breather.'

Jimmy was going to consult someone; that much was obvious. He was reaching for the phone even before Matt was out of the office. Marilyn smirked and looked away as he passed her; her massive boobs and flabby arms were sprawled across her typewriter like an uncontrolled jellyfish. He paused for a second, lost for words, then contented himself with popping a couple of paper-clips down her cleavage.

He rang Angus and fixed up to meet him in the Crown afterwards. Whatever happened at the next meeting, he'd be in no mood to go straight home and face Helen. In any case, Fran still wanted those fifty skins for her new order. Yesterday they'd come away with only two, though twice the ordinary size. He needed to arrange a fresh hunting session in the sewers.

His hand shook nervously as he put the phone down again. He loathed the whole set-up at Television Hall. If your face fitted, if you fell in with the current trend, you were okay; if not, you were merely tolerated. And nothing could be less trendy at that time than worms.

Ironically, he'd have been smothered with honours if he'd found Annie dead or mutilated. Missing children still made good footage. But as it turned out, when he'd driven to the police station with that piece of rag, the desk sergeant had looked at him sceptically.

'Annie, sir? Ah, you must mean Annie Smith, the little girl who ran away from home? Picked up this afternoon at Paddington Station, she was. How she got that far she's not saying. Oh, and ... er, that bit o' rag. We don't want it, sir. If I were you, I'd put it back where you found it.'

Matt didn't bother with a cup of coffee but mooched around the corridors reading the notice-boards until he judged it time to return to Jimmy's office. The atmosphere was cool and formal. Jimmy stubbed out his cigarette. He sat behind his desk, his flushed face serious, almost sad. Bill Roberts was there too, as shop steward.

The decision was that he was to be suspended on full pay pending a formal investigation into his conduct. The charges were clear-cut and Jimmy reeled them off in a neutral voice, passionless: unauthorized absence from duty, borrowing equipment – the Bolex – for his own private use and damaging it into the bargain, sending his privately-shot film to the processing labs at the firm's expense... On the form he'd used the project number of Jacqui's programme, without permission, and it had been spotted. Naturally.

Out in the corridor again, Bill Roberts shook his head disapprovingly. 'You're in the shit, Matt, right up to the eyeballs. We'll give you what help we can, but don't build your hopes.'

But then, Matt realized, your face had to fit in the union too before they'd call out the troops.

In the Crown the bulky landlord exchanged a few words with him as he drew Matt's pint, then returned to a private conversation at the far end of the bar. Matt raised the glass to his lips and supped the top off his drink before going across to their usual corner table. Angus hadn't arrived yet.

Yes, Bill Roberts was right, he thought; he *was* in the shit. Somehow he'd have to tell Helen her 'temping' was now likely to be their sole steady income apart from the bit extra he earned from the worm skins – and Angus took a cut on that.

Of course there were the other TV companies, other outlets. He could press ahead with his documentary, try to place it elsewhere. What was it someone said? *Getting the sack's either an unmitigated disaster or the great opportunity you've always waited for; it's up to you which way you take it.* Maybe that was right.

In his pocket he still had the letter he'd removed from the

file in Aubrey Morgan's office. It was good TV material, so why hadn't they followed it up? The man was a nut-case perhaps, but then so was Columbus, so was Galileo. He took it out and read it again. The writer was a certain Tegwyn Aneurin Rhys whose address was in Hampshire. He'd seen the news film of Matt's face being chewed up and thought viewers might be interested in his own experience of worms. They bred in the open sea, he explained, probably in the deeper reaches of the ocean, arriving along the British coastline in microscopic form but getting larger as they moved up-river in search of food.

But there must be some reason, he argued, why naturalists of earlier ages had never come across them; either they were new to these parts, or to this planet. He inclined to this latter view.

Consequently, he'd made a search of the literature relating to unexplained phenomena and discovered several corroborated accounts of small, dark objects falling through the atmosphere and into the sea in the South Atlantic. Three different ships' logs had independently recorded such sightings on dates between twelve and twenty-four months ahead of the first reports of the worms.

To his mind, the worms were either themselves intelligent life forms from outer space – in which case we should do our best to communicate with them – or they were harbingers of even more sinister creatures waiting to move in and take over.

'Here before me, I see!' Angus stood by the table and threw down his hat on a chair. 'Don't you TV people ever do any work? Fill you up?'

Matt stood up. 'My shout,' he said, and handed Angus the letter. 'Read that while I'm getting them.'

'Worms, is it? Haven't seen any the past few days.'

Matt fetched Angus a pint, with another half for himself. Angus reached for the glass and half emptied it before setting it down on the table again.

'Ay,' he sighed with relief, wiping his mouth with the back of his hand. 'Those sewers stink so bad, you begin to taste it. When there's not much rain it's always like this. I wash my hair every night but I can never get the smell out.'

'What about the letter?'

'Ay, well, you know me. I only believe what my eyes can see an' what my hands can touch. Though he's right about one thing. Up till a couple o' years ago, no one had ever heard of 'em.'

'I'm going to see him,' Matt said briefly. He folded the letter and returned it to his pocket. 'Even if he's wrong, he's studied them. He may know something.'

Angus leaned forward eagerly, his eyes gleaming. 'You've succeeded then? You old bastard, Matt! You've talked 'em into making that documentary after all.'

Matt shook his head. He picked up the half pint, held it steady for a moment, then tipped it into his pint glass without spilling a drop. 'They've sacked me.'

Angus stared at him, disbelieving. 'They can't do that!' he protested. 'You?'

Matt explained. At length.

From time to time Angus nodded. He fetched two more pints, asked no questions, listened thoughtfully and, when Matt had finished, said : 'Sod 'em.'

'That's the way it is.'

'What's the union say?'

'On their side.'

Angus began to get up again. 'A couple o' scotches, Matt, that's what we need. Sod the buggers.'

'No, thanks,' Matt stopped him. 'I have to face Helen, so I'd better not drink any more. It'd only make matters worse.'

'Ay.'

But there's a bright side,' Matt began to tell him, changing the subject; he'd always hated confiding his troubles to anyone, preferring to keep them to himself. 'We've had a big order for skins, and that's the real reason I wanted to see you. When can we go down into the sewers? If I could have regular hunting sessions, maybe once or twice a week—'

Angus interrupted him. 'Ay, but I haven't told you my news, have I?'

Matt waited for him to go on.

'I don't rightly know how to say this, not tonight, not after what you've just told me.' He was rubbing his chin thoughtfully, reluctant to speak. 'Ay, but it's this. We can hunt some tomorrow, an' maybe the day after, but not much longer, Matt.'

'What's gone wrong?'

'They're taking steps to eradicate all the worms. Don't ask me how. We just had this chitty round as from Monday next there'll be a team coming into the sewers wipin' 'em out.'

Matt felt like someone'd just kicked him in the guts with a hobnailed boot, then stamped on his face for good measure. No job, no skins. . .

'Because o' you, Matt,' Angus said.

'How?'

'This inquiry was set up when the worms first attacked you, remember? No, you wouldn't. But it's true – they wanted to know how dangerous they were, what should be done about it, that sort o' thing. And they've decided to clean the sewers up.'

'Months later,' Matt objected.

'Ay, well that's the way these things always go. Take their time. An' I don't mind saying, Matt, I agree with 'em. I work down there day in, day out. The worms've not caused me any bother yet, but it's only a matter o' time – we both know that.'

The two boys sat on the river bank beneath the bridge and checked through the old woman's handbag. She'd been asking for it, Ken giggled. Wally agreed with him. At her age she belonged in hospital by rights. Or the loony bin. Not wandering through the subway with tottering little steps and that silly grin on her face.

They'd blocked her way, saying nothing, their hands thrust into the slit pockets of their mock leather battle-tops. She'd looked scared and tried to go round them, but they'd dodged in front of her again. No need to hit her, not this one. When Ken took the bag she was so eager to let it go, they almost dropped it.

Not until they had dashed on through the subway, leaving

her standing there, had she summoned up enough courage to protest. 'You teenagers!' she'd screamed after them. 'Young hooligans! I'll tell the police!'

The handbag contained keys, a pension book, a couple of hankies, sweets, ten pounds in notes and some loose change. They split the money between them and threw the rest of the stuff into the river; it was no use to anyone.

'Hey, look at this!' called Ken. 'A snake!'

Wally went over to him. It lay in the grass absolutely still. 'Think it's dead?'

'Course it's dead. It's a grass snake, that's what it is.'

'That colour?' It was a sort of purple, tinged with green, and shining brightly like slime. 'I've never seen a grass snake that colour.'

'You've never seen one at all!' Ken scoffed at him. 'Come on, admit you've never seen one.'

'On the telly. What you doing?'

'Gonna tickle it.' He'd picked up a piece of stick from the litter under the bridge and poked at the worm, which was about a foot long. 'Hey, it's alive! Look, Wally, it's alive!'

Wally felt suddenly sick as he realized what it was. 'It's a sewer worm,' he whispered. 'Like the ones that chewed up that cameraman's face. Ken, let's go.'

'You scared or something?' Ken sneered, bending over the worm and teasing it with the stick. 'Let's put it in that old dame's handbag, then let it out in the pub.'

In his concentration he got closer to it, his mouth open, his tongue lolling near his lips. The worm moved so quickly, Wally didn't really see it happen. One moment Ken was trying to coax it to curl around the stick; the next it had shot up at him and seized his tongue between its teeth.

He rolled back, groaning. Wally grabbed the creature's tail and tried to tug it clear, but that only made its worse for Ken who let out a high-pitched, choked shriek.

'Bite it!' Wally yelled desperately. 'Bite it, there's no other way!'

Ken seemed to understand, for his jaws closed. For a moment nothing seemed to happen, but then the worm convulsed once … twice … and went limp. Ken opened his mouth and released the almost severed head; his tongue dropped out with it.

He stared at it horrified, the colour drained from his face, the blood pouring from between his lips. And he fainted.

Matt planned to tell Helen the moment he arrived home, wanting to get it over with right away. But he found her busy with a petition some neighbours were organizing against the long-distance lorries which parked in the streets overnight, waking everyone up at four o' clock in the morning with their revving engines and slamming doors. She invited him to help, so he put off the difficult explanations and spent the evening with her, going from house to house gathering signatures.

It also took his mind off things. Later on, flushed with success at the response, they went over to call on the neighbour co-ordinating it all and sat talking to her for a long time, sipping weak, milky coffee. Her husband had been killed in the Navy during the Korean war, she explained, and she'd brought up their son singlehanded. He was now at Cambridge, studying nuclear physics; a wistful smile tinged with pride crossed her lined, alert face when she mentioned it. Her eyes were a soft, dreamy blue. She showed them photographs of the dead husband and the village in Cornwall where they'd first met. Then Helen began talking about Westport and how they planned one day to go and live there when the right moment came.

At home, as they prepared for bed, Helen brought up the subject again.

'I'm fed up with London, Matt. Pushing through crowds wherever you go. The time and energy you waste trying to get from one place to another. The noise. And Westport would be much better for Jenny too, somewhere she could feel really at home and grow roots. Why don't we?'

'Money.' He still hadn't told her.

'Things work out somehow.' She came around the end of the bed towards him, wearing a flimsy nightdress which was practically transparent. 'Matt, let's think about it, shall we?'

She pulled her arms around his neck and pulled his head down to kiss him. It was the wrong moment to tell her he'd lost his job, he'd broken all the rules by going off in search of worms in the company's time, he'd taken Fran with him. . .

Suddenly he visualized the freckles across the bridge of Fran's nose and the characteristic twist of her full lips. He felt guilty and vulnerable. Trying to blot her out of his mind, he held Helen tightly to him, his hand wandering over her back as they kissed, reaching her bare flesh beneath the short nightdress.

They lost their balance and fell on the bed still clutching each other, laughing at their own awkwardness but keeping their voices down for fear of waking Jenny. Then Helen raised her arms above her head and he lifted the nightdress, peeling it off her. And everything was the way it used to be, long sensuous caressing, a rejoicing in each other's bodies, a sharing of desires and satisfactions, together. Not till much later, when Helen had slipped out to the bathroom, did Matt think again of Fran smiling at him, her eyes troubled.

At breakfast Helen was in a hurry. She let her hand rest on his for a moment, searching for something in his face before she kissed him. He smiled and said he'd see her that evening; he didn't expect to be away. As the door slammed behind her he was very much aware that he'd still told her nothing.

Jenny sat dreaming with a half-eaten plate of cereal in front of her.

'Hey, wake up!' he teased her. 'We must get you to school. Finish your breakfast.'

Obediently she took another spoonful, then said, 'Daddy, I've just been thinking. Next time you go into the sewers to get worms, can I come with you?'

He was startled. 'Why?'

'I like them. I like their colours.'

'So do a lot of people,' he replied drily. 'Hurry up now.'

He dropped her off at the school gate, kissed her goodbye, then drove on to a Do-It-Yourself shop where he bought a length of wide-mesh metal gauze. 'For a garden sieve,' he explained.

The man shrugged, uninterested. 'Just as cheap to buy one ready made.'

Back home he went down to the shed and dug out the butterfly-net someone had once given Jenny. He cut away the net and fitted a scoop of gauze in its place, threading wire through the edges to keep them together. How effective it would be he could only guess, but he put it in the car with a couple of ice-boxes and his usual gear.

Angus was expecting him at eleven o'clock, so he had still plenty of time before he must set out. Enough time to ring Fran. He sat on the stairs in the hall, looking at the phone, unable to make up his mind. It was a matter of business, he argued with himself; he needed to tell her the supply of skins was about to dry up and. . .

No, that wasn't strictly true; it applied only to the sewer. There were still ditches, rivers, the Electricity Board's pond. And if he kept the smaller worms, bred them up?

She'd be expecting a call, though. He picked up the receiver and started dialling the number. Halfway through, he stopped. Oh Christ, after last night . . . the whole thing with Helen had changed . . . only a shit could behave. . . But he'd started something with Fran he couldn't easily drop. Didn't really want to drop.

Upstairs he changed into his oldest clothes, ready for the sewers. 'You are a shit,' he told his image in the mirror. His reddish beard was still short but now it covered most of the scars. 'A shit without a job.'

He went down to ring her – but left the house without doing so.

The following week, as Angus Hume stood watching the extermination squad at work in the sewers, he felt no regret that the worms were finally being flushed out and destroyed. Sure, he'd liked Matt well enough and the money for the skins had been useful, but it would be a relief not having to be constantly on his guard as he went about his daily work.

The squad, eight men dressed in heavy oilskins and gumboots, were emptying the traps they'd set the day before.

'Good juicy meat in them things!' the man in charge had explained cheerfully. He was a small, chirpy Cockney named Len Foster who set about his work with a minimum of fuss. 'Soon get rid o' your worms for you! 'Ere, ever tell your friends you got worms?' Laugh.

Each trap, when opened, was found to be tightly packed with worms, mostly dead. It was easy to see what had happened. The first victim had been tempted in by the poisoned meat; it had died, and then itself become bait to attract more and more into the trap – all intent, as usual, on consuming their dead brother. As though they couldn't tolerate the thought of any morsel of their own flesh falling into alien hands. It was a rum habit, and this time the exterminators had turned it against them.

A few feet away, a short, wheezy man was stooping to retrieve another trap from the effluent when four worms appeared from farther along the tunnel and homed in on him. He'd have been safe enough, Angus reckoned, if he hadn't panicked; but he saw them coming and splashed about trying to climb out to safety. The slimy stonework was treacherous. His foot slipped and he lost his balance.

His shrieks echoed through the tunnels, setting nerves on edge. '*Not me! Not me! Please!*'

Unerringly, the worms made directly for the one exposed area of flesh – his face. They fastened on his ear, his nose, and the chubby meat of his chin.

Within seconds two of his mates had reached him, killed the predator worms and fished him out on to the side, but he was already unconscious and bleeding profusely. They carried him up to the office and applied first-aid dressings while Angus phoned for an ambulance.

Perhaps it was this incident which stimulated the worm population of the sewers into mass resistance. By the middle of the afternoon, hundreds of them filled the effluent, raising their heads to inspect the humans lined up along the sides of the tunnels, out-staring them with their hard little eyes.

'I want every man out!' Len Foster ordered briskly. 'But

move carefully now. Don't go and slip into the shit.'

Cautiously, they filed out, and Angus was glad enough to go with them.

'What now?' he asked. 'Seems they've won this skirmish.'

'Wait 'n' see,' Len Foster answered, making for the phone.

When the men returned to the tunnels about an hour later the worms had still not dispersed. They seemed to be standing guard, or patrolling up and down, determined not to allow any more traps to be set. Len Foster's shouted commands bounced around the vaulted brickwork till the sounds were suddenly muffled by the roar of the half-dozen flame-throwers they'd brought down with them.

Angus watched them from the junction of three tunnels as the men walked slowly away from him, spraying the effluent with fire. The biggest of the worms was no more than two feet long, nothing like the giants Matt had described, but they shrivelled away to nothing as the flame licked them. The sickly smell of their scorched flesh mingled with the arid gases from the sewage.

'You'll set the whole o' bloody London on fire, you idiots!' Angus yelled after them, but they took no notice. He pulled on his breathing gear.

Some worms were diving beneath the surface in an attempt to escape the intense heat; some, perhaps, succeeded in escaping though most died. Angus felt no compassion for them, yet the sight of them burning triggered off deep loathing and disgust at this method of killing. Maybe it aroused in him an uneasy memory of the time he'd used a flame-thrower himself in a Kikuyu village during the Mau Mau uprising. It wasn't a death he'd wish on anyone.

But it cleared the tunnels, no doubt about that. Len Foster came back the following week to inspect them, and there wasn't a worm to be seen.

'Means nothing,' he announced with an air of authority. 'Plenty o' hidden corners in these sewers where they could be breeding a new generation. But this habit o' theirs, eating their own dead – that's where the answer lies! Think I know what to do.'

During the next few days the extermination squad released

several hundred rats and mice into the sewers. Each one, Len Foster explained, carried a minute sachet of cyanide – enough to kill the worm that ate it and any others that joined in the feast.

'These mice and rats can run into corners we can't reach,' he went on. 'Even if they accidentally kill themselves licking the sachets, they're still food for the worms. We're lucky they're not fussy about carrion, unlike snakes. I see you don't believe me, Angus – but two weeks from tonight, I doubt if there'll be a single worm left anywhere in Greater London.'

At that stage, no one realized how wrong he was.

'Come on, you know you can't stay there!' Charlie looked up to see the constable staring down at him, not unkindly. 'Move along now.'

Young enough to be me own grandson, Charlie thought as he sat up on the bench and slowly began to fold the newspapers he'd used to keep warm. P'raps he *is* me grandson, who can tell? What's the point in havin' children if they only turn out to be coppers? Much better not bother.

'Seen you around, haven't I?' the young constable said. 'Could get yourself a bed for the night, you know where to go.'

'Can't stand them places,' Charlie mumbled. 'An' it's a free country, ain't it? 'Cept in them places.'

He shuffled off, glancing back every so often to check if the policeman was still standing there. The bench hadn't been a good idea. Might have known he'd be moved. Best find that spot he'd discovered the other night.

It was in a section of the park normally kept locked after dark, but they had been cutting down a couple of big old trees, excavating the rooots, and had removed a section of railing to get at them.

'Could be me grandson,' Charlie muttered to himself as he scrambled through the gap and trudged over the loose soil in the direction of the pond. 'Bet I've got a grandson by now. Bound to. Tellin' his ol' grandad to move on!'

In the rockery near the edge of the pond the ground dipped comfortably in a hollow where he lay down in his tattered overcoat and arranged the old newspapers around him. Should have come here in the first place, he thought; no one would tell him to move on here. Like home.

He still had something left in that bottle in his pocket. Before going to sleep he took another long swig.

When he awoke it was still dark. Something was slithering over his face and he tried to brush it off. 'Quit foolin'!' he protested. 'Quit muckin' me around!'

Whatever it was – and it felt heavy, like a hand at the end of a thin, supple arm – it passed over his eyes ... his mouth ... explored his throat ... down through the open neck of his shirt, next to his skin...

He could see it now as well: a green, glowing tail waving in front of his eyes. 'It's the drink,' he told himself, lying stiff with fear, not daring to move. 'Must be the drink. Can't be real, not like that.'

A caressing movement on his ribs – that felt real enough. Then another across his boots and ankles, penetrating up his trouser leg. As it bit into his calf he jerked at the sudden agony. 'No, gerroff!' he cried, rolling over and trying to fight back. 'Gerroff!'

It chewed at his flesh. Under his shirt the other worm joined in, tearing at the loose skin. And a third worm caught his lower lip between its teeth. There was a rustling sound as more squirmed over the ground towards him. Shimmers of green approached in the faint light.

The scream welled up inside him, trying to break out, but the only sound he could produce was a long, shuddering moan of anguish as yet another worm gnawed through his cheek, its teeth scratching against his gums. He was sobbing with terror, panting and gasping for air, uncontrollably groaning as the intense pain racked his body and his mind gradually slipped its moorings.

No worms any longer. He was lying again on the Dunkirk sands, riddled with shrapnel, cursing his mates for leaving him behind, cursing the sergeant for getting himself shot, cursing ... cursing...

Cursing.

13

Six weeks later they moved down to Westport.

Jenny was delighted. They found her a place in the local school; to get there she had to pass the little fishing harbour. She never stopped chattering about how wonderful it all was, so much nicer than her old school which had been a modern, neutral building with graffiti-scrawled walls and the motorway feeder running just beyond the playground.

Helen shared her enthusiasm. She went eagerly about the business of converting the holiday cottage into a permanent home, humming to herself as she worked, even smiling whenever she caught Matt's eye. More than once she declared this was the best move she could possibly have made. It was her idea they should start going to the parish church on Sunday mornings to help get them accepted as part of the community.

The worms caused a problem at first.

When Matt brought the first boxes of them down to Westport and tipped them all into the large tank he'd installed, he was surprised at how sluggish they were. He'd never seen them behave quite like this in nature. But then he was only too aware that he understood nothing about their feeding habits and nothing about keeping them in captivity. The whole operation was a gamble.

One day he was late with their food, delayed at the shop by Fran with her constant questions about why he was avoiding her – her searching eyes, her worried look, biting her lip as usual. When he got home he found the worms had made their own feeding arrangements.

He realized cannibalism was not unknown in the animal kingdom. Even hens sometimes eat their own eggs. The larger feed on the smaller – that's normal, but the worms had to do it differently. They'd picked on the oldest and biggest to be sacrificed as food for the rest.

'I suppose there's some horrible logic in it,' Matt expounded to Fran when he told her about it the next day. He was still so shaken that he had to get it off his chest, and Helen refused to listen to anything about his worms. 'My theory is they've a collective will for survival. The group decided which one was to go and I don't imagine there was any resistance even. He accepted his fate, willingly. It's gruesome.'

'We lost a good skin,' she commented critically. She fingered the tattered remains he'd brought to show her. The small teeth had bitten into it in a dozen different places. 'We mustn't let that happen again.'

Matt was touched to the quick at her hardness. 'Fran, I know what you must be feeling...' he began awkwardly. 'It's my fault things have—'

She put her fingers over his lips to stop him. 'I'm over it, Matt,' she assured him. 'Honestly. I don't blame you for anything.'

Selfconsciously they switched the subject back to the worms. She was experimenting with mounting their skeletons on wire. Suitably framed, they might make an additional novelty for the shop. For some time he watched her dextrously arranging the vertebrae.

Outside, the wind was gusty and they could hear the halyards slapping against the masts of the yachts in the harbour.

'I think I'll split up the colony according to size,' he decided before he left. 'Reduce the risks. It'll mean getting more tanks.'

'Do that,' she approved without looking up.

That morning the post had brought his compensation from Television Hall. 'Compensation for what?' he'd demanded when he'd first heard the details of their plan for getting rid of him. It was explained that the disciplinary inquiry had been dropped. In view of his unfortunate experience in the sewers, his contract was to be terminated on medical grounds.

There'd be a handsome hand-out to help him settle in his new life, Jimmy had informed him with the air of a man taking credit where credit was due. Later, in the corridor, Bill Roberts straightened out a few points, emphasizing that he had the union to thank. Then came the farewell handshake from Aubrey Morgan, Acting Managing Director, who'd made it quite plain that all decisions come from the top.

The Acting top.

Goodbye. Good luck. Next please.

The money paid for the timber he needed to construct a long shelf down one side of the shed. The new tanks were spaced out evenly along it, with strip lights immediately above each one.

He bred their food in the smaller of the two sheds. At the start he'd fed them on butchers' scraps, but soon discovered that their skins lost their sheen if they were deprived of living meat. This meant ensuring a steady supply of mice, gerbils and rabbits.

To simplify the feeding process and avoid having his remaining fingers snapped off, he devised a set of boxes to fit over the tanks. The bottom section of each consisted of a sliding panel. He'd only to pull this out, and the live food dropped down to the worms below.

Breeding the worms themselves was a different matter. He watched them day after day, but they showed no interest in reproduction, no sign of young. The only way to replenish his stock was to go out hunting; even catching small ones was useful, as they could be fed up to the right size in a matter of weeks.

'I imagine they're waiting for spring,' said Fran one day when they were discussing it. 'That's when most animals breed in this country, isn't it? Who can we ask?'

He'd written twice more to Professor Jones at the University, but with no reply. He also wrote to Tegwyn Aneurin Rhys. He explained defensively to Fran that, though it was ridiculous to regard the worms as aliens from another planet, at least the man took them seriously and might have discovered something useful. About a fortnight later they received an invitation to go and visit him.

Tegwyn Aneurin Rhys lived in a large Victorian brick-built house known as the Old Rectory. It was set well back from the lane. The wide wooden gate at the entrance to the drive looked as though it hadn't been shut for many decades. A couple of greenhouses could be glimpsed beyond the thick trunk of the old oak tree which dominated the extensive but unkempt lawn.

On the gravel in front of the steps leading up to the porch an oldish Bentley was parked, and Matt drew up behind it. Before they could ring the bell the front door opened and an Alsatian bounded out to investigate, closely followed by a smallish man whose bald head was fringed with grey hair sticking out wildly on each side.

'Heard you arrive,' he said, ordering the dog to heel. 'I'm Rhys.'

Matt introduced Fran and himself.

'Glad to meet you. House is a mess, but come in. Not all that many people take these worms seriously. You've found that yourself, I imagine. A bad to-do you had with them in the sewers, wasn't it? Sorry about that. Been lucky myself, though Barker here lost an ear as you can see.'

The Alsatian looked up at them with knowing eyes, then turned his head sideways to let them see where one ear was missing.

'That's what first put me on to the worms,' Rhys continued, leading the way into a large downstairs room whose walls were heavy with books. 'I'll take you to the river afterwards, show you the scene of the crime. Barker saved himself of course. Bit the worm in half, and they haven't bothered him since. Obviously word got around. Sit down, sit down.' He waved to a lumpy sofa which still bore signs of having been a very elegant piece of furniture in its day. 'Now tell me why you want to breed worms. To my mind we've enough already.'

Matt explained, with Fran filling in the commercial details. Rhys listened intently, his eyes bright and alert, darting across to Fran's face every so often.

'And that's it,' Matt concluded. 'Can you help? Anything you happen to know. . .'

'If anyone deserves to make money out of these creatures, I imagine you do,' Rhys commented after a moment's thought, gazing at the facial scars still visible under Matt's beard. 'It wouldn't have occurred to me, but then I've always had enough money. You've broken your connection with television?'

'I was thrown out. Contract terminated.'

'You don't surprise me. Anything they do... Can't stand those television people. So smarmy. Think they know everything. In fact they know nothing. I wrote to them – you've seen the letter – but no reply. Even sent them some specimens, and not a word of thanks.'

'In a chocolate box?'

'Half a dozen small worms in a chocolate box personally addressed to the managing director, Mary Keating. Used to watch her children's programmes. Excellent. Miles better than all the evening crap. Oh, I read in the paper afterwards she'd been a bit careless opening the box, had a fright, but you'd think she'd say thank you.'

'She was quite seriously injured, wasn't she?' asked Fran, looking at Matt.

'No, no!' Rhys shook his head vigorously. 'A couple of small bites, and whose fault was that? I warned her in the note to take care. Open with care, I said. But you can't tell them anything.'

'Too true,' Matt agreed with feeling. 'Though the truth is, I don't think they found a note.'

Rhys stared at him with uncomprehending eyes. 'Typical!' he snorted. He stood up and leaned against the marble mantelpiece which bore an ornamental clock, several piles of books and journals, and assorted rocks. 'Breeding. You want to know about breeding.'

'Yes.'

'Can't help you, though. Nobody can. Reptiles either lay eggs or give birth to living young, same as we do. But which methods these worms use, that's a mystery. They may be oviparous – lay eggs, you understand – or viviparous, but how can we tell? I've never met a female, have you?'

'I . . . I wouldn't know,' Matt admitted, shamefaced. 'How to tell, that is.'

'If you're planning to breed them, I suggest it would be worth your while finding out,' Rhys observed drily. 'Come with me.'

He led them through to the back of the house, to a room fitted up as a laboratory. Shelves of jars, containing worms, snakes and various organs all preserved in formaldehyde, lined the walls. A freshly dissected worm lay spreadeagled on a piece of fibreboard.

'Invited you here out of self-interest, you know,' Rhys was telling them as they came into the room. 'When you find a female I'd like to know about it. Now, if we look at this worm—' he picked up a scalpel to use as a pointer '—you can see the cloaca here... And this – see? – is the penis. Or hemi-penis, as it's more properly called – or maybe less properly, but that's what they call it anyway.'

'Forked,' Fran noticed, bending closely over it.

Rhys stood aside to let her study it. 'You understand that they are not always forked in this type of reptile, but definitely in the case of sewer worms. And rattlesnakes, of course.'

'Why hemipenis?'

'They've two. Here's the other one. And they use whichever is more convenient.'

Fran's eyes twinkled as she looked up at Matt. 'Jealous?' she teased.

Rhys moved the microscope away from the bench to make room for a second board which he fetched across from another table. 'I prepared this for you as well. It's a slow-worm, quite different in every respect, but it'll help you to recognize what to look for. This is a female. You see? But I've never come across a female sewer worm.' He was quite emphatic. 'One week I took two dozen out of the river, deliberately, and every single one was male.'

'I tried to get in touch with Professor Jones—' Matt began.

Rhys snorted again. 'Jones is a nuts-and-bolts man. He'll tell you all about how a reptile's made, how it's put together, but he doesn't know them as *creatures*. I'm no herpetologist but I've thought it my duty to learn as much as I can in the last eighteen months. How do they fit in with the general scheme of life on this planet? That's the important question. But then I'm one of those old-fashioned people, a natural philosopher. Not many of us about these days.'

He took them down to the far end of the garden to show them the spot on the river bank where Barker, the dog, had first come into contact with the worms. The air was hazy, softening the outlines of the bare branches; dead leaves, soggy from the rain, still covered the grass. Fran took Matt's hand and snuggled up against him, shivering. 'Isn't he a darling!' she whispered. 'Oh, I'm so glad we came.'

There were no worms in the river now, Rhys explained, because it was too cold for them. Being cold-blooded creatures, sensitive to the temperature of their surroundings, they would either hibernate or find a warmer spot. If Matt really wanted to fish some out, there was a tributary stream not more than a mile away which received waste water from a factory on its banks with the result that its temperature was a good two or three degrees higher.

They went there in Matt's car, scrambling over waste ground and through barbed wire to reach the water's edge. Using his home made sieve-cum-scoop, Matt netted four at his first attempt. Then another three, then five very small ones, then one almost as long as his arm.

'Who says they're not breeding?' Matt grinned as they drove back to the Old Rectory.

'Not me,' Rhys assured him. 'In my opinion they're multiplying fast, they're getting bigger, and in short they're becoming a real menace. I've had reports of sightings in Spain, France, Belgium, the Netherlands, and northern Germany. But never a female. Now, explain that away.'

'Let's go back to your lab,' Matt suggested. 'Maybe we've got a mum among this lot.'

In the laboratory they took the larger worms one by one out of the strong metal box he now used as a portable container. Matt killed them himself, then watched as Fran examined them, with Rhys looking on to check and instruct. They were all male.

'It's weird,' she said when they'd finished and the worms were safely locked away in the boot of the car. 'Uncanny.'

'Design, I think,' Rhys commented seriously, for the first time openly mentioning his theory of extraterrestrial origin. 'Unusual features – the colouring, varied sizes, rate of growth, the rapid increase in numbers, and no visible females. I'd like to show you some of the evidence. People think I'm a nut-case, but before you make up your minds – it's dark outside now – I'd like to take you up to my observatory. I've only a small telescope, and it's not too clear a night either, but you should be able to see at least enough to make you wonder.'

They went up to the room he'd converted at the top of the house and took it in turns to stare at the planet Jupiter through his 6-inch telescope. It certainly made the possible existence of other worlds seem more real. Then he showed them reports of objects observed falling from the sky, drew diagrams, and ended by inviting them to look through the telescope once more. 'Not from the solar system perhaps,' he conceded. 'But somewhere else?'

Afterwards they went back to the car, thoughtful though not convinced. Rhys was clearly disappointed at their reaction. 'You'll not forget to let me know if you find any females?' he reminded them. 'That information's vital, wherever they came from.'

Julie had been glad to get out of the disco into the cool fresh air. It was her twentieth birthday and Mum had wanted her to celebrate with the family; there had been a row when she'd told them she'd fixed up to go out with Pete. But how could she invite him home when Mum never had a good word to say for him?

He was already astride the bike, pulling the goggles over his dark eyes, grinning at her. She hitched up her skirt and swung her leg over the pillion, clinging to his black leather jacket as they shot out through the gate and headed for the wood.

Somehow she didn't care whether she ever went home again. The wind rushed past her ears; the powerful bike throbbed and surged beneath her. The thought of that poky living room with Dad grumbling in front of the TV and the china birds flying up the wall made her sick.

They left the road and took the rough path between the trees, but someone else was in their usual place. Another bike stood there; in the undergrowth they caught a flash of white thighs as they rode on, circled, and returned to the main road.

Pete stopped. 'What about that cave I told you about?' he

suggested without switching off the engine. 'Only take us half-an-hour to get there.'

'Then why are we waiting?' she called back.

She hugged his waist as the bike picked up speed. Ahead, the road was deserted, though one or two cars met them coming from the opposite direction. A quick moment of bright headlamps, then they passed.

Beyond an isolated farmhouse Pete turned off into a winding lane. The high hedges on either side ceased unexpectedly, giving way to open moorland. He left the tarmac and they bumped over an uneven track for some distance, heading towards the hillside.

The cave entrance was hidden behind a high crag in a crevice only just wide enough for them to ease the bike through. Inside, it seemed shallow and dark, but at the rear was a low, twisting passage. Pete went ahead with the bike, using its headlamp to light the way; it took a lot of manoeuvring to get through.

'Oh!' Julie cried, delighted, when she emerged into the chamber beyond and saw the richly-coloured stalactites hanging from the rock face like a delicate screen.

Pete had jacked the bike up and was undressing. Julie nodded quickly and pulled her own clothes off. This was a hundred times better than the wood; it was a magic temple.

'Happy birthday!' Pete laughed, as he explored her body with his hard hands. The walls of the cave echoed the words around and around till they disappeared in a whisper.

They made love on the heap of clothes, awkwardly because of the uneven floor, but Julie didn't mind that. She couldn't remember ever having felt so totally happy and relaxed; even the eerie sounds of the cave added to her mood – the occasional drip of moisture, the whispers and slithers. . .

Then suddenly Pete screamed and twisted, throwing her away from him. Hurt, she began to protest, but her words died on her lips as she saw that long, green, snake-like thing squirming across his chest. It glowed like something evil in the half-light as it bit deep into his armpit.

Blood streamed from the wound on his belly just above his

navel where a second green thing was eating into him. A third nuzzled against his buttock. He thrashed about, bellowing with pain and begging her to help him.

But what could she do? The cave was full of them and she stood there panic-stricken, naked, totally vulnerable. It wasn't possible to get her clothes as Pete was lying on them, his blood soaking into them as he weakened and his struggles gradually subsided.

Biting her lip, trying to force herself to stay calm, she backed slowly towards the twisting passage. If only help would come! But she remembered Pete's words: 'No one'll ever find us here.'

A worm slipped over her foot. At the feel of it she lost all control and turned to dash out. Two more worms, slightly larger than the others, blocked the exit. They were half-erect and swaying as though to music; their eyes looked directly into hers, understanding.

One of them wrapped itself around her leg and buried its teeth into the flesh behind her knee; another, from behind, nibbled at her ankle. She heard herself whimpering, not screaming, as though something in those eyes had subdued her; she suddenly realized she was just standing there, allowing herself to be eaten and doing nothing about it.

At that, the spell broke and she screamed out her anger, seizing the first worm and tearing it away from her leg, fighting mad. She flung it to the far end of the cave and stooped for the second; but two others fastened themselves on her, one catching the flesh of her forearm.

Cursing and yelling, she killed one after another and didn't stop even when they forced her down to her knees and attacked her stomach, her full breasts, her cheeks, the softness under her chin. They slid over her naked body, wet with blood, more and more of them as if welcoming the fight, till she lost consciousness and her thin arms – the bones exposed – fell uselessly away.

The weeks passed. At Christmas Jenny played the part of a shepherd's wife in the Nativity at the parish church; she'd made friends quickly and was soon invited to several parties.

Helen suspected that the adults pumped her for information about how Matt earned his living and why the sheds were kept locked. Any idea of having a party of her own at the cottage was scotched by Helen. How could they even think of it with all those worms around the place? Matt argued they could never escape from the shed as they were in solid tanks, but she remained unconvinced.

Boxing Day was particularly uncomfortable. He'd gone to feed the worms and, as usual, became absorbed in watching their behaviour, forgetting all about the time. They'd asked Fran around for lunch – after all, she was a business associate – and Matt only emerged from the shed when he heard her arrive. From the look on Helen's face it was obvious what she was thinking.

After they'd eaten, as they sat in front of the fire, Fran began talking about Tegwyn Aneurin Rhys and soon had Jenny in stitches wtih her imitations of his eccentric way of talking and his bird-like habit of putting his head on one side when he was making a special point.

Helen didn't even smile. When Fran left and Jenny was in bed, they washed the dishes together in silence. When they'd finished he suggested there might be something worth watching on television.

'Anything rather than talk to me!' she burst out at him.

It was their first quarrel since they'd moved down to the cottage, yet they both knew it'd been smouldering for some time. She accused him of having an affair with Fran. That hurt. He'd smothered those feelings almost from the start.

Then she attacked him for the long hours he spent with the worms. True – but they were trying to make a living, he argued back. Not only from skins either. What about those colour transparencies he'd sold to the *Geographical*? That illustrated article to the German paper? Why couldn't she involve herself more in what they were doing? Fran had asked her to help with the book-keeping, to become part of the business, but she'd refused. Why?

'You know very well why!' Helen retorted.

But the storm passed that day and during the next few weeks

neither of them mentioned it. They even made love occasionally, trying to repair the breach. And he cut down the amount of time he spent with the worms and did more jobs about the house. She began to take in typing from the local solicitor and Matt helped her to check the work for accuracy. It gave them an insight into several neighbourhood scandals. In church on Sunday mornings they looked at several members of the congregation with renewed interest.

It was a mild winter that year and spring came early. He checked the tanks daily, hoping the worms might show signs of a courtship dance, anything to indicate a change in their behaviour pattern. They'd still not found any females but Fran had read somewhere that hermaphrodites were not unknown in the animal world. She rang Aneurin Tegwyn Rhys to discuss the idea; he thought it not impossible.

'If only we could breed them,' he explained to Jenny as she watched him dropping food into the tanks one day, 'we'd have more control. Hunting's so uncertain. Hit or miss.'

'You hate it, don't you?' Jenny observed, matter-of-fact. 'I know you do, Daddy, because your mood's quite different when you go hunting. You're all on edge. Mummy notices too. Why don't you love each other like you used to? Is it because of the worms?'

Matt's immediate instinct was to deny it, but then she'd only fall silent as she realized he was lying. 'I don't know, Jenny. People go through these phases.'

They moved to the tank with the largest worms. 'Isn't it beautiful, that one?' she cried out enthusiastically. 'Isn't it beautiful? Isn't it lovely?'

He smiled at her, agreeing, but holding her arm to prevent her putting her hand in to stroke it. The worm regarded them both lazily, opened its mouth to display its teeth, then curled and slid away in an elaborate figure-of-eight to the far side of the tank. Its long back rippled and twinkled with every imaginable shade of incandescent green and purple. Jenny caught her breath with excitement.

'Oh, I love them!' she exclaimed, her eyes bright with pleasure. 'If only Mummy weren't so afraid of them! And they're so intelligent! I'm sure they understand every word we say. Where do you think they come from?'

'Where do we all come from? We're all part of nature, aren't we?'

'Mm...'

14

Helen went down to the main shed reluctantly, hating what she had to do. It was eight o'clock in the evening and still not dark yet, though the pale moving clouds were tinged with red. A sudden breeze had sprung up, swaying the masses of daffodils; it was unexpectedly chilly after the warm spring day.

Matt had said he'd not be able to get back from London that night. A business deal with a lot of money involved – more skins, she supposed – so would she mind feeding the worms just this once? Jenny had been invited out to a birthday party, otherwise she'd have done it gladly.

Mind? Of course she minded. The mere sight of them turned her stomach. That glowing greenish-purple colour, The ripples as they moved. Their eyes.

Time and time again she'd told Matt they were his concern, she was having nothing to do with them, if she had her way she'd incinerate them in their own tanks. So why had she weakened once more? Why?

He'd left everything ready. The specially-constructed boxes he'd designed himself, each clearly marked, were stacked in order on the rough trolley he'd knocked together out of that discarded pram they found on the rubbish tip. He certainly worked hard, no one could fault him on that score. The hours he put in, the labour... Those worms were never out of his mind. At meal-times, while watching TV, even in bed. It was eerie, verging on madness.

As she pushed the trolley down the uneven path the 'food' suddenly came to life, scratching and scrambling inside the boxes. Helen shuddered. Right at the very beginning she'd argued with him about it, voiced her objections. But he hadn't listened. Pigheaded.

Biting her lip nervously she unlocked the shed door and went inside, easing the trolley over the step. Even before she switched on the light she sensed the quick stir of interest in the worm tanks. Sensed rather than heard. She was convinced they had known she was coming and consciously waited for her – silently. That threatening silence inside the shed.

'Well, here's your food! Here it is!' she called out, trying to reassure herself with the sound of her own voice. And failing. *They* knew all about her. Her fear. Her loathing of them. They weren't taken in.

She started with the first of the tanks on the wide shelf down the left-hand side of the shed, the glass aquarium where he kept the smallest worms, no more than three or four inches long. Already they were emerging from the murky water at the bottom and oozing up the smooth rocks he'd placed there; raising their heads, rhythmically waving them from side to side, trying to fix her with their tiny pinhead eyes. But she averted her gaze as she took the uppermost box from the trolley and placed it sideways over the tank, slotting the top edges of the glass walls into the grooves.

When it was firmly in position she opened the catch and drew out the sliding bottom of the box. The two mice inside squealed in alarm and protest; a panic-stricken scratching as they tried to cling to the walls; then they dropped down to the waiting worms. One landed in the water, the other on the largest of the rocks. More tiny screams and scurrying as they tried to save themselves from the sharp teeth.

Sickened, she turned away and went to the next tank. It was much bigger, made of sheet metal, and in the bottom was an evil-smelling mixture of stale water, rotting vegetation and rocks which Matt had collected from the seashore. In the semi-darkness the worms' skins glowed; their eyes seemed to seek hers. She retched, and it was all she could do to prevent herself vomiting into the tank.

Hurriedly she lifted up the next box and fitted it into place. Then the catch ... and the slide. The same frightened squeals from the mice – three of them this time – and the same helpless panic.

'Nature red in tooth and claw,' Matt had always quoted whenever she accused him of cruelty. 'It's their natural food. That's the way all animals live.'

'But in the wild some at least manage to escape,' she'd told him fiercely. 'They're not sacrificed callously, with no way out, to die in terror.'

'Aren't they?' he'd shouted back at her on that occasion, slapping his hand down on the table. 'Aren't they? Look at that hand! Look at my face! I know what it's like to be hunted for food. Remember?'

And she hadn't answered, not knowing what to say.

An agonized high-pitched squeal from one of the mice brought her back to her senses. From the two remaining boxes on the trolley came the sounds of violent but useless attempts to escape. They'd never be able to break through however long they scraped at the wood.

At the third and largest tank on that side of the shed she went through the same routine again, heaving the heavier box on to the top, making sure it was properly in place, then opening the slide to release the living food. She didn't stop to watch, but turned to the biggest tank of all on the right-hand side.

It was a long, deep metal bath covered with safety-frames of heavy wire mesh. This was the tank she feared most. The worms in it were like fully-grown snakes, and at this size they were no longer repulsive but dangerously attractive. Their colouring was more delicate, their movements over the rocks graceful, even elegant. Their eyes too lacked some of the hardness of the smaller worms. They enticed – beckoned...

As she undid the clips at the edges of the frame she became uncomfortably aware that silence had returned to the shed, an ominous silence. Even the poor miserable animals inside the food box were absolutely still. It was as though every living creature was holding its breath, waiting ... watching.

'Don't be stupid!' she told herself, speaking aloud. Her words seemed to hang on the air, rejected.

She grasped the heavy wooden frame at both ends, ready to lift it. Then she noticed, just beneath the mesh, two eyes regarding her sympathetically – and invitingly. She quivered, held by them. The head swayed gently. The long body lay supported against the side of the tank, draped like an expensive scarf in a Knightsbridge shop. She wanted to reach in and touch it, feel its silky smoothness beneath her fingers, stroke it. The urge was so strong, she was on the point of surrendering to it and was tugging the frame to one side when her hand slipped along the edge and—

'Damn!' She sucked her injured finger; the splinter had penetrated deep under the skin. It was nothing too tragic but enough to break the spell of those eyes. The worm, too, acknowledged defeat and slunk back to the bottom.

'You're not going to catch me like that again!' she swore at it.

With a quick impatient movement she swung the frame out of the way and dumped the food box into position. She had to shift it around a little before the grooves engaged, but Matt's design was accurate. The box exactly fitted the space left by the frame. She flicked open the catch and jerked the slide out.

One by one the rabbits dropped into the long tank: scared little creatures with long ears and pink eyes. They crouched there, quivering and twitching, making no attempt to escape as the worms darted at them from all directions, biting through their fur, ruthlessly tearing at the nearest portion of living meat. They didn't kill their victims, nor even attempt to subdue them, but savaged the bleeding flesh remorselessly, gulping down each mouthful.

Helen made for the door, slamming it shut behind her and locking it the moment she was outside. Her stomach heaved. She swallowed great mouthfuls of air. Then, unable to stop herself, she was violently sick.

The quick sweat felt cold on her skin. The garden fence shifted and dissolved before her eyes. Her hand found a corner of the shed to lean against as she coughed everything up, desperately struggling not to faint.

At last the spasm was over and she was able to stand up straight again. Her eyes cleared, her head ached, and her mouth tasted sour. She went back up the garden path towards the house. The wind-blown daffodils brushed against her legs, startling her; for a moment she saw them as a mass of yellow worms swaying towards her and she almost broke into a run in her need to get to the kitchen door.

Once inside, she shot the bolt top and bottom, then turned the key before rinsing out her mouth and splashing handfuls of cold water on to her face.

Oh, that was the last time she'd ever go near those worms. She'd never do it again. If Matt wasn't around to feed them, let them starve to death. She knew she hadn't completed the job. She should have replaced the slides, collected up the boxes and loaded them on to the trolley before withdrawing quietly in order not to excite the worms, switching off the light behind her. Yes, she knew the routines all right, but she hadn't done them. She'd left everything lying there in her panic to get out. The light on too.

He'd grumble at her when he got home. Give her a lecture on how worms only flourished in the dark, how the glands controlling their luminosity became sluggish in the light. And luminous skins fetched the best prices.

Yes, and he'd say it all so gently, carefully explaining every point as though talking to a child, spelling it out step by step till she felt like throwing something at him. But what good would that do? He'd only look at her with hurt in his eyes and later, in an intimate moment, he'd ask where it had all gone wrong, their marriage, and she'd lie to him that nothing was wrong between them; he was over tired, that was all. Over sensitive.

Not true, though. No, not true.

She fetched the whisky from the living room and poured a generous slug, drinking it neat to settle the queasiness of her stomach. Slowly it did its work. She poured another, then sat at the kitchen table and looked down at her clothes. The vomit had splashed over her shoes. On her tights, too, and the hem of her skirt.

No, it was not true. Things she did irritated him; that was only too obvious, though he tried to hide it. Little things, like the way she scratched her nose while trying to work something out, or left her comb in the bathroom full of strands of blonde hair, or used whichever toothbrush happened to be lying there, even if it wasn't hers.

Yet in the early years they'd always shared their toothbrush.

It was hard to imagine now how they'd delighted in each other's body: her excitement at his touch, his face eager and open. Not withdrawn and absentminded, not in those days.

She kicked off her shoes and peeled down her tights to rinse them through in the sink. No worms then, not anywhere. No one had ever heard of them, let alone thought of keeping them in a shed at the bottom of the garden. The sight of it through the window made her shudder; gooseflesh spread over her arms.

After hanging up the tights, she took off her skirt to try and clean off the vomit stains. Then, impatiently, she rolled it up and threw it in a corner. That acrid smell caught in her throat. She wanted to strip everything off, stand for hours under the shower and let it wash away all trace of the worms.

In the bedroom, she took more whisky, leaving the bottle on the dressing-table. She'd protested to him about the worms, then always weakened because it was his obsession. His living. His pride at the way it was all working out.

'Matt,' she whispered involuntarily. 'Oh Matt. . .'

She sat on the edge of the bed, her elbows on her knees, holding her glass with both hands curled around it. They'd all predicted it would go wrong: her friends at the time, her sister. . . It was too improbable, they'd told her – Helen, at the tail-end of a stale affair with the producer she worked for, falling in love with an over-tall, shy, awkward camera assistant who turned out to be a virgin the first time she took him to bed.

Not that she'd minded that part. She'd even felt flattered, wished she could return the compliment. And it *was* a compliment, as she tried to tell him while they lay naked in each other's arms. He'd flushed with embarrassment and she'd sensed his shame, confusion and happiness all inextricably mixed up together.

Emptying her glass she stood up to get more, then changed her mind and undressed for her shower. In front of the mirror she paused and examined her body critically, as though the secret of how their love died might be found in that rounder stomach, or the heavier hips. She no longer had that lithe, girl-ish figure, but she was still attractive surely? The lines were softer, the breasts fuller. . . Men still looked at her.

But it wasn't a physical thing, not only. What had gone was that unbelievable sense of belonging together, being made solely for each other to the exclusion of the rest of the world. If that could come back. . . But how? Never while he remained so taken up with those worms.

She turned abruptly away from the mirror and went into the bathroom. At least the shower was working efficiently since he'd fixed it. Pulling the waterproof curtain across, she adjusted the flow of water before stepping into the bath and letting it pour over her. Its force against the back of her neck and shoulders slowly released the tensions. She abandoned herself to it.

After some minutes she began to soap her body, moving her hands sensuously over her skin . . . her arms . . . sides . . . ribs . . . breasts . . . the way his hands used to in those first months when they took their shower together.

'Oh, Matt. . .'

He'd been so ambitious at that time, talking about the sort of films he dreamed of shooting, critical of his own work but optimistic. But then the opportunities had gone to others, and with them the international prizes, the recognition he so desperately needed. He'd been left behind. Of course he'd said nothing, never spoke about it, but bottled it all up inside himself.

And now the worms. Even under the warm water, caressing and comforting her as it washed the soap away, she couldn't help shivering as she thought of them. What were they doing to him? That fanatical look in his eyes whenever he enthused about them, the look verging on madness. They had such a hold on him; she couldn't even bring herself to be jealous of that woman with the shop – Fran or whatever her name was. She couldn't even imagine he was being unfaithful to her. They probably sat there and talked worms – for hours on end, nothing but worms.

A plan began to form in her mind. It would mean going back inside the shed for one last time. She'd need extra paraffin, several gallons of it, but that would be no problem; she could hide the cans under the tarpaulin at the side of the house. Then a generous dose in each tank, splash it over the floor and up the walls, throw in some extra wood – the logs he'd cut which they hadn't used after all – and old newspapers. And the worms would know what she was about. They'd watch her. She'd have to avoid their eyes.

Then the quick roar of the flames as they surged through the entire shed, licked up the walls and along the shelves, until *whoosh* ... *whoosh* ... *whoosh* ... the tanks ignited, each one separately...

She bent down under the shower to soap her legs with the rich white scented lather, and the water splashed on her back and streamed down off her shoulders Ever since they'd moved into the cottage he'd been going to fix that plug-hole, a round yawning outlet with no little chrome grid in it to prevent things falling through.

At that moment, as she stooped, she saw two hard little eyes looking up at her.

'No!' She caught her breath in a quick gasp of fear and stepped back.

Then she told herself it must be imagination, a trick of the light. Worms couldn't possibly ooze their way up inside a narrow drainpipe – or could they? She forced herself to look again.

Purposefully and calmly, the worm was emerging from the plug-hole. It lay there on the white enamel of the bath, staring at her without moving.

Helen knew she mustn't panic. She worked out what she must do: draw the shower curtain aside, step out of the bath carefully, quietly – no quick unexpected movements which might upset it...

The curtain was slippery with soapy water and her fingers couldn't get a grip on it. It seemed ridiculous, but her hand slid over it. She backed towards the rear end of the bath.

'It's fear,' she told herself, 'and I mustn't show it. I can't close my hand but the worm mustn't know that. Once they realize you're afraid...'

A second worm was wriggling up through the plug-hole. It

lay alongside the first and they both watched her.

'Stay there,' she begged them, 'Oh, please, stay there. Don't come any closer.'

With a great effort of will she grasped the shower curtain, but the wet plastic material seemed to cling to her arm and hamper her. She wanted to pull it out of the way, yet she seemed paralysed. A third worm had appeared at the plughole; the first two started slithering along the bottom of the bath towards her.

Desperately she tugged at the curtain; it ripped, falling down in folds around her. She struggled to escape from it, then felt her foot slipping on the soapy bath. Her arms waved wildly as she tried to regain her balance.

As she half fell, half slid into the bath, the first worm buried its teeth into the full flesh of her inner thigh. She shrieked in agony and tried to pull it away, but at the same moment the second worm began to feed hungrily on her calf.

'No ... no ... no, don't!' she sobbed as she tried to defend herself, still thrashing around in the folds of the shower curtain. 'I shan't do it, I shan't burn you, I promise...'

Once again she felt the first worm's sharp teeth as it moved higher up her thigh. But there were more worms now. God, where were they all coming from? They squirmed all over her legs, her abdomen, taking their time as they selected parts they fancied. Hysterically she screamed for mercy, begged them, as though they could understand her.

Then one moved between her legs. She covered her vagina with her hand, shuddering with terror. 'No, not there, not there!' The worm bit into her wrist and another joined it, moving down over her belly.

They were exploring her neck. Reaching for her cheeks...

Again she shrieked out. And again.

Her mind snapped into insanity but she remained cruelly conscious as they devoured the flesh from her face, under her chin, her breasts, her stomach, buttocks, legs... The pain shocked through her body from every part.

Then everything became suddenly quiet. Vaguely she realized she'd been the one making all the noise. Now, as her blood seeped away, she lost the strength even to scream. They were still feeding on her, in silence. Only the champing of jaws. As their incisors ripped out each mouthful of her flesh, even the pain seemed less.

Distantly, she realized at least one worm had finished with her surface meat and was burrowing into her intestines. But she hardly felt it; her nervous system was practically paralysed already.

Then at last she slipped away into uncomprehending death.

15

Matt and Fran left Cy Steinberg at the Dorchester at about eleven-thirty that evening and continued on foot to their own hotel near Baker Street. The meeting had been more successful than either of them could have imagined. Steinberg, Inc. supplied most of the more exclusive New York fashion houses with accessories. They'd expected a single large order for belts and possibly handbags; instead, they were offered a five-year deal for as many items as they could produce. On a quick reckoning, Matt estimated this should bring his income up to four times his old Television Hall salary.

'If only we can get hold of the skins,' he mused as they went up the steps to the revolving glass door. 'I phoned Angus this afternoon. He's seen a few back in the sewers, but not all that many.'

'They killed the golden goose, now they must lie on it!' Fran declared, crossing to the desk. And giggled. 'If you get my meaning. Matt, let's not talk business any more. I think I had too much champagne. Did you notice our American friend's technique? We did all the drinking while he drove the bargain. I wonder how much he stands to make?'

'Rooms 395 and 399, please.'

'Quite a packet, I bet,' she went on.

Matt picked up the keys, said goodnight to the porter and guided her towards the lift.

'My, aren't we masterful?' she murmured, glancing shrewdly at his face. 'Don't misinterpret my little confession.'

'Wouldn't dream of it.'

In the lift, Matt pressed the button for the third floor, but as the doors were closing a man dashed towards them and squeezed in. '*Ja, danke, danke,*' he breathed, his face flushed. Beads of sweat rolled across his bald head. He took a handkerchief from his pocket, carefully unfolded it and wiped them away.

Fran grinned at Matt mischievously. The tip of her tongue played across her lips. Her foot tapped the floor. '*Gute Nacht*,' she said to the sweating man as they went out.

Matt followed her along the quiet corridor of closed doors. When they came to her room he turned the key in the lock, then stood hesitating on the threshold till she caught his hand and drew him gently inside.

As they kissed he thought of Helen. And Jenny. He hated the idea of hurting either of them, yet Fran belonged in the picture too. Somewhere.

She broke away from him and put her hand to his cheek. 'What's the matter?'

'Nothing.' He kissed her again.

She kicked off her shoes and reached behind for her zip, but he took hold of it, easing it the full way down till her dress slipped from her shoulders. She stepped out of it and threw it across a chair. He fumbled with the rest of her clothes but she laughed and told him to get his own things off. Then she lay there on the bed, naked, watching him.

'That's better, we're the same height now,' she whispered when they were lying side by side, his hand wandering over her hips, her belly, her small breasts, the pale freckles spreading down from her neck.

He raised himself on his elbow and looked down at her, kissing her face, her lips. Her straight, dark brown hair tumbled about her head on the pillow. Gently she guided him and he felt himself being drawn into her; it was like a return home after all those months. They made love quietly, unhurried, as if exploring the experience afresh, then gradually with greater intensity and—

The phone rang shrilly, cutting into the moment.

They looked at each other, shocked. It rang a second time. Fran rolled from beneath him and sat on the edge of the bed.

'Who can it be?'

Matt looked at her uncertainly. 'Cy? Changed his mind?'

She took the receiver. 'Yes?' Trying her best to sound sleepy; putting on an act. Her expression changed. She looked taken aback. Scared. 'It's for you. Jenny.'

The childish voice was hard and clear through the crackles on the line. 'I hope I haven't disturbed you in the middle of sex,' she said unemotionally. 'I thought I should tell you Mummy is dead. If you're interested.'

'Jenny, how. . . ?'

'The worms are eating her.'

Before he could question her properly she'd rung off. He stared at the phone, unable to believe her; yet something terrible must have happened to make her behave that way. He dialled the number, answering Fran's urgent questions with half-phrases.

'We'll see what Helen says.' But the line was engaged.

'She's left it off the hook more likely,' Fran observed. She reached for her handbag and began to finger through her address book. 'Who else can we ring? Frank's number's here.'

'You get dressed while I call him,' Matt said, taking the booklet from her. Frank was the solicitor who paid Helen to type his case notes; he had three children of his own, including a daughter of Jenny's age. 'If he can't go round himself, at least he might get in touch with the Westport police. It'll take us hours to drive back there, even at this time of night.'

He let the number go on ringing till Frank's irritated voice answered. When he heard who was calling, he sounded even more annoyed at being dragged out of bed.

Matt told him quickly about Jenny.

Yes, he would go round there right away and see what was wrong. It was perfectly in order for Matt to ring him – what else were friends for? Now he was not to worry. Everything would be looked after till Matt got back.

Fran was ready by the time he'd finished the call. He pulled on his clothes, went to his own room for his still unpacked bag, and then checked out. He'd been on the point of warning Frank to watch out for the worms when he went to the cottage, but then thought better of it. Jenny was probably inventing the whole thing.

The hotel had its own underground car park which was dimly lit and filled with silent rows of cars. Their footsteps echoed loudly; the few words they spoke were whispered back at them from odd corners. Fran watched him, concerned, as he unlocked the passenger door.

He took her into his arms and kissed her, holding her close. 'I'm sorry.'

'Not your fault.'

'I don't believe for one moment that Helen is dead, but Jenny's obviously going through some sort of crisis. I only hope Frank can manage.'

'You realize he'll charge you for it – personal services? Come the end of the month, his account will be in the post. He's known for it.'

The London traffic at that time of night was sparse but erratic; cars shot away from the lights, swerving across the lane unpredictably, skidding around corners without warning. Matt was relieved when he reached the motorway. He kept up a steady eighty, his headlights eating into the blackness.

'It can't be the worms,' he commented after a very long silence. 'They could never get out of their tanks, not by themselves.'

'Let's wait till we get there,' she said.

Her hand rested lightly on his shoulder as if to reassure him. But he continued to turn it over in his mind. He could see no reason why anything should have gone wrong. Not with the worms.

In his rear mirror he spotted the headlights of another car and dropped his speed slightly just in case the police were on the prowl. At this time of night they had no one else to pick on.

'You were saying the worms are back in the sewers,' Fran started. 'You rang Angus?'

'This afternoon. Told me it was like a massacre last autumn. They used traps, flame-throwers, poisons, even mice with cyanide on them. According to him there wasn't a single worm left anywhere in the sewers. Not anywhere.'

'And then?'

'Slowly they came back.'

'Since when?'

'He spotted the first about four or five weeks ago. Their

numbers have been building up every day. Big brutes, he said. He also mentioned if we want any, we'd better get there quickly. The men are threatening a strike if the worms aren't exterminated properly.'

He slowed down to turn off the motorway into the network of B-roads which would take him to Westport. The other car sped past him; it hadn't been the police after all.

By the time they arrived it was almost four o'clock. Lights were on in several houses and Matt thought he heard a shot from somewhere in the distance. Entering the lane leading up to his own cottage, his headlights picked out the shape of a man hurrying off in another direction. He didn't recognize who it was.

'Oh Christ,' he muttered to himself, gripping the wheel. 'Oh Christ, they've got out.'

Fran's fingernails dug into his shoulder. 'What are we going to find?' she whispered. 'Matt. . . ?'

'You'd best stay in the car till I fetch you some boots. They could be anywhere in the long grass, on the path. . .' He drew up behind the police Rover, leaving his headlights on. The doctor's car was parked a little farther up the lane. Every window of the cottage was lit. 'Pray God, Jenny's all right.'

He swung his legs out of the car and dashed across to the back door, watching the ground sharply for worms. Dr Davies and the burly, uniformed police sergeant looked up as he burst into the kitchen.

'You got here, then?' the sergeant commented brusquely. 'It's not nice. I'm sorry, Mr Parker, it's not nice at all.'

'Where's Jenny?'

'Jenny's going to be all right,' the doctor said in his unctuous bedside manner. He was a thin, sickly-looking man with straight dark hair which he wore too long. Matt had never taken to him. 'Frank has taken her home and I've had to put her under sedation.' His tone was reproachful.

'Was she attacked?'

'One of her fingers. Only a small bite. Nothing to get upset about.'

'I'm afraid Mrs Parker is dead,' the sergeant intervened. 'You've heard about that already, I believe. Nasty business.

We haven't moved her yet. I'll come up with you for formal identification but you'll excuse me if I don't go in. I've seen the body once, that was enough.'

'In the shed?' Matt asked, not understanding.

The sergeant looked at him blankly, then led him up to the bathroom, standing to one side to let him pass.

Smears of blood on the wall tiles. And on the shower curtain which lay heaped on the floor. Helen's eyes stared up at him from the bath, unblinking; most of her face was a raw, red, distorted mess; her legs, torso and arms had been crudely ripped open. With her in the bath were the remains of several worms – battered to death by a police truncheon, he was told later. But not before they'd gorged themselves on her flesh, torn it away in greedy mouthfuls to expose her bones, dropping pieces in their savage eagerness.

Matt looked numbly at the scene as though paralysed. Then a scream broke from him as his mind began to comprehend what he was seeing. *His* worms had done this. It was *his* fault, no one else's. The agony welled up inside him. He relived that experience in the sewers, felt the sharp teeth once again, and knew Helen had gone through the same hell before she died.

In despair he hid his face against the bathroom wall, hammering against it. 'No, no. . .'

'Doctor, come up, would you?'

Matt stumbled down the stairs, brushing past the doctor with his syringe ready. 'Fuck your sedation!' he snarled. 'I'll show you who's responsible. Give *them* one of your jabs.'

In a few strides he was down the garden path and at the door of the main shed. As he fumbled in his pocket for the key he thought vaguely it was odd the light was still on. He was filled with fury against the worms, ready to charge in there and hack them to death. Doctor Davies and the burly police sergeant fell back a pace as he opened the door.

Silence.

He'd half-expected to find worms spilling over the floor, slithering along the bench and the shelves, maybe poised above the door jamb. Instead, everything was in order. The food boxes were still over the tanks but otherwise. . . Mechanically he checked them, pushed in the slides again and returned them to the trolley. The worms looked up at him lazily. They'd never been out of their tanks.

'There must be others,' Matt was desperately explaining when Fran appeared in the doorway.

'I thought you were going to bring me some boots,' she greeted them sarcastically. 'Can somebody tell me what's happening?'

Matt turned on her savagely. 'Why the hell didn't you stay in the car?' he yelled at her. 'The place must be crawling with worms. They've killed Helen.'

'They got out?'

'Not these, but their kind. Their kith and kin. They got into the bathroom, God knows how. They. . .' His voice broke; he leaned against the door and covered his face, sobbing uncontrollably. 'Helen. . .'

Fran took charge and coaxed him back to the house where she sat him down in the kitchen and made some fresh tea. Doctor Davies fussed about with his syringe, but Matt said no and Fran told him sharply to put it away. The doctor took offence; his thin lips tightened.

'He'll need his wits about him,' Fran said briskly. 'We all shall. Don't you understand? Matt knows more about these worms than anyone else in the whole country. What use is he going to be if you knock him out with that stuff? They may be anywhere – drains, ditches, streams. . .'

'You know then?' the sergeant demanded heavily.

'Know what?'

'That this isn't the only incident involving worms in Westport tonight.' He took out his notebook and turned over its pages, though obviously more for effect than because of any need to refresh his memory. 'We've been flooded with calls. A few typical ones: Mrs Penhaligon's dog – yesterday evening, this was – rooting around in a stream. They bit his eyes out.'

'She was in hysterics when I called,' Doctor Davies joined in. 'I had to sedate her.'

'A young couple out for a cuddle in Lover's Wood – we've all been there in our time – but they ended up in the cottage hospital, the girl with leg injuries and the boy suffering from shock. Your worms, Mr Parker. A farmer reports one of his pigs savaged and killed. Another farmer hears one of his cows in distress and goes out to investigate. It's being devoured by these worms of yours, and they've already started on a second cow. No way of saving them, he has to shoot them both. Oh, and he says his dog's also injured. They're everywhere, all over the place.'

Matt gulped the hot, sweet tea Fran had put before him. He was gradually regaining control of himself as he listened to the sergeant. 'How big are they, these worms?' he demanded.

'Getting on for a yard long, the dead one I saw.'

'And they're all that size?'

'If they're biting chunks out of your leg you don't stop to measure them.'

'Nor if they're attacking your pet dog,' Doctor Davies contributed nastily.

'I came here in the first instance to ask you to help us round them up,' the sergeant told him, 'and then to get the answers to a few questions. But when I arrived I found this ... er ... this situation with your wife ... and ... well, if you don't feel up to it, that's understandable.'

'There's none missing from the shed,' Matt insisted stubbornly.

'How can you be sure?'

'Go and check them yourself. There's a tally sheet on the wall above each tank. Count the numbers, see if they correspond. They do. It's not my worms causing this trouble.'

'Mr Parker, these things are dangerous—' the sergeant began ponderously, but Matt interrupted him.

'Do I need you to tell me that?' he said bitterly. 'With my wife lying dead upstairs, almost unrecognizable? And how d'you think I got these scars on my face, lost these fingers? I don't underestimate them, I can assure you.' He stood up to go to the cupboard where he kept his waders. 'Fran, you're too exposed in that dress. You'd better put some jeans on – you'll find some in the bedroom – and gumboots.'

Doctor Davies stood up as well and snapped his bag shut. 'If these worms aren't yours,' he queried, without attempting to disguise his hostility, 'how is it we never saw any before you arrived to live here? Why do they suddenly appear now?'

Matt pulled on his waders with difficulty. He felt worn out, beaten to the ground; it took a great effort of will to reply politely. 'It's spring, isn't it?'

'So?'

He remembered an expression Angus had used on the phone. 'Their spring offensive.'

'Ridiculous!' the doctor sneered. 'In my opinion, Mr Parker, in breeding these worms you've acted irresponsibly, endangered life and limb—'

'Breeding them?' Matt exclaimed. 'What makes you think anyone knows how to breed them? You ignorant bugger, you understand nothing, do you?'

'Now, Mr Parker,' the sergeant expostulated. 'I don't think this is going to help us at all.'

'You're right, it isn't. They don't normally bite through thick clothing, or rubber boots, or that sort of thing. Not in my experience. And keep gloves on if you're anywhere near them. I'd like to see where these cows were killed, so let's start there. I imagine it was somewhere near a stream or a pond?'

'That's right,' the sergeant confirmed.

'I'll take some equipment with me, but. . .' He left the rest unsaid, his fear that the worms might really have started a spring offensive as Angus suggested, that they might find not five, ten or twenty, but hundreds of them. What then?

Fran came downstairs again. She'd changed into Helen's jeans and sweater; Matt pointed out her gumboots. It hurt him seeing her in Helen's clothes, and she realized it. She touched his arm and looked into his face, as if trying to say something. He nodded unhappily; it had been his own suggestion after all.

Outside, the sky was pale and slightly streaked with cloud. The tree-tops were thick with birds; on any normal morning he'd have stopped to comment on the dawn chorus, but this time the shrill twittering jarred his nerves. As though they were singing in triumph, he thought; reminding him that human beings were in a minority on this planet.

'I'll drive first and you follow behind,' the sergeant was saying. 'Don't wander off on your own. And Doctor Davies, I don't think we need detain you any— Oh Christ, look at that!' His voice dropped almost to a whisper.

As the early morning sun rose above the crown of the hill its rays caught the supple, multi-coloured worms which had gathered around Matt's car. There must have been at least thirty, some curled in the high grass of the rough lane, others stretched along the parallel strips of exposed soil which had been hardened and worn bald by the tyres. One was draped like an ornate figure 6 over the boot of the car, with its head guarding the lock. Another, shifting position every few seconds, displayed itself on the roof.

They stopped dead. 'It's beautiful!' Fran breathed.

For a few seconds Matt's hatred dissipated. No existing film stock could capture those colours. Their scales broke up the light, heightening the natural luminescence of their skins.

'You'll have to do something,' Doctor Davies was burbling, his voice strained with fear. He clutched his bag in his right hand like a weapon, his knuckles whitening. With his left hand he nervously brushed some of his long hair back from his face. 'We can't stay here all day. We must get away.'

A few worms moved, aware of the presence of human beings. They raised themselves, arching their heads as they swayed. Perhaps they were merely taking pleasure in the warm sunlight; or perhaps they were co-ordinating their attack.

'Oh, yes,' Matt agreed. 'What d'you suggest?'

'You're the man with all the experience,' the sergeant commented steadily. 'They're mostly gathered round your car, so if we risk trying to reach mine and. . .' He stopped.

'Give them what they're after.' Fran sounded strange – not afraid, but as though she'd just discovered something about the worms she'd not understood before. 'They want the skin samples.' She paused. 'Or you.'

Matt's anger flooded back. Maybe it was something about her face, white and drawn after their sleepless night. Or the fact she was wearing Helen's brown, polo-neck sweater. He looked at her, seeing Helen. The worms were trying to get at him through his own weak spot, he was convinced – his emotional tangle, Helen-Fran. He flushed hot with fury.

'The sergeant's right.' He drew on his gauntlets. 'You all keep back while I deal with them. Who else?'

The worms watched him, almost warning him that they

could predict what he was about to do. He hated everything about them – the threatening way they slithered through the grass towards their victims, their tiny eyes, those beautiful, evil skins, the deadly jaws with their sharp teeth.

The only weapons he'd brought from the cottage were a heavy walking-stick and his sheath-knife. They'd be sufficient. He waded in among them.

Two or three worms wriggled out of the way as he approached; once he'd passed them, though, they closed in again behind him. He was completely surrounded.

Swinging his stick viciously at the nearest, he heard the skull crack. His right arm rose and fell rhythmically, like a reaper with a sickle. The worms snapped back at him, crowding around his legs. He ignored them. This time he was not hunting skins; he was killing with cold deliberation.

A worm slid over his foot and he tried to stamp on it, almost losing his balance. He'd only to fall, he knew, even stumble back against the car, for them to be able to reach his face.

Something moved up his leg, curling around it. At the same time the worm on the boot lid launched itself at him, twining about his right forearm.

'Stay calm,' he muttered to himself; fear gripped him. 'Never panic. . .'

In his left hand he grasped the sheath-knife. It was razor-sharp, honed every day. The worm on his arm tightened its coils. It was already raising its head to strike at his face when he slipped the point of the blade into its throat.

A sudden hiss. The rippling body slackened and he shook it off.

The worm on his leg dodged the blade twice, then caught it between its teeth, holding on like a vice. As Matt pulled it clear, the sharp edge cut into the corners of its mouth. Something gave way – maybe the blade had entered the brain – the coils loosened and it fell.

Another worm slithered lazily across the top of the car, dropped down on to the carcase and began to eat it.

Breathing heavily, as much from shock as from his exertions, Matt heard something behind him and swung around. Fran had joined him. She'd armed herself with a spade and was ferociously chopping down on any worm that approached. Grimly he renewed his own attack, laying about him with the heavy stick, till suddenly he realized they'd won.

They must have killed between fifteen and twenty altogether. Those that remained were too busy feeding on the bodies of their fallen comrades to show any further interest in Matt or Fran. They were gulping down great mouthfuls of flesh. Two had been cut in half by the spade; in each case they ate their own shorn tails.

Matt brought his stick down hard on the heads of three more, spattering them across the ground. Fran decapitated others, grinning with joy as each head fell.

'Intelligent?' Matt cried with scorn, whacking at yet another one. 'Rhys must be off his rocker if he thinks these are intelligent. They're just asking to be killed.'

'Are they?'

Something in her voice made him glance at her sharply. Her face glowed with the effort, all traces of tiredness gone. But what had she meant?

Near her feet was another worm. She slammed her spade down at its head, but missed and severed its tail. Once again it twisted back on itself to investigate and then began to swallow the amputated section.

Fran shuddered as she watched it.

But it wasn't until afterwards in the car – he was following the sergeant to the farm – that she revealed what was on her mind.

'Don't you see, Matt?' she pleaded with him anxiously. 'They eat their own dead every time, and their own tails, as if they're afraid of samples of their flesh falling into the wrong hands.'

'Or simply hungry.' He was remembering that later in the morning he'd have to face Jenny. What could he say to her? She would accuse him, hurt, and he'd be able to deny nothing. If he hadn't gone to London with Fran, Helen might still be alive.

'Another thing,' Fran was insisting, 'it was the skins brought them to our car in the first place. They wanted them back. To eat them. Don't you see what that means?'

'We can't possibly know,' he said wearily.

'All the women wearing our belts, gloves, handbags...
they're in danger if they go anywhere near a worm. It's true,
Matt, and you know it.'

Matt didn't answer. He was still thinking of Jenny, trying
to work out what to say to her and absentmindedly sucking the
wound on his finger.

'You're hurt?' Fran asked.

In the heat of the fight he hadn't noticed it happen. One of
the worms must have caught him with its teeth, tearing through
the artificial leather of the glove.

'Thought you said they didn't bite through clothing,' she
was going on.

'That's right.' It had tasted his blood, he realized; its mind
would have flashed the message back.

'So?' she demanded.

'So they do now.'

16

Little knots of people stood around in the steep cobbled streets and on the harbour walls of Westport, talking it over, swapping experiences. That morning they'd opened their newspapers and switched on their radios expecting to learn that other towns had also been affected. No mention of any. It seemed this small fishing port had been the only one.

Everyone had a story to tell. Mrs Phillips had been about to fill the kettle when she'd discovered a worm exploring her kitchen sink; it had oozed its way up to the draining-board where she'd killed it with a bread knife. Old Jack Ridley, up early as usual, had been startled when one suddenly reared up at him as he was about to use the outside lavatory. Others had been seen lying alert on the low corrugated iron roof of a lean-to bicycle shed. In a lobster pot. In a bucket. Coiled around the milk bottles on a doorstep. Lurking among the washing Mrs Cornish was about to hang on the line.

Most people had put on thick protective clothes and tucked their trouser legs into gumboots. Many carried some sort of weapon: a heavy stick, or even a shot gun. They'd no doubt who was to blame. Only one man could be responsible, the man who'd brought the worms to Westport in the first place.

Matt and Fran left the police station and threaded their way back to the car. Everyone had heard by now of Helen's death but there was no word of condolence, no look of sympathy. Matt felt relieved when at last they reached the car and got in, slamming the doors and starting the engine. People moved out of their way as they drove off.

Maybe they were right, he thought. If he hadn't brought the worms here. . .

Helen was dead. Three more people were in hospital in addition to the young couple mentioned by the police sergeant.

One of them was a child who'd gone out early that morning to meet her father off a fishing boat returning to harbour. In the estuary the body of a young man in swimming trunks had been found; a worm had gnawed its way into his intestines. And the toll of animals was not yet fully known: at least two cows, several sheep, a mare in foal, pigs, dogs, hens, geese... But no cats. Not yet.

Thank God Jenny was safe, though she refused to see him. Frank had tried to be diplomatic on the phone. 'Shock,' he'd said. 'Doctor Davies has been around again. Maybe it's best she stays on with my kids for a day or two, don't you think?'

What choice did he have? Where could he take her – back to the cottage where she'd returned from a birthday party to find her mother dead in the bath, with the worms still feeding on her? He could hardly invite her to Fran's flat over the shop. Over and over again he heard that hurt little voice on the phone: 'I hope I haven't disturbed you in the middle of sex, I hope I haven't disturbed you in the middle of sex, I hope I haven't disturbed you in the middle of...'

Fran was looking at him. His hands gripped the steering wheel as the car rocked over the uneven lane leading up to the cottage. 'Oh, hell.'

The undertakers' van was already there. As he pulled up the men manoeuvred out through the back door carrying a long narrow container covered by a waterproof cloth. He stood in the garden and watched them. No sign of the worms now, not even of those he'd killed earlier that morning, but this was their moment of trumph. Killing Helen, and in that particular way, hit him harder than anything else they could have done. The police constable watched him impassively. Fran stood near him, anxious. He felt empty, and suddenly alone.

Motorcycle engines shattered the silence, several of them roaring up the lane as the undertakers' van pulled away. A gang of teenagers in full black leather gear with silver studs and white-painted Nazi insignia rode into the garden, round and round, revving aggressively, through Helen's flower beds, flattening the daffodils and churning up the vegetable patch he'd sown only a few days earlier.

The policeman made no attempt to stop them, but stepped

back into the shelter of the kitchen door and began to speak urgently into his radio.

Fran clutched Matt's arm. 'What are we going to do?'

'Nothing.'

One by one the bikes stopped, splitting the eardrums with their revving before the engines finally died. The boys dismounted and gathered in a group. Six of them. He recognized two or three, though he couldn't see their faces clearly through their helmets. One was the telegraph boy. Another he'd seen working on a fishing boat. They looked towards him, arguing amongst themselves.

'Now, lads, be sensible. Leave him alone,' the policeman warned them, trying to assert his authority though he couldn't have been more than four or five years older.

'Who touching 'im?' the burliest of them sneered. He went to the door of the main shed and started kicking it in with the flat of his foot till it burst open. ' 'Ere they are!'

Matt dashed across with a warning to be careful, the worms were dangerous, but they brushed him aside and began to carry cans of paraffin into the shed. When the young policeman tried to intervene, one of the boys stood in front of him with a crowbar in his hands, blocking his way.

'Yer wan' them worms dead much as we do, don' yer?' he threatened. 'We're gonna clean this place up, kill every bloody worm. Why don' yer jus' look the other way at the pretty view? Jus' leave us be.'

The policeman glanced at Matt, who said: 'Let them. Why not? They're doing my job for me.'

Bitterly.

Through the open door he watched callously as they poured paraffin into each tank and set it alight. The worms thrashed about trying to escape the flames but he felt no pity. The largest succeeded in knocking away the safety net from the top of their tank; then their heads appeared above the edge, swaying as they burned, their eyes seeming to seek his. He didn't move. Let them fry. The fire crackled and the sick smell of scorched flesh mingled with the stench of paraffin.

Fran joined him. 'It's the end, isn't it?' she whispered, her lips quivering. 'The end of all we planned.'

It hardly seemed credible that only the previous evening they'd been having dinner with Cy Steinberg, negotiating the contract for worm skins which could have made them rich. Drinking champagne while Helen fought for her life. And lost.

The boys kicked open the door of the smaller shed, overturning the cages and whooping with delight as the mice ran over their feet. The white rabbits cowered fearfully against the walls. They shooed the animals out and set fire to that shed too.

One mouse headed for the far end of the garden where the grass was high; Matt had been intending to clear it that summer and maybe plant potatoes or parsnips. But before it could reach shelter, loping over the vegetable patch, a long worm appeared slithering towards it. The brilliant sunshine brought out the full splendour of its colouring. It stopped for a second as though posing to be admired, then shot out to catch the mouse between its teeth.

Simultaneously the boys spotted it. They scrambled for their bikes, shouting to each other, kicking the engines into life and roaring off towards the rough grass. The worm was too slow in sensing the approaching danger; it died, squashed beneath the wheels of the first bike. Up and down over every inch of ground they rode like Furies, making sure no worms escaped. Matt looked on, accepting the punishment. Blaming himself.

'You're sure you don't wish to lay charges, sir? They're making a bit of a mess of your place.' The policeman watched them nervously, uncertain how to handle the situation.

Both sheds were burning fiercely; the roof of the larger one cracked and swayed, on the point of falling in. The garden was unrecognizable, scored with deep tyre-marks where the bikes had skidded round, the plants broken and mauled.

'Quite sure,' he said.

The policeman nodded and went over towards the lane where Matt saw him talking into his personal radio, away from the noise of the bikes. Requesting instructions, maybe.

One worm broke cover, slipping across the earth at an amazing speed, changing direction several times, playing games with the bike pursuing it. The others stopped to applaud and encourage, taking sides. Then it made a mistake; the rider swooped on the worm, catching it by the tail and swinging it around his head.

He let go. Matt dodged as it flew through the air towards him, and it landed on Fran's blouse. She screamed in panic, trying to brush it off.

'Stay still!' he shouted.

It slipped, then seemed to steady itself as it prepared to strike up at the flesh beneath her chin. In the background Matt could hear the boys laughing, enjoying the sight. He grabbed the worm with his bare hand just below the head but instead of squeezing he turned and walked towards the one who'd thrown it, still sitting astride his bike with his helmet off, grinning, running his fingers over his close-cropped hair.

'You threw this?' Matt demanded.

At first the goon didn't flinch as Matt held the worm close to his face. He was the son of the timber-yard owner, in his mid-twenties, with a reputation to keep up among the tougher element. Matt had often seen him with his hangers-on in the pub down by the harbour. He moved the worm an inch or two nearer; it strained forward to bite, its jaws opening.

'You're mad! Get that thing away from me!'

'You shouldn't have thrown it,' Matt told him. The fury simmered inside him. If it had landed only an inch higher its teeth would have been buried in Fran's neck, perhaps severing the jugular. 'You'd better take your friends out of here, or I'll let it feed on your face.'

He was in a tight spot, he knew. The others had gathered in a circle around him, still on their bikes, the engines ticking over. One false move and they'd ride straight at him. Beyond them, he could see Fran had armed herself with a garden rake.

'Tell them to go,' Matt ordered. 'But you stay here till they're all away.' To emphasize the point he brought the worm closer to the goon's scared face again.

'You bastard, I'll get you for this, see if I don't!' The goon twisted his head to avoid being bitten, but the worm's sharp teeth sank into the lobe of his ear. Just the tip of it, but enough. The blood trickled down the side of his neck.

'That's just to whet its appetite,' Matt threatened. 'So tell them.'

His hand was steady. The worm didn't struggle but its jaws opened again as Matt brought it nearer.

'All right!' The goon surrendered and told his companions to get to hell out of it, he'd meet them down by the harbour. At first they hesitated, perhaps hoping to see how far Matt would go. Then, one by one, they roared out of the garden and down the lane.

Matt waited till the sound of their engines had died away in the distance. The goon's eyes were on him, apprehensive. And on the hungry worm in front of his face. Holding it still within an inch of his nose, Matt produced his knife and speared it through the soft skin below the jaw. He felt it slacken as the tip of the blade entered the brain.

Still holding it on the point of his knife, he stepped back. 'Move,' he commanded quietly. 'In future, keep out of my hair.'

The goon didn't need telling twice. A quick rev of the engine and he shot off clumsily, his rear wheel digging into the ground and throwing up a shower of topsoil before it gripped. Matt watched till he was out of sight before flinging the dead worm from him.

They stayed at the cottage only long enough to tidy up and pack some fresh clothes for Matt. He insisted on being alone while he cleaned the bathroom. The police had taken the dead worms; he could visualize them gingerly placing the remains in labelled polythene packets ready for laboratory reports and the coroner's court. There'd be a post mortem on Helen too, what was left of her. Her smeared blood had dried on the sides of the bath and on the wall-tiles; it felt sacrilegious to be wiping them away. The bathroom should be left untouched, as a memorial.

But he went over it thoroughly, the way Helen would have wanted. She'd always been a stickler for a clean bathroom. It was almost an act of homage to her.

Fran was ready when he went downstairs again and they left immediately for her flat above the shop. Neither of them spoke. As soon as they arrived he tried to ring Tegwyn

Aneurin Rhys while she cooked some lunch. There was no answer.

He'd told her he wasn't hungry but the smell of the lamb chops sizzling in the pan reminded him he'd taken nothing since the previous evening. His mouth tasted sour; his whole body was aching and tense.

'What am I going to do about Jenny?' he asked, mooching around disconsolately as Fran prepared the meal. 'I'll have to talk to her, but what can I say?'

The potatoes had boiled long enough. He watched her as she carried the pan to the sink and poured away the scalding water in a great cloud of steam.

'I'll ring Frank,' he decided.

But Frank said in his usual smooth, professional manner that Jenny still refused to see him, which was understandable, wasn't it? She needs time, old man. In any case, she'd expressed a desire to go to stay with her aunt in Devon and it had all been agreed.

'I phoned her this morning to explain matters. Couldn't have been more helpful. Of course she was shocked about her sister's death and the fact you'd not told her anything, but I was able to smooth things over, I think. We're driving down there this afternoon.'

Matt was bewildered. The whole thing was out of his hands. He was on the point of protesting that Jenny was *his* daughter, *he* should be taking the decisions, but what was the use? If Jenny wanted it that way... So he tried to be gracious and began expressing his thanks, only to be cut short.

'As your solicitor, old man, I regard it as my duty.' Frank sounded increasingly pompous. A whiff of the magistrates' court about him. 'You'll be getting my account in due course.' Before ringing off, he added: 'I'm surprised you're not out with one of the parties hunting these worms. It's a serious problem. In my opinion we're all in danger.'

Fran put his meal on the table and ordered him to sit down and eat it. The day wasn't over yet, she pointed out, and they were both going to need all their strength. In her opinion, it would be best for them to leave Westport right away and make for somewhere safe. He told her about Jenny.

'Best thing for her,' she commented. 'You can keep in touch by phone and go to visit her when. . . Well, when she's ready for you.'

'Yes.'

'Matt. . .' She put down her fork and laid her hand over his. 'I can guess what you must be going through. If you want to. . . I mean, you've only to say the word and I'll go out of your life completely.'

'Is that what you'd like?'

'You know it isn't. But if it helps. . .'

He shook his head. 'No.'

From downstairs came a crash of glass and the sound of raucous voices shouting and laughing. Matt dashed down into the shop in time to see a group of youths and girls running away. They'd smashed the main window with a rock and paint-sprayed the words WORM-LOVERS over the door. Fran looked strained and pale as she surveyed the damage.

'They've taken a handbag and a couple of belts. I'll phone the police.'

'Would you like me to?' he offered.

'If you want to help, collect the rest of the stock out of the window,' she instructed him. 'We don't want the whole of Westport taking what they please. There are some cardboard cartons in the room at the back.'

But when she put the phone down again she shrugged her shoulders in despair. 'They say they'll try to come round later but they're too busy right now. It was that sergeant again; he's still on duty. He said one of the hunting parties ran into trouble. Found themselves surrounded; hundreds of worms, he said. One man is dead and three others are in hospital. They're blaming us.'

'Why? For Chrissake, why?' But he knew the answer already.

'No other town has had them, not in these numbers. Only Westport and the farms around.'

They packed the stock into several cartons, but only the more valuable items, nothing else, and only as much as they thought they could carry in the two cars. Anything made from worm skins, including the belts she'd been working on, they left behind. No point in inviting trouble.

As for clothes, Fran limited herself to one case. While she sorted through her wardrobe Matt made another attempt to contact Tegwyn Aneurin Rhys. The number rang for some time before it was answered.

'Rhys – yes?' the voice barked at him, irritated. But when he understood it was Matt his manner changed. 'Oh, my dear fellow it's you! Aren't you watching the Boat Race?'

The question took Matt by surprise. He'd even forgotten it was Saturday. 'Boat race?'

'It's on now.'

Faintly in the background he could hear the TV commentator's voice. 'I'm sorry,' he apologized, and as briefly as possible he explained the situation – Helen's death, the multiple attacks on Westport, the other deaths, the casualties in hospital. Rhys puctuated his account with expréssions of concern and sympathy which sounded very genuine.

'People here think Westport has been singled out,' Matt began to explain, 'because. . . I think you know.'

'It's possible,' Rhys admitted. 'Especially if my theory of their origin is right. Equally, there may be other cases that we don't yet know about and—' He broke off. His voice rose almost to a scream of astonishment and horror. 'Good grief, look at that! On TV, man! Matt, switch your TV on – *now*!'

17

Aubrey Morgan stood cramped in the back of the Outside Broadcasts van, watching the monitors intently. He felt hot in his yellow waterproof anorak which he'd bought while ski-ing in Switzerland earlier that year; he'd have slipped it off if there'd been room. His glasses were steaming up and tiny beads of sweat were gathering on his scalp under his thinning hair.

Fifty pounds he'd put on the Oxford boat, a token of loyalty to his old university, but Cambridge already led by three lengths.

'Cambridge are approaching Barnes Bridge now; they have about a mile to go,' the commentator confirmed, 'and when they get round Barnes Bridge I expect them to put on the real pressure and try to increase their lead with a really high rate of striking . . . Oxford are three, no – almost three and a half lengths behind, well over on the Middlesex shore at the moment . . . and Cambridge are. . .'

Aubrey clenched his fists and leaned forward towards the small monitors. His fifty pounds was disappearing before his very eyes. The next commentator took up the story.

'. . . and Cambridge are making for the centre arch of Barnes Bridge, the white flag is up . . . and as they shoot past Barnes Bridge their time is. . . Yes, they're through, the flag is down! Fifteen minutes ten seconds, no record again this year, and Oxford is a good twelve seconds behind. . . There's something in the water just behind the Cambridge boat!'

'Get a close-up of it, quick!' Aubrey snapped in the van.

The cameraman on Barnes Bridge responded immediately. He let the boat go out of frame and zoomed in on the object. The picture on the monitor became hazy for a split second as he adjusted the focus.

'Looks like a . . . periscope?' Bill Hayes, the director who was also doing the vision mixing, held his fingers poised above the buttons, ready to punch it up to transmission. 'Two of 'em!'

'Stay with them,' Aubrey instructed.

The Great British Public could not see them yet. The transmission monitor still showed the Cambridge boat. Their rate of stroke had faltered as the crew, all but the cox, saw their Oxford rivals heading straight for the giant worms.

Aubrey was calm and fully in control of himself. He waited as the Oxford boat entered the frame, cutting through the water towards the worms, before giving his command: 'Okay, let the world see it!'

The worms seemed to rise out of the water and throw themselves across the boat, each curling around its chosen victim. The long oars which only seconds before had been gracefully and rhythmically dipping in and out of the water in unison were now in disarray like split matchsticks. Even on the small monitors in the O.B. van it was obvious the worms were making no attempt to kill their victims but were tearing off mouthfuls of raw flesh from their thighs and arms.

Bill stumbled out of the director's seat, his face ashen, and staggered to the door of the van to be sick outside. Aubrey slipped into his place. He told the helicopter to get as low as possible over the scene. The flotilla of boats which always followed the race were obscuring the sight-lines. The Oxford boat had sunk and the men were struggling in the water, but the Barnes Bridge camera only caught the occasional glimpse of them. He cut to the commentator on one of the launches with the order: 'Keep talking. Tell us what's happening, however sick you feel.'

The camera on board the helicopter showed two men jumping into the water from a launch to help the Oxford crew. One died immediately as a worm bit into his throat; his blood spread around him. But the second managed to offer some assistance to the cox, Dick Simmonds, and another Aubrey couldn't recognize.

'. . . and they're being pulled on board now,' the commentator was saying, 'and I think they're . . . yes, it's Phil Smith and the cox, Dick Simmonds . . . I'll see if I can have a word with them later on but in the meantime down there in the river there are still at least four men alive. The water is stained with blood and the worms ... three of them now, or four maybe, yes ... yes, I think it's four worms feeding on the bodies of those unfortunate crew members ... the Oxford crew ... and this is a Boat Race which has ended in total disaster ... and I can't ... I can't go on.'

Aubrey expected no congratulations over the broadcast but he knew he was right. Worms, earthquakes, wars, hurricanes, riots... No one wanted disasters, but it was television's role to report them whenever they happened and that's all he'd done. He remembered Mary Keating's fear of causing a nation-wide panic if they transmitted the film of Matt Parker being attacked by worms in the London sewers; much smaller worms they'd been, too, unlike these monsters in the Thames. But if people panicked, he'd put that on the screen as well.

He made his way through the excited crowds to the side-street where he'd parked his light green Lotus. No sign of panic among these folk. They might almost have enjoyed watching the worms demolish the Oxford boat, like ancient Romans in the Colosseum eager to see the lions crunching their way through that week's supply of Christians.

Two boys stood by his car, admiring it. He murmured a faint 'Excuse me' as he pushed between them to open the door and drop into the driving seat. Before pulling away from the kerb he let them hear a burst from the purring engine, just to whet their appetites.

The main road was jammed solid with traffic, though the police were keeping one lane clear for the ambulances whose sirens screamed urgently as they approached. Impatiently, Aubrey turned into another residential street, roared down it as far as the intersection, and took the next road on the right. At one time he'd had a flat round these parts and he still remembered the short cuts.

Back at Television Hall he checked on the latest situation report. Three of the Oxford crew had died, as well as the man who'd jumped in to rescue them. Of the others, two were badly injured. They'd all been taken to hospital and a bulletin would be issued shortly. Farther up-river at Richmond a boy angler had been attacked on the river bank; passers-by had gone to his aid and killed the worm, but the boy was dead by the time the ambulance arrived.

Other reports of incidents involving worms were coming in from several different parts of the country. A Cambridge undergraduate had taken his girl-friend for an outing in a punt; she'd trailed her hand in the water and it had been bitten off. An actress at the Shakespeare Memorial Theatre at Stratford had decided on an early morning dip in the Avon; her chewed-up remains were discovered two hours later drifting by the river bank. Two families living on houseboats on a canal near Droitwich had found they'd unintentionally caught some worms when they'd filled their buckets with water for washing-up. Both suffered minor injuries – bitten hands, arms and legs. One of the women lost a thumb.

The worst-hit area was the seaside town of Westport. According to the news telex, it had suffered 'a plague of worms' during the past twenty-four hours and the casualties included several dead as well as many in hospital. The people of the town had organized worm-hunting patrols to try to exterminate the menace, but they'd discovered such large concentrations of worms they had given up. The authorities had just announced the town was to be evacuated.

Westport...

Thinking it over, Aubrey remembered vaguely that Matt Parker had gone to live there. Or somewhere with a similar name. Maybe he'd have some film...

He rang Al Wilson, Head of News, who told him a news team was already on its way to Westport.

'But that's not the only seaside place,' he added grimly. 'It's the worst so far, but God knows what tonight will bring. They've been seen in practically every part of the country – Scarborough, St Andrews, Chichester, Newton Ferrers, St Ives, Polperro, Blackpool, Morecambe, Troon ... you name it! Since the Boat Race the lines have been jammed with calls. Every two-bit journalist in the country thinking his story's the only one. We're trying to get a statement out of the Home

Office, but they've clammed up on us. Won't even tell us where the Minister's spending the week-end. As for the Ministry of Agriculture, they've closed shop till Monday.'

'You'd better keep me in touch,' Aubrey said, and gave him the address where he'd be staying for the night. 'Carole's engagement party. I promised to be there.'

'Carole?'

'My secretary. They're making an honest woman of her.'

'Must be a brave man,' Al commented. 'Like marrying an iceberg.'

'All fire underneath, I can assure you,' Aubrey smirked, and added: 'You'll not forget to get in touch if there's anything important?'

Tall, slender Carole, daughter of a retired major-general with a hush-hush background in military intelligence, had become – or rather, *was* to become that evening – engaged to a muscular, rugger-playing investment-trust manager with talent for making money. He had an impeccable background, of course; no doubt he'd end up in the House of Lords one day, if he didn't kill himself hang-gliding or skin-diving first.

The engagement party was to be at her uncle's place in Kent. Aubrey went to his flat in Chelsea to change into evening clothes before driving down there. He chose his dark blue dinner suit with a pale frilled shirt. If anything, he told himself as he checked his appearance in the mirror, he felt flattered that she'd asked him. Their relationship had been ... ambiguous. But not without its moments. From time to time. She was one of those girls who administer their private lives with the same cool efficiency as they run the office.

She'd given him precise instructions on how to reach The Priory and he followed them implicitly. As he pulled up on the drive she came down the wide steps towards him and pointed out where he was to park. Her evening dress was a long sheath of olive green, and she looked elegant in it.

The sound of laughter and conversation filled the house. Aubrey murmured something complimentary, pressed her hand, kissed her cheek, and then she opened the double doors and led him into the main room to introduce him around.

Clearly he was one of the last of the expected guests to arrive. Eyes turned towards him and looked puzzled till someone – maybe it was the Fiancé – mentioned the word 'television'. Recognition. Questions, which he answered suavely as usual, sipping his gin.

A voice said, 'The Boat Race.' A shock-wave surged through the room. More questions – he'd been there, hadn't he? Wasn't it terrifying? But what *were* these creatures? Was anyone safe from them? And those poor men in the boat, what must their families be going through? But what was the Government thinking of, letting these things live in the rivers? They'd been seen in other places too, hadn't they? It wasn't safe any more to go skin-diving, or water-skiing, or anything.

Carole allowed the topic full rein before intervening. She managed her parties as she managed everything else in her life. Taking Aubrey's hand and drawing him out of the circle of people surrounding him, she announced: 'There's someone I want you to meet. Her name's Lady Cynthia, and I invited her specially for you.'

'I'd not put it past you.' He imagined a dowager aunt who needed to be flattered. 'One of your family?'

Carole smiled her usual superior smile but didn't answer. She took him to the far end of the room. 'There she is, by the fireplace. Lady Cynthia. She's longing to meet you.'

She was in her early twenties, short in comparison with Carole, and deeply sun-tanned. Her face was puckish and lovely; her eyes wrinkled as she smiled, holding out her hand to take his. Although her long, auburn hair had been elaborately arranged for the evening, it looked as though it should really be floating freely over her brown shoulders. She wore a flimsy dress which barely concealed her nipples.

'She's just back from the Bahamas, lucky thing!' Carole was saying. 'I'll leave you two together.'

Aubrey stammered a few polite remarks, lost for words. So this is what Carole had planned for him – a consolation prize! Lady Cynthia seemed to be laughing at his embarrassment.

'Oh, drop the "Lady", please!' she told him. 'That's just Carole's joke.'

'Not genuine?'

'Yes, it's genuine okay, but I don't like people calling me that.'

'You're an actress,' he guessed. She had the starlet look about her. Topless in St Tropez.

'Research student. I'm doing a doctorate at Edinburgh. In mediaeval history.'

'Dressed like that?'

Carole had arranged that they sat next to each other at dinner. They pretended to be surprised when they saw the place cards, laughed, sat down, and continued the conversation. From time to time he became aware that the Fiancé was looking pointedly in his direction, but he ignored him. Whatever Carole was up to, for once Aubrey didn't mind. When the time came for the announcement of the engagement and the toasts, Cynthia was telling him about the dissolution of the monasteries and he was listening intently. What was more, she hadn't once asked him how she could get into television; that was refreshing.

They danced together most of the evening, hardly giving a thought to anyone else. The band had their amplifiers turned up to full volume and the sound was deafening. Occasionally they mouthed words to each other but then gave up, laughing. Once or twice the thought of the worms entered Aubrey's mind; some extensive coverage would be necessary, interviews with the victims in their hospital beds, dig up the material he'd prepared when Matt Parker had his set-to in the sewers. . . But all that was really a problem for Monday morning. He grinned at Cynthia and pretended to mop his brow.

'Hot?' she bawled against the steady *thump-thump-thump* of the music.

It was cooler out on the terrace. They perched on the stone balustrade with their drinks. The ruins of the old priory appeared almost ghostly in the moonlight. Cynthia said she planned to explore them in the morning, she'd been told there was a section of wall dating back to the Anglo-Saxon period with a cross and runic lettering carved into one of the stones.

'Probably a Holy Place long before Christianity,' she commented. 'That may have been why they built the first church here.'

The heavy sound of the music pumped out through the open windows. Over in a corner of the room some horseplay was going on – they couldn't see what – and there was loud laughter. Aubrey made some remark about it being the last wild party before civilization crumbled, and started talking about the worms. Seriously.

'They're in every river all over the country. Every stream. And they're spreading. Soon we'll not be able to go near a drain, or even step over a gutter in the street, without being in danger. Even your own bathroom at home, or your kitchen. That cameraman, Matt Parker – I did him an injustice. He was right.' Another crazy burst of laughter from indoors. 'Let them celebrate while there's still time.'

He was surprising himself. Up till that moment he'd thought only in terms of programmes. His job was to *report*. Put the facts before people. But now – perhaps it was the moonlight, or he'd had too much to drink – he saw it all differently.

'Surely we can get rid of them somehow,' she objected. They were sitting close together on the balustrade. Her voice was low.

'I'm not so certain.'

'We exterminate other – well, rodents.'

'It's a much bigger problem. People will have to change their habits, take a lot more care, no swimming, no strolling around. And the Government will need extra powers which it may not want to give up afterwards.'

'What kind of powers?'

'They've already evacuated one town. By tomorrow morning maybe there'll be another.'

She didn't answer. It was getting chilly but neither of them made a move to go inside again. They sat there, toying with their empty glasses, staring at the moonlit ruins through the trees. Suddenly she stood up.

'Let's offer them a sacrifice!' Her face was mischievous; she held out her hand to him. 'This is a Holy Place, isn't it, where our ancestors came when they were in trouble? And it's full moon tonight.' She deepened her voice mysteriously, teasing him. 'Maybe there's something down there in need of a prayer or two.'

He laughed and allowed her to pull him up. 'D'you really believe that?'

She shook her head. 'I believe in neutrons, electrons, and radio-carbon dating,' she informed him; then wrinkled her eyes at him. 'But it's worth a try. Come on! I wanted to see the place anyway.'

Her car was parked on the drive just below the terrace and she stopped to get the torch out of the glove compartment. In her eagerness she half-ran down the sloping lawn towards the gaunt, broken walls of the priory. As they got closer he caught a glimpse of water.

'The old fish pond,' she explained when he pointed it out. 'They went in for fish farming, those old monks.'

Enough remained of the main walls of the church to make them drop their voices. Part of the pointed gothic arch of the main window was still in place, sharply outlined against the sky. They stood quietly for a moment, staring up at it, then drew closer together, his arm slipped around her shoulders, and they kissed. At length she broke away from him and looked at his face almost seriously.

'Now you've pledged yourself to me,' she said, mockingly. 'This is consecrated ground, and with that kiss—'

'I thee cherish,' he interrupted her lightly. 'Let's find the writing on the wall.'

She shivered. 'What a way to put it!'

They walked over the grass down the main body of the church towards what must once have been the high altar. Now only a couple of fallen slabs marked the place. He sensed her mood changing; she was becoming more tense. In the corner was an arched doorway hidden in shadow. She played the torchlight over it. Worn stone steps led down into the darkness, broken and uneven.

'It's a section of the crypt which was excavated only ten or fifteen years ago,' she whispered. 'And that's where they found the stone with the carvings. I'll go down first. I hope you don't mind spiders.'

There were more steps that he'd imagined and they began to curve, with one or two sharp corners. She moved very slowly ahead of him, aiming the torchlight so they could both see where they were putting their feet. Steadying himself against the side wall his hand became tangled in a cobweb which clung to his fingers; trying to get rid of it, he dislodged a pebble which bounced down the steps, echoing hollowly, till suddenly it stopped. His ears strained against the sudden silence. Was that a scratching he heard? Or merely his imagination?

Her hand groped over his body, feeling for his. 'You all right?' she breathed.

'Yes. And you?'

The sound of their voices seemed to spread and dissolve in the emptiness.

They continued down the crumbling steps, one by one, till they ended in front of a low arch. She went through, then exclaimed in surprise; he followed, grazing his hand painfully against the stonework. The air smelled damp. Something scurried away in a far corner, he couldn't see what.

It was a long, narrow chamber with a floor and walls made of great stone slabs. A broad shaft of moonlight flooded in from above, illuminating a ledge cut into the end wall; above it, also carved in the stone, was a cross set in a circle. The runic signs were beneath it, faint and time-worn.

For a long time she stood silently before it, holding his hand tightly. 'Don't you feel this is a Holy Place?' she said at last. 'Perhaps at first, thousands of years ago, it was just a grove, a fissure in the rocks. Early human beings came here, experienced that sense of awe and mystery... I thought we might make love down here, but it's too sacred. Isn't it?'

As she turned to look up at him, her face earnest in the moonlight, he stooped to kiss her but she twisted away. Then a gasp; she backed against him. Lying in a patch of moonlight on the stone floor, its head raised, watching them intently, was a large worm. Its deep green skin seemed to glow in the dim light. He reckoned it was about a yard long, its body elegantly curved and coiled.

'That's what you were talking about,' she whispered, her voice trembling only slightly. She picked up the torch from the ledge. 'D'you think there are more?'

She swept the torch beam around the long, narrow room, into the darker corners not reached by the moonlight, and they counted six worms all staring in their direction.

'Oh, Christ!' The words burst from her lips; she was terrified. The torchlight wavered, then she switched it off. 'Oh, Christ, what are we going to do?'

Aubrey tried to say something, but the spittle rasped in his throat and he couldn't speak the words. Those twisting stone steps were the only entrance to this chamber – the other hadn't been excavated – and to get there they'd have to pass two of the worms.

'We. . .' The words wouldn't come. He shook his head as if to shake the fear out of his brain. His stomach cramped up and he found it hard to breathe.

The worm in the patch of moonlight moved. It slithered towards them across the stone slabs with an effortless grace, then stopped again. Its eyes were hard, betraying nothing. In spite of himself Aubrey stared at them. He was gulping the air, swallowing, gasping for breath.

He felt Cynthia tugging at his sleeve. 'Lift me,' she begged, 'lift me on to the altar where they can't reach.'

She meant the ledge cut into the wall. He tried to help her, despising himself for his own cowardice, forcing himself to breathe more slowly. His arms shook as he grasped her to take some of her weight; but she was halfway up already and she managed to scramble on to it.

'There's room for you too,' she said.

'No.'

The ledge was narrow and she sat on it with her legs drawn up, her knees touching her chin. In that skimpy dress she looked only too exposed. A sacrifice – that's what she'd said, wasn't it? He took the torch from her. It was the only weapon they had, that and his bare hands. When they'd attacked Mary Keating he'd plucked them off her and killed them with a mere flick of his fingers. But they'd been small, no longer than earth worms; these were the size of rattlesnakes. More of them now, too. In a circle around him. Watching.

'Cy—' His mouth was dry and he knew he was shaking. It

would be different if he could lash out at them with his fists, if they were something solid he could hit. But these long, ribbon-like things wriggling towards him, the movement passing like waves down their sinister green bodies, getting closer to his feet, his legs. . . It was a re-run of every nightmare he'd ever had.

One of them touched him. Reared up and lashed into him, its teeth missing his flesh but tearing his trouser leg at knee level. He recoiled. The edge of the altar hit the small of his back. The bile rose inside him and he spewed.

The nearest worm caught the full force of the vomit. It's mouth opened as if it enjoyed the stuff. The sight of it caused Aubrey's stomach to heave again. Once more he retched, and once more the worms advanced.

Somewhere, he thought distantly as they bit into the calves of his legs, he'd heard they didn't attack through clothing. That was wrong. He wondered at the way his mind functioned with an apparently cool logicality while they gnawed at him. Certainly he was screaming, he could hear himself, and lashing out with the torch, trying to batter their brains out, but inside – in the very eye of his dying – was a calm centre.

The pain was intense at first as their teeth found his flesh, but then it began to slip away. He was lying on the hard stone floor and one of the worms was coiled over his eyes, feeding on his cheek. Somewhere he could hear Cynthia sobbing – or was it Carole? – and he wanted to say her name. If only he could have had her on that ledge-like altar beneath the Saxon cross. Fertility ritual by the light of the full spring moon . . . moon . . . moon. . .

A scream bounced around the excavated walls of that death chamber, coming closer, a shrill scream – not his – penetrating his ears like hot needles. Something struggling and heavy fell across him, writhing in agony, screeching as her flesh was torn and their blood mingled. As they'd wanted to mingle, he thought. As they'd wanted to.

18

On board the fast Royal Navy command craft, Matt scanned the Westport quayside through his binoculars but saw no sign of life. The evacuations had obviously been thorough. Normally on a day like this there would be a good scattering of people about. The fresh breeze put white crests on the waves and caused the neglected sailing dinghies to bob up and down at their moorings. The fishing nets on the harbour walls were equally unattended, the roads deserted.

'Can't see any worms,' he reported, shouting against the breeze.

'Let's put in!' Tegwyn Aneurin Rhys called back. His bald head was sun-tanned and his fringe of grey hair stuck out even more wildly than usual. 'If we can't get as far as your house we might at least reach the shop. You said you keep some of your pictures there.'

The bronzed, bearded lieutenant gave the order and the boat began to edge forward again. He'd shown no curiosity about his two civilian guests; in fact, he'd hardly spoken at all.

Matt and Fran had left Westport the previous Saturday afternoon before the police had decided on evacuation, so they'd missed the long traffic jams. On arrival at the Old Rectory they'd found an official black Rover 3500 parked in the drive. Rhys had bustled out to greet them with firm handshakes and the comment that he was tied up for the moment, so could they look after themselves for an hour or so?

He'd shown them upstairs to a large room containing a wide marital bed and a couple of thousand books. Fran declared Matt could read if he liked; she was going to soak in the bath. Then, only a few seconds later, she'd unexpectedly reappeared, a towel in her hand. She'd stood uncertainly in the doorway.

'What's wrong?' he'd asked.

'I'm scared to.' All the colour had gone from her face. 'I've remembered Helen. I don't think I'll ever be able to have a bath again.'

She'd contented herself with a wash while he kept guard, just in case. If Rhys agreed, he thought, he'd fit wire mesh over all the outlets.

Two hours later they'd heard voices in the hall as Rhys said goodbye to his guests. Car doors slammed discreetly. Wheels crunched gently over the gravel as the Rover 3500 pulled away.

Rhys had come bounding up the stairs, apologizing profusely. 'Of course, I've known the Minister since we were both at Cambridge,' he'd explained. His Alsatian had looked up at him with understanding eyes, then sat down to scratch itself. 'The situation's serious. Reports of worm attacks are coming in from all over the country, especially seaside places and rivers. The Prime Minister intends to seek powers from the House of Commons on Monday to declare an official State of Emergency. Several areas are being evacuated already. The army's been using flame-throwers in an attempt to contain the menace but, as I told the Minister, we need to know a lot more about these worms if we're not to be completely overrun. A scientific advisory committee has been established under Professor Jones.'

'But he's never seen one alive!' Matt had exclaimed.

Rhys had grinned. 'Wait for it, Matt. I've involved you two. You're to give evidence. We're going to need all the film you took, the still photographs, everything.'

As their craft moved alongside, a young rating – he couldn't have been twenty years old – jumped smartly ashore and tied up. For a few seconds no one else moved. Westport seemed unnaturally empty and quiet. The masts of the yachts and fishing boats swayed in a strange, gaunt dance. Rows of gulls sat on the telephone wires.

'Risk it?' asked Matt uneasily.

'It's what we came for.' Rhys turned to the lieutenant to explain they might be wanting to get away in a hurry, so. . .

'We'll watch out for you, sir.' Laconic.

He's probably wondering what the fuss is about, thought Matt.

They went ashore, Matt first. The moment he felt the firm stone of the quayside beneath his boots he could sense their presence. They were in the town somewhere, though they weren't visible. He grasped his usual heavy walking-stick; in addition, he had two knives in his belt. Rhys had armed himself with a vicious-looking knobkerrie.

'Ready?'

Matt nodded. He was as ready as he'd ever be. Under his thick clothing he also wore a rubber skin-diving suit, remembering how the worms were no longer deterred by clothes the way they had been when he'd first met them in the sewers.

'Rhys, if we come face to face with them, we retreat.'

'My dear fellow, it shall be as you say. You're the man with the combat experience. So lead on.'

The cobbled shopping street was as quiet as death. So often he'd walked along here with Jenny running and chattering at his side, greeting the shopkeepers and others, but now there was only an eerie silence. They kept cautiously to the centre of the road. It was like entering a war zone after a neutron bomb attack, with all life exterminated though the buildings remained.

This sensation was reinforced by the sight of Fran's craft shop with its broken window. He stooped to look inside. His mouth went dry.

Worms lay in loops across the counter, lazily explored the display shelves and squirmed over the floor. They were mostly about four feet long, though a few were shorter, and they moved sluggishly, ignoring the two men staring in at them.

'Like an army of occupation,' Rhys whispered ecstatically. 'If only we could communicate with them.'

'You can,' Matt told him sourly. 'One step inside that door, you'd get the message right away.'

The butcher's next door had also been taken over. There was no meat in sight, only worms. Sleeping in the window; coiled up on the scales. And in the outfitter's they'd draped themselves langorously over the mannequins, their colouring in vivid contrast with the sailing jackets and white sweaters. One worm eyed them lethargically from amidst a disarray of underwear.

'They don't see us as a danger any longer,' Rhys was saying excitedly. 'They feel they've won their battle. Here we are, strolling among them like tourists almost! Matt, I'm sure we could reach some understanding with them if...'

'Try reaching some understanding with a cobra!' Matt retorted contemptuously. 'They're not attacking us because they've gorged themselves silly already on all the livestock that used to live round here, the pigs, sheep, hens, cows, ducks, dogs, cats, rabbits... If you don't believe me, you stick around till they're hungry again.'

But maybe they *could* get to the cottage safely, he thought. Pack his films and stuff into a couple of rucksacks and get back before they changed their minds. It was risky, but...

He led the way through the narrow lane. The clear stream tumbled and gurgled as it had always done, littered by the same soggy cigarette packets and empty beer cans. The mongrel which had always barked at him from the end garden was no longer there, nor was the old woman he'd so often seen at the open window of the third cottage.

'It's uncanny,' Rhys commented, his voice now a little unsteady. 'Seagulls on the rooftops, and nothing else.' He pushed open a rickety garden gate and crossed the tiny patch of grass to peer in through the front window. 'St Christopher and all the saints!' he murmured.

Matt joined him. Through the spotlessly-clean pane he saw the raw carcase of old Dave Trewin with several worms still feeding on it. The dead man's stomach gaped open and a worm was emerging from it, streaked with red, gripping a large section of intestine. Part of his face was gone, though enough was left to recognize him; his crutches too lay on the floor beside him. Twenty years earlier he'd been injured helping to rescue the crew of a Dutch freighter driven on the rocks; he was well-known in Westport pubs, spinning yarns to holiday-makers in exchange for drinks.

Something moved.

A quick slither on the tiles above.

Matt dodged back instinctively even before his mind had registered the danger. The worm slipped over the guttering and fell with deadly accuracy on to Rhys's shoulders.

It didn't bite immediately. It first steadied itself, then pulled its head back as if wanting to examine its victim's face before selecting which portion to feed on. Rhys's eyes bulged with terror. He opened his mouth as if to scream, but there was no sound. Only a rattle in his throat.

The worm was on the point of striking when Matt's hand gripped it just below the head. It whipped about furiously this way and that, trying to fix Matt with its eyes, then twisting its neck in a vain attempt to bite his wrist. He held it steadily and stared back, asserting his own superiority. Gradually the worm's resistance slackened. Now he need only tighten his fingers slightly. . .

'Don't kill it!' Rhys's voice had returned. 'We'll take it back for Professor Jones. A present from Westport!'

'It's asking for trouble!' Matt protested.

'Why?'

'The others. . .'

'Half-asleep, most of them,' Rhys scoffed. 'The rest are too busy.' He added triumphantly: 'So you do admit there's communication *between* them?'

Matt didn't argue. Still holding the worm in front of him, he marched back into the cobbled street, abandoning all idea of visiting his own cottage. It had been a crazy notion anyway. If there was one place in the whole of Westport which would be crawling with worms, it would be his cottage.

In the shop windows he caught the occasional glimpse of eyes watching him. They were following his progress back to the quayside, yet not obviously moving. He thought at one point he heard something, swung around. . . Nothing.

'You're getting nervous,' Rhys observed, his confidence now fully restored.

Matt stopped, irritated. He thrust the worm's head towards Rhys's face and felt the ripple of interest passing through its body as its jaws opened. 'Would you like to carry it?' he demanded.

'My dear fellow, I didn't mean to offend you!' Rhys backed away. 'Let's just get it back to the boat.'

Rounding the corner at the foot of the cobbled street they came to the wide quayside where he'd often been with Jenny to buy lobster or mackerel from the fishermen unloading their catch. It was crowded with worms, some lying with their heads flat on the cobbles, though others raised them in that interested, periscope-like manner which had become so familiar.

'What d'you suggest now?' asked Matt cynically. He felt weary and realized he no longer minded dying, though he'd prefer it to happen quickly.

'They want their friend back, that's obvious!' Rhys squeaked with delight at this confirmation of his theories. 'So if you place him carefully on the ground. . .'

'And have it take a piece out of my nose?' Matt refused scornfully. He was sickened by the whole expedition. Twenty yards off the boat was waiting for them, standing wisely a couple of feet away from the quayside. But to get there they'd have to pass the worms. 'There's only one way out of this mess, Rhys.'

'What mess? Don't you see. . .'

But Matt wasn't listening. He tightened his fingers around the worm he was holding, squeezing it to death, and then threw the body into the centre of one of the thickest groups a few feet away. As usual, they fell hungrily on their dead brother.

'Now make a dash for the boat!' he shouted at Rhys as he transferred his stick to his right hand. 'Keep over to the right by those boxes. Move!'

'But' Rhys started to argue. A large worm slid rapidly towards him at that moment and reared up to strike at his thigh.

'Go!' Matt pushed him, bringing his stick down on the worm's head at the same time.

Rhys forgot all his theories and sprinted for the boat. Something was happening on board but Matt was too busy to watch. Out of the corner of his eye he saw one of the ratings had jumped on to the quayside to help Rhys aboard. It seemed to take ages, but what was the difficulty?

The worms were coming at him from three sides now. Viciously he hit out at them, cursing and yelling. As he killed each one others began to devour it. Somehow he'd have to edge his way round towards the point where he could start running.

Then came a burst of automatic rifle fire from the rating on the quayside. Chips of stone flew up where the bullets hit.

'That's no use!' Matt cried out to him, but his words were drowned by another burst of firing.

One bullet found its mark. One only. The rating would have done better with a stick in his hands. The other worms changed direction and sped over the stones towards him. Matt shouted a warning but he was too late. His shots went wide, breaking a window, as the worms fastened their teeth into his legs and hands.

By the time Matt reached him the rating had fallen to his knees. A four-foot worm was on the point of biting into his neck when Matt's stick dashed its brains out. Another rating jumped ashore and together they got the wounded man on board. He was groaning incoherently. At least three worms were still feeding on him.

With his gloved hand Matt seized the nearest by the neck, forced its jaws apart and tossed it into the sea as the boat pulled away from the quayside, gathering speed. Rhys and the lieutenant helped with the other two. A fourth, which had been clinging to Matt's own clothes, dropped to the deck. He stamped on it.

'I'll not feel safe on board this boat again,' said the bearded lieutenant when they'd killed all they could find. He ordered a search in case they'd missed one.

'They didn't seem to bite you,' observed Rhys wonderingly.

Matt looked down at his legs. His trousers had been torn to rags by their teeth but the composition rubber of the frogman suit beneath was still whole.

'It worked this time,' he agreed doubtfully, 'but sooner or later they'll chew through it. They learn from experience.'

The meeting next day took place in a high panelled room decorated with dark oil paintings in ornate frames. About twelve people were there, the civil servants both male and female dressed in nondescript suits, the academics ranging from sweaters and denim at one extreme to Professor Jones's nineteen-fifties sports jacket with leather elbow-patches at the other.

Matt was left to cool his heels outside for the first hour and when eventually they called him in he was given a place at the foot of the table. But they listened attentively enough as he described his various encounters with the worms and his observations on their living habits.

'But you found no females?' Professor Jones demanded confirmation. 'You regard yourself as competent to make such a positive statement?'

'Of course he is!' Rhys objected in a loud voice. 'Taught him myself.'

'Nevertheless, he's hardly qualified. . .'

A heated argument developed between the two men during which Rhys accused the Professor of being less a zoologist than a mortician.

'God's creatures live and move and have their being,' he declared hotly. 'We can learn more from watching them in nature – as Matt has done – than on a dissecting table. I'll tell you why we've seen no females. Sewer worms reproduce in the sea, probably in the depths of the ocean. They reach the estuaries, develop lungs – the old tadpole-frog pattern – swim into the rivers and streams, into the drains and sewers. . . Now d'you understand?'

Unexpectedly, Professor Jones shot out a question at Matt. 'Do you understand, Mr Parker?' he asked. 'From what you've seen of them?'

Matt thought for a moment before he replied. 'What about salmon?' The idea had occurred to him several times over the past months. 'They spawn in the upper reaches of rivers, the quiet waters, then swim downstream to the ocean, getting bigger all the time, till in due course they reverse the process and swim upstream again to lay eggs for the new generation.'

'I don't see the parallel,' Rhys announced stubbornly.

'Nor do I,' said the Professor drily. 'Rhys's theory is consistent with the behaviour of eels, but yours. . .' He shrugged.

'It would explain the big variation in size,' Matt ventured, feeling out of his depth. 'Of course I'm no expert.'

'Quite.'

Two or three of the other academics took up the concept and argued about it for the next quarter of an hour or so till a woman civil servant, whose name Matt hadn't grasped, turned to him and said: 'D'you know where to find these spawning grounds?'

'I think so,' Matt answered cautiously.

'You may be wrong,' she told him kindly, 'but we should follow up every lead. I'll see to it arrangements are made for you to go there.'

19

Rain spattered against the windscreen as Matt swung over into the fast lane of the motorway and pressed his foot down hard. The old Landrover supplied by the Ministry of Agriculture still had a good turn of speed. Fran sat next to him, silent, not even looking out.

'I managed to contact Angus,' he said. 'I was worried about him, but he's quite safe.'

'Are any of us?' she remarked gloomily.

The radio played a diet of light music interspersed with hints on how to make your drains worm-proof. According to one news flash, several wealthy families living near the Thames were offering to pay luxury rents for council flats in high-rise blocks. In the past forty-eight hours the prices of Welsh mountain-side cottages had tripled.

Matt hardly listened. He was leaning slightly forward as he drove, keeping his eyes on the road and wondering what he should do about Jenny. He'd phoned again that morning and asked to speak to her. Point-blank refusal.

'I'm coming down to see her,' he'd said.

'Matt. . .' As Helen's older sister, Sue clearly felt she held a position of authority. 'It's not that I don't want you to see her, but. . . Well, you know what's upset her, don't you? It's not only Helen and the way she died, it's. . .' She hesitated. 'Do I need to spell it out?'

'She's got the wrong end of the stick.' Matt had tried to justify himself. 'It was business. We'd spent the evening with our American associate, arguing the details of a contract. When Jenny rang we'd only just got back. Naturally we'd a couple of points to talk over but. . .'

His voice tailed away. Though Sue had made no comment he could sense her disbelief. Helen had once told him he was the world's worst liar. She'd been right.

'She's very hurt,' said Sue. 'Upset about Helen, but hurt too. I don't know if she'll see you. I'm not going to force her if she doesn't want to.'

'She might at least give me a chance,' Matt had replied, unable to disguise the bitterness and pain. He'd rushed on: 'What about the worms? Are you all right?'

'We've still not seen any round here. We keep her in the house, of course. It'd be stupid to let her play outside, but no one in the village has come across them yet, not even the farmers. They seemed to be mainly on the coast.' She'd sighed, worried. 'Matt, remember she's only a child. I realize how much you need her, but ... well, she has needs too.'

The rain stopped and suddenly the sky was blue. Bright sunlight reflected off the wet road surface and glistened among the trees. Fran reached forward and switched the radio off. At first he hadn't wanted to take her with him at all, saying there would be no point. This was a preliminary recce, nothing more. He was going to scout around, film anything interesting, and then report back.

'You'll need someone to watch your back,' she had said, dismissing his excuses. 'And when you're visiting Jenny, I'll stay in the background. That's what you're really worried about, isn't it? But she'll not know I'm there. If it goes wrong – your visit – I want to be within reach to make sure you do nothing stupid.'

'Such as?' he'd challenged her.

She shook her head, grimacing at him. 'You'll not draw me that way.'

They checked into a hotel on the edge of the moor some ten miles away from where Sue lived. After a wash and a quick meal they discussed where to start. Fran had been studying the ordnance survey map and she pointed to an area of marshland where the blue lines of the streams and rivers seemed to peter out. He nodded.

'That's what I had in mind,' he agreed.

He had no very great faith in his theory, only a deep-seated conviction that Rhys was wrong and this might be one way to prove it.

The road across the moor was a straight, bleak ribbon of tarmac, totally deserted and stretching as far as the horizon where it seemed to terminate sharply as though on the very brink of the world. They followed it for about five and a half miles on the clock before pulling off on to the gravelled verge.

Matt switched off the engine and got out. The wind hummed across the telephone wires which were strung on high, lonely poles spaced regularly along one side of the road. A distant bird call, persistent. Whispers through the swaying furze, its masses of yellow flowers brilliant against the dark green spiny plants.

The surface was very uneven, full of little hollows and hillocks; the vegetation was thick and tangled. It might be teeming with worms, slipping easily through the ravel of roots, alerted to their arrival. Both he and Fran had been issued with specially reinforced overalls and flying boots but he still felt vulnerable. When asked what he thought would be the safest clothing, he'd answered simply, 'Chain mail.' He hadn't been joking, either.

'No rabbit droppings,' observed Fran suddenly.

'What d'you mean?'

'The ground's usually covered with rabbit droppings. I used to come here with my husband. Takes me back.' She looked around wrily. 'No worms in those days, though,' she added. 'Pity.'

Matt suggested she might prefer to stay in the Landrover but she told him crisply not to be daft. She was going to stick with him. They chose a path and struck out across the moor, Matt going first and keeping a sharp watch out for worms. He felt very nervous, as though some primeval instinct were warning him of danger lurking among the furze. When the path unexpectedly ended he begged Fran again to go and wait in the Landrover, as there was no point in them both taking risks, but she refused and they went on.

Another five minutes and the ground became wet, dipping into a hollow. They could no longer see the road, nor the top of the Landrover. If it hadn't been for the stark, granite tor about a mile ahead he'd have lost all sense of direction. His foot suddenly sank into the morass.

'U-urgh!' He pulled back, trying to keep his balance. The mud sucked at his boot as if trying to swallow it; there was a squelchy phlut! as he succeeded in freeing himself.

He examined the marshy patch in front of him. Parts of it were smooth water, reflecting the constantly-shifting clouds and the blue of the sky; other sections were like a thick soup of mud, seemingly solid – treacherously so, as he discovered when he probed them with a stick. Clumps of grass and reeds formed a scattering of islands; if they wanted to go on they'd have to step from one to the next, hoping each was firm enough to hold them.

'Where are they?' Fran demanded. 'The worms?'

'This is where we'd expect them,' he agreed.

When he'd asked the Ministry for a bottle of blood there had been a few raised eyebrows and someone had asked, 'Pig or cow?' He'd said it didn't matter so long as it was fresh. Before he'd left that morning, they'd handed him several flasks. He unscrewed the top of one of them now and splashed the blood over the miry ground.

Fran watched him apprehensively, glancing around every so often to make sure nothing was creeping up on them from the rear.

'Blood attracts them better than offal,' he explained. It steadied his nerves to talk about it. 'Can't imagine why. Must be some reason.'

She glanced around again, jumpy. 'Not working this time, is it?' That odd note in her voice was almost one of relief.

'I think that's clear water over there, isn't it?' he asked, feeling very uneasy and needing some excuse to move. 'If we work our way round to it. . . I'll go first again, but keep your eyes skinned.'

'No need to tell me that,' she responded fervently. 'Come on, let's go over there. This spot gives me the willies. Don't understand why, there's nothing here, nothing I can see, nothing tangible, but. . .' Trying to lighten her tone, she added: 'But maybe it's the pixies. Dartmoor was always like this. Human beings are very transient, aren't they? Insignificant, really. I often felt it up here. And we could easily be replaced by some other dominant life form.'

'You've been listening to Rhys,' he scoffed, deliberately.

'Oh, not from space! That idea's just zany. But the dinosaurs died out, didn't they? And civilizations have disappeared.' She shuddered. 'D'you think the worms could do that to us?'

They reached the clear water whose otherwise calm surface rippled under the wind. The mood of the moor was darkening as heavy rainclouds gathered; dramatically, the sun's rays passed through a single gap to illuminate the distant tor.

'Try the blood sacrifice!' Fran half-joked. 'Or better still, let's get away while we can.' She looked behind her and around in every direction, scanning the ground through her binoculars as well as with the naked eye. 'They're here somewhere,' she announced, quite convinced. 'But I can't see them.'

Matt didn't try the blood immediately. Instead, he assembled the fishing net on the end of its extending rod and let it drag through the water. His catch was disappointingly small – hardly more than a few leaf fragments and a couple of insects which had been dancing on the surface – but he transferred it to the specimen jar, adding more water, then going through the same process again.

When he'd finished, he fitted the lid and returned the jar to his bag. It was time for the blood again. The flask was still half-full and he emptied it completely into the water. If he expected worms to swim suddenly into sight as they'd done in the sewers, he was mistaken. The water discoloured, and that was all. He scooped some up into his second specimen jar, fished around with his net, and finally – feeling empty and dissatisfied, as though he'd wasted his time – said he was ready to go.

This time Fran led the way, crashing through furze and fern, stumbling when her foot caught in the tangled vegetation, kicking herself free impatiently, whacking the plants with her stick to warn any hidden worm of what to expect if it dared confront her.

But none did. They arrived back at the Landrover on the roadside without having seen a single one.

Back at the hotel Matt found a message waiting for him from Sue; she'd taken Jenny out to a tennis party at a friend's house. It would do her good to see some new faces, but he was welcome to call after breakfast the following morning if he wished. He showed it to Fran without comment. When she passed it back to him, she merely said she was glad she didn't have to spend the evening alone after all.

He fetched the microscope from the Landrover and for the greater part of the evening they peered through it at drops of water from the specimen jars. They were neither of them very skilled, nor too certain what they should be looking for, though Fran had used a microscope before at college.

A despatch rider had been detailed to collect the jars for laboratory tests, but he was late. When he eventually arrived and they'd handed them over, they went down to the bar for a drink. Only two other people sat there, both local, and the landlord grumbled that the worm-scare had killed the holiday trade. He'd had ninety per cent cancellations, yet he'd still not seen a worm. It was ridiculous.

But at ten o'clock when it was time for the TV news they all gathered silently in front of the set. Southgate, Clacton, Eastbourne and Colwyn Bay had been added to the list of towns to be evacuated. Army patrols had been out again, trying to clean up some of the worst-infested areas. The colonel they interviewed admitted that the best weapon against worms was a good strong stick; flame-throwers had been tried, but there was always a risk to property. The Ministry of Agriculture was also experimenting with various poisons in spite of conservationists' protests that this would only result in the extermination of most of the country's wild life and would permanently upset the ecological balance.

The death toll for the day was high, including several children, two soldiers and two Ministry of Agriculture inspectors.

'I can hardly believe it,' said the landlord. 'I don't know about you, but I can hardly believe it.'

Next morning Matt drove the ten miles to Sue's house. It was built on high ground well away from the village, a generously proportioned Edwardian house with a glass-covered conservatory along one side and stables at the rear. When Matt arrived he noticed their two ponies grazing in the adjacent meadow. A mud-splattered Volvo estate car stood on the drive.

He'd never seen much of Sue during all the years of his marriage to Helen. Perhaps a brief annual visit, just for the day. Or less than that, once every eighteen months, though Jenny had been invited down there every so often for a week's holiday with her cousins. They'd still be at boarding school, of course. Sue's husband was managing director of an engineering firm with a strong export record which meant he was away from home a great deal. She was on several important committees, as well as the county council.

As he parked the Landrover by the spread of rhododendrons, which were in full bloom, she came across the drive to meet him.

'Gorgeous, aren't they?' were her first inconsequential words. 'Particularly lovely this year. It's ironic.'

She was a good ten years older than Helen and the first lines had already appeared on her neck, under her cheeks, beginning to indicate how she would look in middle age. Her hair was short and practical, mouse-coloured, as Helen's had been before she'd decided she preferred it blonde. But then Helen would never have worn those clothes, that thick sensible tweed skirt and sweater, the flat walking shoes.

'How's Jenny?' he asked.

'Better this morning. Taking her out did her good.' Her tone was crisp, almost medical. 'She's decided to see you, but go easy, Matt. I've promised there's no question of you taking her away.'

'I'm very grateful to you,' he said, lost.

'It's the least I could do.'

He followed her into the house where they found Jenny in the rear sitting room, staring out of the window. She looked around slowly, her face set, as though determined not to betray any emotion. As usual, she wore jeans, and her long blonde hair covered her shoulders.

'Hello, Jenny,' he tried.

A pause before she answered. 'Hello.'

'Are you . . . all right here?' What the hell could he say? However he'd attempted to put his feelings into words, going over it again and again as he drove here in the Landrover, he'd always known in his heart she'd react against them. Yet there was so little time.

'Yes. There was no need for you to come, I'm all right.' Brittle; the words carefully chosen to hurt. 'Don't know why you bothered. I'm living with Auntie Sue now.'

'I'm staying with Tegwyn Aneurin Rhys. I told you about him. Westport's been evacuated, and a lot of other places too.' Stick to the facts, he told himself. Don't lie; don't try to disguise anything. 'The Government's given me a job which keeps me very busy.'

She looked at him, unmoved, as though patiently waiting for the visit to end.

'I hear you were playing tennis yesterday.'

That didn't work either; she said nothing.

'And you go riding, I imagine.'

'No!'

It was an outburst; her face flushed with hostility. She stared at him, her eyes dark with hatred. He stood there uneasily, awkwardly, in front of his ten-year-old daughter and didn't know what to say next. She broke the silence.

'You're back with that Fran,' she accused him. 'You're glad Mummy's dead, aren't you? Both of you? Now there's nothing to stop you. You're glad.'

'Don't be silly,' he told her quietly. 'You know very well that's silly.'

'When I got home I didn't know where she was. I called out for her just to say I was back. I knew she was around somewhere 'cos the lights were on. So I looked upstairs in case she was lying down. She'd been drinking whisky. Then I heard water from the bathroom and I went to look and. . .'

'Don't, Jenny. Don't.' He moved to put his arm around her but she flung away from him.

'They were eating Mummy, your worms. In the bath. There was blood, and they were eating inside her.' She backed towards the door, her lips quivering, but her voice hard and undramatic. No tears either. 'I turned off the shower and I went to phone you. Mummy had the number of the hotel written down on the pad. They said you were back but there was no answer from your room. Then I thought, he's with *her*, that's what they're doing. Like Mummy said once. So I asked for her room, and you were. Daddy, I despise you. D'you understand? I don't want to see you again.'

She turned and walked out of the room, closing the door behind her. Matt wanted to rush after her, hold her, rock her as he used to when she was smaller, tell her that everything was going to be... But it wasn't. And she was right.

'I did warn you,' Sue commented briskly. 'I only hope your visit hasn't set her back. The doctor said she was to be kept quiet and allowed to adjust at her own pace. When's the funeral?'

'Funeral?' He was startled.

'Helen's,' she said patiently. 'I imagine you'll be there. If Jenny insists on going, it'll be unavoidable that you two...'

Matt tried to explain that Helen's body was still at Westport, together with the others who'd died there. Since the town had been evacuated, there was no question of arranging funerals or anything else. But Sue didn't seem to understand. She repeated her question slowly, trying to get through to him.

'How d'you mean, no funeral? Of course Helen must have a funeral.' It sounded more like an accusation than a statement, implying that she'd always known Helen had married beneath her but there were family standards to be upheld. 'It's your duty to start making decent arrangements as soon as you possibly can.'

He was hardly listening to her. Through the window he'd just seen someone on a pony galloping across the meadow and jumping the hedge at the far end. 'Isn't that Jenny?'

'Where? Oh! Oh, now you've done it!' she snapped. She tugged the window open. 'Jenny! Jenny, come back!'

'She mustn't go on the moor!' Matt cried.

He ran out of the house to the Landrover, started the engine and reversed to get out of the drive, grazing the side of the Volvo estate. Luckily the road was clear. He shot along it, taking the first turning off to the left, a narrow lane, and praying it would lead in Jenny's direction. It skirted the meadow where the second pony was patiently chewing; then the hedges grew high and he could see nothing more. The lane began to wind and twist; he lost all sense of where he was heading till suddenly it joined a wider road and he found himself on the very edge of the moor, fairly high up, with a good view of the farmland behind him.

Jenny was nowhere to be seen.

Leaving the door of the Landrover open, he balanced on the sill to give himself extra height and searched the country-side through his binoculars. Cows, trees ... a house ... the rooftop of ... yes, that must be Sue's house... But no Jenny. She could be concealed among the trees somewhere, or maybe she'd reached the moor first and...

But it was hopeless. She could be anywhere.

Half a mile or so up the road he spotted a phone box. He drove up to it and called Sue, thinking that Jenny might have changed her mind and gone back. No answer. He rang Fran at the hotel, told her what had happened and asked her to wait there; he'd get in touch the moment he had any news. Then he tried Sue again, but there was still no reply.

The next hour he spent driving through the network of lanes between the moor and Sue's house, stopping at every gate to peer into the fields beyond, enquiring of the one or two people he met if they'd seen a girl on a pony, or without a pony, a ten-year-old girl with long blonde hair down to her shoulders...

At last he found himself back at the phone box and once again dialled Sue's number. She was at home. 'Have you found Jenny?' he asked anxiously the moment she answered.

No, she hadn't. She'd been out on foot and in the car, but there was no trace of her. She'd rung all their friends, places where she might go, but they hadn't seen her either. If she'd gone on to the moor... Well, it wasn't the first time she'd stayed here and the pony knew its way home, but it was very worrying. She'd been thinking of calling the police.

Matt said she should remain where she was in case Jenny returned. He'd ring her every hour or so, but in the meantime he'd organize a search. Then he got on to Fran again, explained the situation and asked her to call the Ministry.

Within fifteen minutes he was back at the hotel where he found her putting on her protective overalls and flying boots. The Ministry had responded immediately, she said. They'd contacted the Navy and a helicopter was on its way. If Jenny was anywhere on the moor they'd have a better chance of spotting her from the air.

'It's not far across the fields from Sue's house,' he reasoned as he changed his clothes. This time he wore his skin-diving suit under the overalls. Better safe than sorry. 'It's much farther round by road.'

They were outside selecting the gear they needed from the Landrover when the large Navy helicopter arrived, its down-draught swirling litter and dust into the air as it landed on the level patch of moorland opposite the hotel. A brisk young officer jumped out smartly and introduced himself.

'Lieutenant Smythe,' he said with a quick salute. His keen blue eyes rested on each of them in turn, summing them up. 'How can we help you?'

With Lieutenant Smythe and the pilot was a tough-looking leading seaman who leaned out through the open door to give them a hand up. He commented that they'd all three encoun-tered worms before – 'And put a few out of their misery' – while evacuating the more isolated villages along the coast, so they knew what to expect. They'd brought a variety of arma-ments with them, including a box of grenades, a couple of automatic rifles and a flame-thrower.

'Hit 'em with everything we've got, that's my philosophy!' the lieutenant bawled as they swooped across the moor, keep-ing the road in sight till they reached the phone box Matt had used earlier.

They began a methodical search of the moor and the border-ing farmland. Twice they thought they'd found her but a closer look through binoculars proved them wrong. In the fields they saw several horses and ponies; they went down low to make sure she hadn't dismounted or been thrown. But there was no sign of her.

After half-an-hour or more they landed in the meadow be-hind Sue's house, scaring the one remaining pony into gallop-ing to the far corner where two hedges met. There it stood trembling its wordless objections at them. Matt ran over to the gate where Sue met him, eyeing the helicopter and his space-era clothing with equal dislike.

'She's not back?'

'No.' She looked more annoyed than worried. 'She's gone off somewhere to be alone for a couple of hours. There's no need to panic. I've been thinking it over. Helen was just the same as a girl. She'd disappear for hours on end. Always turned up again when she was hungry.'

'In those days there were no worms about.' He left her standing there by the gate and loped back to the helicopter whose blades were still turning with a slow, steady rhythm. When he'd scrambled on board, he said: 'Let's concentrate on the moor now. Maybe she got farther than we thought.'

They took off once again and almost hedge-hopped towards the moor. Nowhere did they see either a rider on a pony or a child on foot. The constantly-broadcast warnings were having their effect, and people were keeping their children indoors. On the moor itself even the usual sheep were missing. It was in one of its sombre moods. Here and there the sun broke through the clouds to bring the yellow furze to life or emphasize the darkness of the black mud. The oil pipeline cut across it like a wound on those long stretches where it was above the surface.

'Something down there!' exclaimed Fran, pointing.

'I saw nothing.' The lieutenant squinted through his binoculars. 'But let's go round again, just in case.'

The pilot swung the helicopter round, then slowed down, hovering above the spot. The bog-grass and rushes danced violently beneath them.

Matt adjusted the focus of his own binoculars, trying to get a sharper image of the object. 'What is it?'

'A dead pony,' Lieutenant Smythe judged. 'Forelegs stuck in the mud, head partly obscured by vegetation. Lots of ponies on this moor.'

'But it might be Jenny's!' Fran's voice was sharp.

'Can't see her!' The lieutenant called back above the insistent engine, but he gave the pilot a sign to go lower.

Indicating what appeared to be a firmer patch of ground a

few yards away, the pilot took the chopper towards it. As he came down the lieutenant, armed with one of the rifles, sprang out as if he were on a combat mission.

'Okay!' he yelled, waving.

Matt followed him. It was a bald expanse of moor where the soil and moss barely covered the smooth granite. Towards the west, moorland and cloud dissolved into each other.

The dead pony lay just below them about two hundred yards away, its hide apparently undamaged. Beyond it was some low shrub, and then one of the smaller tors looking like a man-made tower of massive rock-slabs rising gauntly out of the ground.

'I'm going down there,' Matt decided on impulse. 'Alone.'

'What d'you expect to find?' the lieutenant enquired. 'No worms anywhere near that pony. Died of natural causes, I imagine. But if you'd like us to accompany you, that's why we're here.'

'I'd prefer you all up here. Any sign of worms—'

'I'll fire a shot,' the lieutenant told him. 'And here – use this radio if you need help.'

Matt nodded and began to make his way off the broad granite shoulder to the softer ground, deliberately ignoring Fran's unspoken pleas to go with him. He could still observe a good area of moorland around him – his greater height gave him that advantage over the others – but it was treacherous underfoot and he was forced to move slowly. Playing safe, he took a step at a time, from one tussock of grass and rushes to the next.

It helped him, too, to feel that the others were still up there by the helicopter, watching him, though he was too busy to look back in their direction.

One more little island and. . .

Yes, he was right. He could see only the tail of the worm protruding from the dead pony's side but that luminescent green was unmistakable. Slowly it wriggled back till he saw its head emerge, grasping a large piece of raw meat in its jaws. As it withdrew he spotted a second worm, then a third. No wonder they'd not noticed them from a distance. They were all entering from underneath the carcase, or from the side, into the soft under-belly.

But they weren't eating. He watched them closely to make sure he wasn't mistaken. No, he was right – they were taking the food away! Relays of worms, each about the size of those which had originally attacked him in the sewers, were approaching the body to fetch mouthfuls of meat and carry it off into the undergrowth.

So far they hadn't observed him. He held well back and began to move as quietly as he could from one islet to the next, trying to keep them in sight. On every other occasion they'd always eaten on the spot, so why were they behaving differently now?

He reached firmer ground and was able to get closer. Two lines of worms, squirming across the balding rock near the foot of the tor, busily going to and from their food source... He followed them round the base of the tor, carefully, still making sure he didn't get too close.

At the side of the tor he saw them head for what appeared to be a bright green quilt laid out on the ground, quite flat and about ten feet across. It was a beautiful thick, soft layer of moss and as treacherous as the worms themselves. The moment he saw it he felt sick in his stomach. If Jenny had come this way and thrown herself down on it to rest, not realizing that she'd sink to her death in the muddy ooze underneath...

As he watched, the matted moss on the surface broke and a head rose above it, the head of the largest worm he'd ever seen. Its eyes were partly closed, its features bloated. Though he couldn't see its full length, its neck alone must have been almost a foot in diameter. Oblivious of his presence, it laid its head on the edge of the green quilt and opened its mouth lazily to be fed.

A gasp came from behind him – Fran! She clutched his arm and whispered something, but too low for him to understand. He knew they had only to make the wrong move and the worms would turn on them. This giantess – he was convinced it was female – had probably laid eggs in the mud; this could be the only reason why the others were feeding her. She was like a queen termite in the centre of a colony: protected, but also co-ordinating the tasks of her offspring, sending out those waves of intelligence he'd so often experienced. A queen worm, the telepathic centre of her empire.

He freed his sleeve from Fran's fingers and turned, intending to ask her to leave. If the worms did attack – and those visiting the pony's corpse must be the soldier-hunters of the tribe – he'd need to be unencumbered. But then he heard a low whimper from the direction of the tor.

'Daddy!' The voice was so soft, hardly distinguishable from the whine of the wind through the stones, that he thought at first his ears were deceiving him. 'Daddy. . .'

'Jenny! Jenny, where are you?'

Then he saw her. She had climbed on to the lowest of the great hunks of rock which made up the tor and half-knelt there, pressing herself into a narrow cleft. One slip, one split-second of tiredness, and she'd drop down among the worms, perhaps even rolling over into the jaws of the queen herself.

20

Between Matt and the tor stretched the soft quilt in dazzling light green, enticing him to set foot on it. The queen worm had withdrawn and the only reminder of her presence was the ruffling of the thick moss where she'd poked her head out. The soldier worms too went, one by one, as if it were now their turn to feed, though Matt knew they had not returned to the dead pony for he caught glimpses of their luminescent skins here and there among the vegetation.

'Waiting to see what we do,' he told Fran.

'As though they can read our thoughts.' She shivered.

'Jenny,' he called out, attempting to sound unrushed and confident, 'I want you to stay where you are a bit longer. You're quite safe there. I'm going to find a way of reaching you. Can you hear me all right?'

'Yes.' Her thin voice trembled a little, but then she took courage and spoke louder. 'Yes! Oh, hurry, Daddy!'

He explained – still keeping his voice as steady as possible – how he was going to try and work his way round the side of the tor. She seemed to understand. Then he unclipped the radio from his belt and called up Lieutenant Smythe to tell him what he intended.

'Sounds crazy to me,' came the reply, 'when we can pick her up from the air.'

'Not with that amount of overhang, you can't.'

'So what d'you want us to do?'

Matt spelled it out.

'Okay, Matt, it's your neck. If that's the way you want it, we'll stand by till you give the signal. Good luck!'

Fran refused to return to the helicopter, saying yet again that she had no intention of letting Matt out of her sight. If there had been more time he would have argued with her, insisted, but he had to get to Jenny as quickly as he could. Already three worms had appeared from somewhere and were slipping towards the foot of the rocks where they stopped and raised their heads, moving them gracefully from side to side.

'Jenny, don't look at them!' he warned, speaking encouragingly. 'Turn your face towards the rock . . . that's right . . . now close your eyes and keep them tight shut. . .' He glanced at Fran. 'Ready? Okay, let's move. And have your stick ready. If only that moss were as solid as it seems we'd be over there and. . .'

'The locals call it a feather-bed.'

He hardly listened. They skirted the edge of it, testing the ground carefully whenever they were in doubt. More worms were gathering, though they'd gone no closer. Not yet. So long as Jenny didn't get caught by their eyes she'd be all right. He could keep them off long enough with his stick for her to get on to his back, he reckoned. Risky, but safer than any other way.

The moment they were clear of the 'feather-bed' he knew his plan was hopeless. The ground was soggy right up to the edge of the rock. The patch where the worms waited was like a firm island cut off from all sides.

Through the bright green moss the head of the queen worm protruded once again, regarding him with half-lowered eyelids. Even if he could get safely across the morass – and somehow Jenny must have managed it – his retreat was too difficult under full worm attack.

'Over the rocks,' said Fran. 'It's the only way.'

The great outcrop of rock was much more extensive than they had first imagined and only a trained climber with all his equipment would be able to get to the top. Matt examined it carefully. There was a ledge, and if they could get on to it, perhaps working their way round. . . Yes, that might be possible.

He gave Fran a leg-up first and handed her both the sticks to look after while he pulled himself up beside her. Once again, his height and longer reach were an advantage.

They tried edging carefully around the rock face but unexpectedly the ledge narrowed and there were no more handholds, so they went back again to find a spot where they could climb up to a higher level. This time they succeeded in working towards the point where they could overlook the 'feather-bed'. Jenny was somewhere below them.

Matt spoke to her quietly, telling her not to move, they were not far away and they'd soon be with her. She mustn't look up, he repeated twice; just keep her eyes closed.

With some difficulty he managed to lie down full-length on the rock and peer over the edge while Fran held tight to his legs. At first he couldn't see Jenny at all. Either she'd pressed herself more deeply into the cleft or else the rocks overhung more than he'd estimated. Then he caught a glimpse of her shoes.

It was an impossible situation. Even if he brought the helicopter overhead and had himself lowered on a cable he'd most likely not be able to reach her because of the overhang. Yet from the ground level, where ten or more worms were patiently looking up at him, he'd be able to stretch out his arms and lift her clear.

He wriggled back to a more secure position.

'There's a spur sticking out about half-way down,' he explained to Fran who crouched precariously on the edge of the rock beside him. 'I'm going to see if I can reach Jenny from it. With any luck, I might be able to hoist her up here – that's if you can take her off me when I'm ready.'

'I'll try. What about the helicopter?'

'Here. . .' He unclipped the radio and gave it to her. 'Call them up when I give the word. But not before, because I could be in trouble if the down-draught catches me at the wrong moment.'

'If only we had some rope!'

'We'll have to do our best without it. But keep the sticks handy, I might need one.'

He took a breath and looked around. Great banks of white and grey cloud moved across the sky, blotting out the sun and causing wide areas of dark shadow to creep over the moor. *Glory be to God for dappled things!* he thought, remembering the poem.

But not for green worms gathering at the rock's foot.

And not for queen worms lurking like giant serpents in the mire. Maybe these were the monsters of ancient legend come to life again after centuries of lying dormant. Yet there, not half a mile away, was the oil pipeline leading to the new refinery. Surely the whole world would have heard the news if there'd been worms on the moor when they'd laid it only three or four years ago?

'You know what to do?' Matt asked.

Fran nodded. 'Be careful,' she begged. 'Don't . . . do anything. . .' She stopped and looked at him, her eyes filled with concern, as though she were suddenly convinced she'd not see him alive again.

Slowly he crept backwards towards the edge, feet first, feeling his way blindly. The ledge was too narrow for anything else. Gradually he eased himself over till his legs were hanging free. Instinctively he felt for a foothold, though he knew there was none. He would have to lower himself over completely till he was supporting his weight on his arms before his feet could find that jutting piece of rock he'd noticed.

His legs waved wildly in the air as he searched, but then his boot kicked against it. The real question was whether he'd be able to stand firmly without slipping or the rock giving way. Cautiously, he tested to discover if it would take his weight. It did, and he breathed in relief.

The next stage – this was the way he'd planned it – was to bend his knees till he was almost squatting on his heels and could reach out to Jenny beneath the overhang. It wasn't going to be easy. The rock face was so close, angled outwards as it got higher, he might well lose his balance. He looked down to check his position.

A worm was moving purposefully up the cleft towards Jenny, whose ankles and feet he could just see. Another, farther off, was approaching along a parallel route. A sudden shaft of sunlight caught them as the clouds above shifted; they looked like flowing rivers of shining emeralds.

'Stick!' he called urgently to Fran.

She handed it across to him.

Grasping it in his right hand and steadying himself against the rock face with his left, he began to crouch . . . slowly . . .

carefully ... knowing that if he fell the worms beneath would be on him without mercy.

At last he stopped, wanting to move his feet, to adjust his balance, but at the same time feeling the risk was too great. He could just about reach it now perhaps, if he stretched out.

The fingers of his left hand found a slight fault in the granite, just enough to give him a better grip. Holding on firmly, he reached out with the stick towards the worm in the cleft. There'd be no chance of beating its brains out as he'd like to, not from this distance, but if he could flick it away... The metal ferrule at the end of the stick slipped beneath it, but he was too slow. As he tried to dislodge the worm, it draped itself in festoons over the stick. Taken by surprise, he tossed away both worm and stick together.

'Fran!' he yelled up. 'Fran, get the helicopter! Quick!'

The second worm was joined by others, and two more had appeared in the cleft. There would be no way of fighting them off. Jenny was trapped higher up the cleft where it widened. On hearing his voice she turned and saw him.

'Daddy...' Her eyes were wide with fear.

'Jenny, listen,' he urged her. 'I want you to be sensible and brave. Keep quite still for a minute till I get a bit closer to you. Then I'm going to lift you out. We're going up, not down – remember? Whatever happens, there's a helicopter on its way to get you out of here.'

As he was speaking he tried to crouch down even farther, leaning over in the direction of the cleft. The handhold he'd found was no longer any use to him and he had to steady himself against the bare rock. Then he noticed a small fold in the granite which offered about an inch for his foot. He'd have to risk it.

Jenny screamed, but he begged her to hang on whatever pain she felt. A worm was biting into her bare ankle, just below the leg of her jeans.

His foot found the fold of granite. Reaching across, he was able to grasp Jenny around the waist with his right arm and swing her out of the cleft towards him, still screaming and sobbing. For a second or so he was convinced he would lose his balance and they'd both plunge down to the giant queen worm's lair in the 'feather-bed', but at last he managed to get both feet back on to the firm spur of rock.

Somewhere, he couldn't see where, the helicopter was hovering. The roar of its engine filled his ears, but without drowning Jenny's screams which cut into his very soul. Still holding her tight against him, he manoeuvred into a position where he could support himself against the rock face, freeing his left hand to grip the worm just below its head. He squeezed relentlessly till he felt the bones crack between his fingers and the jaws slacken.

But as he dropped the dead worm he sensed something pressing against his legs, winding itself around and between them. Another explored his boots and ankles. Jenny's blood, he thought. It's attracting more of them. He looked down. They were coming at him from all directions, wriggling along every crack and fissure in the granite tor. And below, as if in command, the queen worm had risen to the surface of the 'feather-bed', breaching the moss carpet in several places, the thick loops of her body glistening green in the sunlight. Over towards the pipeline he saw more speckles of green and it seemed he was totally surrounded.

'Matt!'

At first he hardly heard the voice above the noise of the helicopter, and Fran must have screamed his name several times before he looked up. She was lying on the rock only a foot or so above his head, holding out her arms ready to take Jenny from him.

'Okay!' he shouted back.

The worms were crawling over his legs, unhurried. Their teeth had not yet met his flesh but he'd felt the thick material of his overalls tear in several places.

He shifted his grip on Jenny and tried to lift her high enough for Fran to take her, but she clung to him hysterically. Nothing he said could make her let go. Then she squealed in sudden desperation, an unnatural, high-pitched squeal, and her fingers loosened their hold on his clothing. He swung her up to Fran who caught her under the arms and began to haul her to the safety of the higher ledge. It was only then he saw what had made her squeal – a second worm, gnawing at her ankle. Its tail slapped against Matt's face.

The helicopter was immediately above and someone was being lowered. It looked like the leading seaman. His feet kicked against the granite as he came down, narrowly missing Matt. He grabbed Jenny and gave the signal to be taken up again, hugging her close to him but with the worm still dangling from her ankle.

But something else was happening up there too. He couldn't see what it was, though from Fran's shrieks he could guess. Then he heard the thwack of the stick against the hard rock and realized she was screaming anger and hate. Once more something hit the rock with a sharp crack! and he found himself grinning, feeling the worms had met their match in her.

And Jenny was safe. Whether he lived or died didn't seem to matter any more. At least Jenny was all right.

He caught the head of one worm which was moving up to his abdomen and squeezed the life out of it. How long he could carry on like this he had no idea. So far they hadn't succeeded in doing more than rip his clothing with their sharp teeth, but sooner or later they'd find a way through those lined overalls, Ministry-issue, and that would be the end. There wasn't much time. The helicopter would pick up Fran first, winch her to safety, and by the time they returned for him. . .

He snatched at another worm but his arm became entangled in its writhing body. Holding it as far away from his face as possible, he tried to shake it off. Unsuccessfully. Its head was pulled back ready to strike, its eyes watching him. Hard. Knowing. Almost as though it recognized him.

This was it, he thought. Above him, he realized the leading seaman was being winched down again to fetch Fran whose high-pitched yells were still audible above the engine. He felt uneasy. Something was wrong – voices, shouts, a couple of shots. . .

The sound cleared his mind. He'd been so taken up with the danger of his own position, so convinced there was no hope of getting off these rocks alive, that he'd been acting like an idiot.

With his free hand he tugged the knife from his belt and

slashed at the worm just as it was shooting its head towards him, impaling it on the sharp blade.

He shook it off and peered upwards to see what was happening to Fran. A drop of blood splashed on to his face.

'Fran!' he yelled out. 'Fran!'

The leading seaman swung free on the end of his cable with Fran's body strapped to him. She was unconscious. One leg of her overalls was in shreds and she was bleeding profusely. On the other leg was what appeared to be a long ribbon of luminescent green.

The remaining worm on his own leg shifted. Viciously he jabbed down at it with his knife, risking the blade going into his knee but just avoiding it. The worm, injured but not dead, dropped away. Another immediately took its place, slipping rapidly over the rocks towards him and trying to bite into his boots. A third raised itself to investigate his leg and took a mouthful of overall, which it let go again. A fourth swung down from the ledge of rock above and fell across his shoulder.

He heard a bellow of horror, quite involuntary, escape from his own lips as he attempted to shake it off, brushing it away with his hand. Miraculously, he almost succeeded. It slipped sufficiently to make it feel insecure. It squirmed and wriggled to regain its balance. Those few seconds were enough for him to get hold of it and sling it away.

A shot whined close to him. Fragments of rock showered against him. Then another shot. And another.

Glancing up he saw Lieutenant Smythe kneeling in the open doorway of the helicopter, calmly picking off the worms around him one by one. Stupid bugger, he thought. How many does he think he can kill that way? If he had any compassion he'd put a bullet through me, finish me off before the worms do it.

Another tear at his leg, and this time they drew blood – not deep, but enough to whet their appetites. He caught one in his hand and hammered its skull against the rock.

More shots. 'Christ, that was close!' he shouted up resentfully. 'If you want to kill me, do it properly!'

The leading seaman was only a couple of yards above him. As he came closer the firing ceased. Matt killed another worm by the same method, dashing its head against the granite. Then he turned to find his rescuer face to face with him.

He took two worms with him up to the helicopter, but Lieutenant Smythe was ready to deal with them the moment he was hauled on board. He plucked them expertly off the tattered overalls and threw them out.

In several places the worms had bitten through the composition rubber of the frogman suit Matt wore under his overalls. Blood oozed out and began to drip down his legs.

Jenny lay on a stretcher, whimpering and hardly aware of where she was. Her eyes were open but she stared straight in front of her without seeing anything.

If possible, Fran was in an even worse state. She was unconscious and her right leg was soaked in blood. The lieutenant had applied a tourniquet.

'Right! Let's go!' he ordered brusquely.

'Wait!' Matt still had one job to do. They were hovering directly above the tor next to the bright green of the 'featherbed', its surface now broken by the giant coils of the queen worm. He crawled to the box of grenades, then back to the door. Gripping the metal ring of the pin between his teeth, he pulled it out and tossed the grenade down to her. It exploded in a shower of moss and mud. 'An Easter egg for the bitch.'

'Suppose you find your seat and get strapped in!' the lieutenant snapped, asserting his authority. 'Keep your vendetta for another time. We must get these people to hospital.'

21

Jenny was asleep under heavy sedation but at least he'd spoken to her. She'd smiled up at him, her face almost as white as the hospital pillow case, and held out her arms. 'Sorry, Daddy,' she'd murmured drowsily in his ear, 'but it's all right now, isn't it?'

Was it?

Fran wasn't expected to live, that much was obvious. When they'd taken her into the operating chamber there'd been a flurry of people around, doctors and others, consulting in hushed voices. A heavy, deep-jowled, pasty-looking man had arrived after about half an hour. 'Mr Griffiths,' they'd whispered. Everyone gave way in deference as he strode through the hospital and Matt understood that this was the surgeon on whose skill Fran's life depended.

Matt himself had shrugged off all attempts to persuade him to remain in hospital as a patient. Once his minor injuries had been cleaned and dressed he sat about in the waiting room, hoping for news of Fran and coldly thinking about the worms. The Ministry had been informed. He'd spoken to Rhys personally and no doubt the committee was meeting at that very moment, deciding on a course of action. But they would do nothing till the next day, Matt was convinced, so he still had a few hours left in which to settle his own account with them.

A friendly nurse came to ask if he'd like something to eat. He shook his head impatiently. 'When . . . when she comes out of there,' he wanted to know, 'assuming she's . . . all right. . .'

'Of course we hope she's going to be all right,' the nurse reassured him hurriedly. She was auburn-haired and had freckles, like Fran's, across the bridge of her nose. 'I think you *should* eat something. Do you good.'

Mr Griffiths, the surgeon, came into the waiting room in his shirtsleeves, carrying his jacket which he put on as he spoke. 'You're Mr Parker, are you? Rhys phoned me about you. We're old friends. Hear you've found the worms' nursery. Congratulations. First positive news we've had about this affair.'

'How. . .?' Matt began.

'She's as well as can be expected. I'll be blunt. You know what these worms can do, perhaps better than anybody. Loss of blood – considerable. They severed an artery. Shock – a key factor. As well as the leg, they'd also started work on the lower abdomen. Now you have it, straight.'

'But will she live?'

'I don't know.' Mr Griffiths sat down next to him and put a hand on his arm. 'I've told you all this because Rhys said you like to know the facts, unadorned. That makes two of us. Now the best thing you can do is let them give you a bed and something to help you sleep.'

'I'd rather get some fresh air.'

'That's your decision.' He stood up and buttoned up his jacket. 'But don't do anything silly, will you? You've something to live for. Your daughter's going to need you whatever happens. Don't forget that.'

Matt left the hospital and walked down the hill into the town. The remains of the overalls flapped about his legs in the breeze and the uppers of his boots were lacerated in several places. He'd need fresh clothing, that would be the first step, something strong enough to keep the worms at bay till he'd done all he intended. Another frogman suit too; they'd cut through the first at the hospital to get at his wounds more quickly. If only Fran had been wearing one.

It was already late afternoon but there were still several hours of daylight left. Long enough, anyway. He passed a butcher getting ready to close up, clearing the meat out of his window. In front of an outfitters he paused for a moment in two minds, then went on. That wasn't the sort of thing he needed. A woman came along the street towards him and he tried to ask her advice; she gave him one look and walked away, probably frightened by his odd appearance – his unusual height, his clothes in rags, his missing fingers, his scars and beard.

But turning a corner he found what he wanted in a large, double-fronted shop whose windows were filled with motorcycle accessories and camping gear. He went in.

A lean, hard-bitten man – ex-Navy by the look of him – looked up from his newspaper. 'Been in the wars, skipper?'

'Accident,' Matt said briefly. 'Need some new clothes.'

'You can say that again,' the man commented. 'What takes your fancy?'

Matt hunted around among the motorcycling gear, selecting the thickest he could find in his size, black imitation leather lined with sheepskin. The man let him change in the storeroom at the back.

'You look more human now. What about a helmet?'

He produced a cycling helmet with a visor on the front and a row of studs around the bottom edge for a cape which could be tucked into the top of a jacket. 'Keep the wind out.'

And the worms, thought Matt approvingly. He told the man to add it to the bill, as well as a new sheath-knife.

'Skin-diving stuff?' he enquired.

'Snorkels, masks. . .' The man pointed to the other side of the shop.

'A rubber suit?'

'Sorry, not your size. Don't know where you'd get that. Nowhere round here.'

While he was making out the credit card slip, Matt asked him where he could hire a car. 'Or a bike,' he added.

'If it's a bike you want I might be able to help. Where are you camping?'

'Not far. About five miles.' No point in disillusioning him. 'I could bring it back tomorrow.'

'That's up to you.' The man handed back his credit card and led him through the shop to a side door. It opened into a lane leading to a garage and workshop. 'He may be able to fix you up. Tell him I sent you. He's my brother, and just about the biggest motorcycle dealer you'll find in these parts. But don't get into any more accidents, or you won't be too popular with him.'

Twenty minutes later Matt rode back down the lane on a shining 500cc bike. At first the garage owner had been suspicious, wanting to check his licence and demanding a deposit, but when Matt pointed out that the scars on his face had been inflicted by worms, he'd suddenly snapped his fingers and said, 'You're that cameraman! Saw your picture in the papers!' It was the old routine, and it never failed. 'Ask me, it's all these nuclear power stations are to blame. They're the cause of changes in nature – the weather, the worms. . . Well, if you're trying to do something about those worms, you can have a bike with pleasure.'

Matt had one more stop to make as he headed back in the direction of the moor. As they'd come in by helicopter he'd spotted a quarry just off the main road and by now, he reckoned, the workmen would all have gone home.

He found it without too much difficulty. As he'd hoped, it was deserted. A squat, stone building stood isolated from the rest; he guessed this was what he was looking for. He rode up to investigate. The door was strong and firm, securely locked.

Over on the other side were three wooden huts, one obviously an office and the others possibly toolsheds. He chose the smallest and tore away the padlock with a wrench from his saddlebag. The tools were stacked neatly inside.

Taking one of the picks, he rode back to the stone building. It needed quite a few blows before the woodwork around the lock splintered and gave way.

The explosives were in boxes neatly ranged along the shelves inside. Here, he felt uncertain. Some years ago while he was still a camera assistant he'd spent three days filming at a quarry. He could still remember some of the details – how to prepare the primer, connect up the exploder. . . But he knew only too well he might blow himself up before he got anywhere near the worms.

He took one or two boxes down and looked inside. Detonators, cartridges of dynamite. . . But the sight of them began to bring it all back.

Still hesitating, he looked in several other boxes before making up his mind. Then he selected some No. 6 electric detonators, a carton of dynamite and a small exploder which he could hold in his hand, packing it all as carefully as possible into the side-bags of his bike. He was about to leave the quarry when, as an afterthought, he went back for a length of connecting wire.

His mouth tasted sour as he kicked the starter. It needed only one tiny thing to go wrong and his bike would blow up underneath him with all that explosive packed in its saddle-bags. But the engine growled gently and he eased the bike over the rough ground towards the road. Then he opened her up and sped along the smooth tarmac, eating up the miles towards his appointment with the worms. 'Don't do anything silly,' the surgeon had said to him, but there was nothing silly about fighting for survival – and that's what this battle was all about.

The worms knew this instinctively, just as any wild animal knows it. That was where Rhys was so wrong-headed, assuming the worms could reason when in fact they were merely behaving in accordance with their genetic programming. Matt had shot enough educational film to understand that much. But if some other life-form tries to overpower you and take over your territory – whether it's tigers, alligators, driver ants, cockroaches or anopheles mosquitoes – you hit back and kill them.

As the road crossed the moor the wind buffeted him and in response the bike seemed to buck beneath him. He felt exhilarated, almost happy, but then he took control of himself again. The hatred hardened within him. He stopped, consulted a map, and then swung off the road on to the moor. The ground was uneven, rising and dipping unexpectedly. Once more he slowed down almost to a crawl, conscious of the cartridges of dynamite he was carrying.

The entire moor was a nursery – that's the word the surgeon had used – and with one blow in the right place he could destroy a whole generation of worms. And die while doing it, perhaps.

From time to time he caught glimpses of the pipeline cutting across the moor, dead straight, a scar on the face of nature. At least it meant he was heading in the right direction. Over to the west the fleeting clouds were tinged with pink as the sun sank lower in the sky; how much more daylight he had it was hard to guess. Half an hour perhaps. An hour at the most.

Then, when he least expected it, his front wheel gave way and sank almost to the axle in mud. His rear wheel slewed around violently.

But he didn't come off. He managed to keep the bike upright and kill the engine. After a struggle he succeeded in coaxing the front wheel out of the mire and on to firmer ground. This was as far as he could get; now he'd have to continue on foot. He left the bike where it was and made for the nearest hillock to look around.

The oil pipeline was not too far away now and he could actually see the point where they'd taken it underground 'to preserve the beauty of the environment'; that was before money ran short. To get to it he would have to cross a wide expanse of treacherous ground, part mire, part rivulets and streams, where each tussock of grass or rushes might collapse beneath him. Or might conceal a whole posse of soldier-hunter worms.

But he had no choice; he had to do it.

He returned to the motorcycle and prepared the dynamite, trying to remember all he'd learned during those three days of filming years earlier. One thing he hadn't collected from that squat building was a pricker, but he made do with a pencil instead, pushing it into the end of the dynamite cartridge. Drawing it out carefully, he inserted one of the electric detonators, cap first, then half-hitched the leg wires around the cartridge.

Underneath his heavy motorcycling gear he was sweating like a pig. He wiped his face with the back of his hand, desperately trying to work out what to do next. Checking that the shunts were still in place on the wire ends, he placed the primed cartridge back into the saddlebag and began to pack the rest of the dynamite around it. It made quite a tidy little bomb. When it was ready he unstrapped it from the bike. Then he pulled on his gloves and adjusted his helmet.

If the worms chose to attack too early, he thought, he'd be helpless, with the spool of connecting wire and exploder in one hand and the dynamite-filled bag in the other. He longed for the comforting feel of a good firm stick.

He walked slowly, taking great care over where he placed

his feet. Whether he made it back to the bike afterwards or not didn't seem to matter. His mind was intent on that one satisfaction: the big bang. It worried him that he knew nothing about the oil inside the pipeline. What was its flashpoint? Would it ignite, or merely spread over the swampy ground in one vast dark slick?

His foot slid forward into mud which sucked hungrily at his boot. He almost panicked, almost dropped the bag, but then he righted himself and pulled his foot slowly out again. The mud was reluctant to let him go.

Still no worms, though. Somewhere over that dark moor he was convinced they were gathering. Or was that merely his terror of them painting devils in his mind? He stopped and stared around, trying to pick out the tell-tale green. No. Nothing.

Unexpectedly, he reached a stretch of firm ground with solid soil and rock underfoot. He was almost there. The pipeline was only a few yards away. They were the most difficult yards so far, with luscious grass concealing hollows filled with thick black mire, then sudden streams. He floundered across, slipping and skidding, his feet unable to find any firm foothold, till he stumbled into gently running water. That was the answer, of course. The stream bed offered a much better footing than the soggy land.

A worm darted at him but he ignored it. A second, then a third appeared, all three worrying at his boots and leggings. When he left the stream they accompanied him. A few more joined them, wriggling swiftly over the ground, their shining green bodies tinged with red from the setting sun.

'Glory be to God!' he exclaimed fervently, not for the first time that day, as he reached the pipeline.

At that point it passed over several rounded boulders of rock protruding above the surface like islands in the midst of the swamp. It couldn't have been better. He laid the bag of dynamite carefully on the ground, then eased it into the gap between the pipe and the exposed granite.

The worms flung themselves at him, biting into his sleeves and the shoulders of his thick jacket, smacking against his helmet, across the visor, on the neck covering. Again and again they attacked, always from the same side as though trying to goad him into moving on.

How long it would be before they succeeded in chewing through his new clothing he'd no idea, nor any intention of sticking around to find out.

Once the dynamite was in place he stood up and began to pick the worms off one by one, fiercely squeezing the life out of them, crushing their skulls. As always, most of the others broke off their attack and slithered across the ground to feed on their dead comrades. It gave him a few seconds' respite.

He stooped to snatch up the leg wires. One insistent worm slashed at him but he dodged back, its teeth only inches from his eyes. It it hadn't been for the helmet he'd have been blinded immediately.

Fortunately the wires were quite long and he was able to stand back while he took off his gloves to remove the shunts. He attached the bared ends to the connecting wires, covering the join with a couple of makeshift twists of insulating tape.

One of the worms bit through the motorcycling gear; he felt the scrape of its teeth against his left calf. A shock of panic tingled through his nerves. Looking down, he saw it lying between his feet, its body betraying that slight tautness he'd often noticed when they were feeding.

He stamped down on it, hard; the vertebrae cracked beneath his boot.

But the worm didn't die immediately. It recoiled without opening its jaws, taking a piece of his skin with it. Then it lay jerking unpleasantly on the ground till he kicked it away from him.

Now that they'd drawn blood he knew it was only a matter of – oh, perhaps no more than a few minutes till they overcame him. He was quite resigned to the thought. After all, he'd been living on borrowed time ever since he'd first met them in the sewers. But he would complete his job first. He swore that much.

He began to unwind the connecting wire from the spool, following the pipeline for a few yards before heading away in the direction of a large outcrop of rock. The tufts of grass were uneasy underfoot as he crossed the mire and he was forced to make several detours.

The worms went with him. He became aware that they were no longer biting, not as long as he kept moving. Experimentally he stopped a couple of times, only to be nipped again. It was a new behaviour pattern, something he'd never met before; it made him cold with apprehension.

Then they left him, withdrawing to the edge of the mire, where they kept watch like guards drawn up in pre-arranged positions. He looked around, puzzled. Then, glancing down at his feet, he noticed the ground heaving beneath him.

The thick coils of a queen worm rose above the surface of the mud and one great loop caught him behind the knees. The exploder and spool of connecting wire flew out of his hands as he slumped forward. Another loop embraced his hips as the queen's head emerged, towering above him.

Instinctively he drew the knife from his belt but there was no way he could use it. He thrashed about in the mud; only the bubble of air trapped inside his helmet kept him from suffocating.

Had the queen chosen to tighten her grasp, as a python crushes its victims, he'd have died within seconds. Instead, she held him up and darted at him with her massive head, unable to understand why her teeth couldn't penetrate the helmet.

Then she dragged him down. Mud seeped into his clothing and began to fill the helmet. Another few seconds, and he would choke to death on it. But she hauled him up again and made another attempt to bite through the perspex visor.

This time she suceeded in dislodging the helmet slightly. He slashed out with his knife, wildly, blindly, but hit nothing. Again he tried, kicking, struggling, feeling himself immersed in the mud, then raised up once more by the giant worm. He was weakening now. His efforts were feeble, though suddenly his helmet was off and he could at least breathe.

He saw her eyes, hard and unmoved. He was helpless against the power he could feel rippling through her body as she tossed him this way and that, held him, then struck once more at his face. It was a slim chance, but he drove the knife upwards with all the force he could muster. She bellowed – a long wailing note – as the point of the blade went into her jaw from underneath and emerged through her eye.

She writhed and coiled in agony, then straightened like a catapult and threw him off. He landed some distance away from her, with his legs and hips still in the mire. Immediately it began to suck him down. Desperately he clawed at the firmer ground. His fingers found a jutting piece of rock. He held on, then gradually managed to tug himself out.

He spat out mud and gasped in deep lungfuls of air, trying to recover enough strength to stagger to his feet. The most he could manage was to crawl away on hands and knees.

The mud covered his eyes too. Through it he could just see the queen worm as a vague form rising high into the air, then plunging down again into the mire, wailing plaintively in her death throes. Any second now, he knew, the other worms would get to him, thirsting for revenge.

His hand hit against something small and hard – the exploder! He groped around and found the spool with a few turns of wire still on it. First attempting to clean his fingers on the moss, he took the two bared ends and fumblingly fixed them to the terminals, cursing at his own clumsiness.

The exploder was a No. 10 twist-type which he could hold in his hand, with a strap around his wrist to keep it steady. He grasped the handle and twisted it firmly.

He'd imagined a bigger explosion and looked up in despair, wondering what had gone wrong. Then he saw the pipeline was spewing out fire, a fierce sheet of flame which spread rapidly across the swampy moorland on each side. He struggled to his feet, holding on to a rock for support.

'Christ!' he breathed, awe-stricken.

Rising in the midst of those flames were more queen worms than he could count, seeming to perform an exotic dance of death as the intense heat tortured them. Until now he'd assumed there would be half a dozen queens at most, never this number. He felt sick with terror.

The scene was like some old, nightmarish painting come horribly to life. A medieval madman's vision of hell. A Medusa's head of convulsing snakes.

They sang their death agonies in a ghastly, moaning chorus far worse than any coven of banshees; but gradually the sound became thinner as one after the other they succumbed to the fire. At last they fell silent.

He watched the flames consume them. The air was thick with the stench of burning oil and roasting worm flesh. A black pall of smoke gathered above the fire which continued to burn steadily, fed by the pipeline. Through the apertures in the rocks the wind howled.

22

'As chairman of the committee Professor Jones is to receive a knighthood,' Rhys explained blandly, his voice betraying no hint of sarcasm.

They were sitting on the Old Rectory lawn some months later, drinking a weird mixture which Rhys called Plantation Punch. The recipe was his own, he boasted; the result of many years' experimentation. A few yards away, Jenny was playing under the trees, watched over by the Alsatian who thumped his tail on the ground with pleasure whenever she spoke.

'But I'm afraid you, Matt, narrowly missed being prosecuted for setting fire to the moor, causing wanton damage and destroying the pipeline.'

'If it hadn't been for Matt, none of us would be here!' Fran protested strongly.

'Fortunately the managing director of the oil company agrees with you. His own son was attacked by worms, and badly mutilated.'

'But isn't Matt to get any recognition?' she demanded.

'As much as any other member of the committee. Collective recognition.'

Matt laughed at him. What the hell did it matter anyway?

They'd come out of it alive, that was the main thing. He and Jenny had moved back to Westport. Fran now lived at the cottage. It was a little awkward at first but Jenny had come to see it was the only way. She even helped out in the shop on Saturdays.

Helen lay buried in the Westport parish churchyard as she would have wanted. None of them felt comfortable using the bathroom at the cottage; they planned to have it stripped out and install a new one. One of the TV companies had offered Matt the position of lighting cameraman on a new film series.

The money would pay for the alterations.

'Of course, your hunch was right,' Rhys was saying as he topped up the glasses. 'The sewer worms' social organization is not unlike that of ants or termites, with a queen who lays eggs and exercises a co-ordinating control over her offspring. Several features foxed me at the time.'

'Including UFOs?' Fran asked innocently.

'Oh, I admit I may have been wrong!' He waved his hand dismissively. 'Yet who knows where they came from? And when? Remember all those ancient legends about monsters? Serpents. Dragons. St George, perhaps – was his dragon really a queen worm? Or Beowulf's battle with Grendel? I could take you to a place locally known as Grendel's Mire. Even the serpent that tempted Eve – was *that* the knowledge of good and evil?'

'But we got rid of them,' said Matt simply.

'*You* got rid of the queens,' Rhys acknowledged. 'Most, at any rate. There were far fewer on the other sites where we found them. But I don't suppose you heard the news at midday? It seems our worms have reached the United States. Two people seriously hurt in New York. The familiar pattern. . . Maybe they'll call you in, Matt, for consultations.'

'No, thanks! All I want now is to see Fran out of this wheelchair. Now let's find out what Jenny's up to, shall we?'

A few minutes earlier she'd disappeared somewhere among the trees, and the dog with her. These days it always made him feel uneasy if she went off anywhere out of sight. He stood up, slipped off the brake, and began to wheel Fran across the lawn.

Rhys followed.

FICTION

HORROR/OCCULT/NASTY

☐ Death Walkers	Gary Brandner	£1.50
☐ The Howling	Gary Brandner	£1.50
☐ Return of the Howling	Gary Brandner	£1.50
☐ The Sanctuary	Glenn Chandler	£1.50
☐ The Tribe	Glenn Chandler	£1.10
☐ The Black Castle	Leslie Daniels	£1.25
☐ The Big Goodnight	Judy Gardiner	£1.25
☐ Rattlers	Joseph L. Gilmore	£1.25
☐ The Nestling	Charles L. Grant	£1.75
☐ Slither	John Halkin	£1.25
☐ The Unholy	John Halkin	£1.25
☐ The Skull	Shaun Hutson	£1.25
☐ Pestilence	Edward Jarvis	£1.50
☐ The Beast Within	Edward Levy	£1.25
☐ Night Killers	Richard Lewis	£1.25
☐ Spiders	Richard Lewis	£1.25
☐ The Web	Richard Lewis	£1.10
☐ Bloodthirst	Mark Ronson	£1.00
☐ Ghoul	Mark Ronson	95p
☐ Ogre	Mark Ronson	95p
☐ Deathbell	Guy N. Smith	£1.00
☐ Doomflight	Guy N. Smith	£1.10
☐ The Lurkers	Guy N. Smith	£1.25
☐ Manitou Doll	Guy N. Smith	£1.25
☐ Satan's Snowdrop	Guy N. Smith	£1.00
☐ The Beast of Kane	Cliff Twemlow	£1.50
☐ The Pike	Cliff Twemlow	£1.25

SCIENCE FICTION

☐ More Things in Heaven	John Brunner	£1.50
☐ The Proud Robot	Henry Kuttner	£1.50
☐ Death's Master	Tanith Lee	£1.50
☐ Electric Forest	Tanith Lee	£1.25
☐ The Dancers of Arun	Elizabeth A. Lynn	£1.50
☐ A Different Light	Elizabeth A. Lynn	£1.50
☐ The Northern Girl	Elizabeth A. Lynn	£1.50
☐ Balance of Power	Brian M. Stableford	£1.75

WESTERNS – Blade Series – Matt Chisholm

☐ No. 5 The Colorado Virgins		85p
☐ No. 6 The Mexican Proposition		85p
☐ No. 8 The Nevada Mustang		85p
☐ No. 9 The Montana Deadlock		85p
☐ No. 10 The Cheyenne Trap		95p
☐ No. 11 The Navaho Trail		95p
☐ No. 12 The Last Act		95p

FICTION
CRIME – WHODUNNIT

☐ Thou Shell of Death	Nicholas Blake	£1.25
☐ The Widow's Cruise	Nicholas Blake	£1.25
☐ The Worm of Death	Nicholas Blake	95p
☐ The Long Divorce	Edmund Crispin	£1.50
☐ King and Joker	Peter Dickinson	£1.25
☐ The Last House-Party	Peter Dickinson	£1.50
☐ A Pride of Heroes	Peter Dickinson	£1.50
☐ The Seals	Peter Dickinson	£1.50
☐ Sleep and His Brother	Peter Dickinson	£1.50
☐ Firefly Gadroon	Jonathan Gash	£1.50
☐ The Vatican Rip	Jonathan Gash	£1.50
☐ Blood and Judgment	Michael Gilbert	£1.10
☐ Close Quarters	Michael Gilbert	£1.10
☐ Death of a Favourite Girl	Michael Gilbert	£1.50
☐ The Etruscan Net	Michael Gilbert	£1.25
☐ The Night of the Twelfth	Michael Gilbert	£1.25
☐ Silence Observed	Michael Innes	£1.00
☐ There Came Both Mist and Snow	Michael Innes	95p
☐ Go West, Inspector Ghote	H.R.F. Keating	£1.50
☐ Inspector Ghote Draws a Line	H.R.F. Keating	£1.50
☐ Inspector Ghote Plays a Joker	H.R.F. Keating	£1.50
☐ The Murder of the Maharajah	H.R.F. Keating	£1.50
☐ The Perfect Murder	H.R.F. Keating	£1.50
☐ The Dutch Shoe Mystery	Ellery Queen	£1.60
☐ The French Powder Mystery	Ellery Queen	£1.25
☐ The Siamese Twin Mystery	Ellery Queen	95p
☐ The Spanish Cape Mystery	Ellery Queen	£1.10
☐ Copper, Gold and Treasure	David Williams	£1.75
☐ Treasure by Degrees	David Williams	£1.75
☐ Unholy Writ	David Williams	£1.60

NON-FICTION
WAR

☐ The Battle of Malta	Joseph Attard	£1.50
☐ The Black Angels	Rupert Butler	£1.50
☐ Gestapo	Rupert Butler	£1.50
☐ Hand of Steel	Rupert Butler	£1.35
☐ Legions of Death	Rupert Butler	£1.75
☐ The Air Battle for Malta	Lord James Douglas-Hamilton MP	£1.50
☐ Auschwitz and the Allies	Martin Gilbert	£4.95
☐ Sigh for a Merlin	Alex Henshaw	£1.50
☐ Hitler's Secret Life	Glen B. Infield	£1.50
☐ Spitfire into Battle	Group Captain Duncan Smith	£1.75
☐ Women Beyond the Wire	Lavinia Warner and John Sandilands	£1.95

FICTION

GENERAL

☐ The Patriarch	Chaim Bermant	£1.75
☐ The Free Fishers	John Buchan	£1.50
☐ Midwinter	John Buchan	£1.50
☐ A Prince of the Captivity	John Buchan	£1.50
☐ The Eve of Saint Venus	Anthony Burgess	£1.10
☐ Nothing Like the Sun	Anthony Burgess	£1.50
☐ The Wanting Seed	Anthony Burgess	£1.50
☐ The Other Woman	Colette	£1.50
☐ Retreat From Love	Colette	£1.60
☐ Prizzi's Honour	Richard Condon	£1.75
☐ The Whisper of the Axe	Richard Condon	£1.75
☐ King Hereafter	Dorothy Dunnett	£2.95
☐ Pope Joan	Lawrence Durrell	£1.35
☐ The Country of her Dreams	Janice Elliott	£1.35
☐ Secret Places	Janice Elliott	£1.35
☐ Letter to a Child Never Born	Oriana Fallaci	£1.00
☐ A Man	Oriana Fallaci	£1.95
☐ Rich Little Poor Girl	Terence Feely	£1.75
☐ Marital Rites	Margaret Forster	£1.50
☐ Grimalkin's Tales	Gardiner, Ronson, Whitelaw	£1.60
☐ Who Was Sylvia?	Judy Gardiner	£1.50
☐ Lost and Found	Julian Gloag	£1.95
☐ La Presidenta	Lois Gould	£1.75
☐ A Sea-Change	Lois Gould	£1.50
☐ Black Summer	Julian Hale	£1.75
☐ Duncton Wood	William Horwood	£2.50
☐ The Stonor Eagles	William Horwood	£2.95
☐ The Man Who Lived at the Ritz	A.E. Hotchner	£1.65
☐ The Fame Game	Rona Jaffe	£1.50

NAME ....

ADDRESS ....

....

Write to Hamlyn Paperbacks Cash Sales, PO Box 11, Falmouth, Cornwall TR10 9EN.

Please indicate order and enclose remittance to the value of the cover price plus:

U.K.: Please allow 45p for the first book plus 20p for the second book and 14p for each additional book ordered, to a maximum charge of £1.63.

B.F.P.O. & EIRE: Please allow 45p for the first book plus 20p for the second book and 14p per copy for the next 7 books, thereafter 8p per book.

OVERSEAS: Please allow 75p for the first book and 21p per copy for each additional book.

Whilst every effort is made to keep prices low it is sometimes necessary to increase cover prices and also postage and packing rates at short notice. Hamlyn Paperbacks reserve the right to show new retail prices on covers which may differ from those previously advertised in the text or elsewhere.